The Gift

By

Verda Foster

THE GIFT

ISBN 1-933113-03-0

THIS TRADE PAPERBACK ORIGINAL IS PUBLISHED BY **INTAGLIO PUBLICATIONS**, GAINESVILLE, FL USA

FIRST PRINTING: OCTOBER 2004

CREDITS

EXECUTIVE EDITOR: STACIA SEAMAN

COVER DESIGN BY DONNA IRENE ROBERTS

Other books by the author

Graceful Waters

The Chosen

These Dreams

Crystal's Heart

Infinite Pleasures
An Anthology of Lesbian Erotica

Acknowledgements

Donna Roberts created the cover for this book. Thanks, Donna, I love your work.

Next I would like to thank my wonderful technical advisors. These women were invaluable help and I really appreciate their input. Radclyffe, for her medical expertise. Patty Schramm and Susan Keith, for their advice on EMT procedures. Sheryl Low for checking over the physical therapy scenes. These ladies helped to make The Gift a much better book.

Laney Roberts and Stacia Seaman are the wonderful editors I had the great pleasure to work with on this book. Thank you ladies.

And a special thanks to Kathy Smith and StarCrossed Productions.

I would also like to thank Shirley Smith who proofread two of my previous books and I meant to thank her and forgot. So, thank you, Shirley.

I would also like to thank the wonderful women on my list. Their encouragement and beta reading expertise is always appreciated.

Last, but not least, I would like to thank my sister Vada, for proof reading this book, and her wonderful partner Gypsy who put up with having a dog named after her.

Verda
VHFoster@AOL.com
http://verdas-kaleidoscope.womenwhoroar.com/

This book is dedicated to my wonderful family. I love you with all my heart.

CHAPTER ONE

The afternoon was pleasantly warm, and a soft breeze ruffled the leaves of the old ash tree in the small neighborhood park. Lindsay Ryan sat in the cool shade watching people go about their business. Her shoulder-length red hair was a mass of curls, and with her fair skin, dimples, and a generous dusting of freckles, she looked like an older, Irish version of Shirley Temple. Her youthful appearance always gave people the impression that she was younger than her thirty-six years.

Lindsay couldn't help but smile as she watched two little girls playing a game of kickball. They seemed to be having a good time, and their cheerful laughter was music to her ears. The older girl was much more coordinated and had no trouble keeping control of the ball. The grin never left the smaller girl's face even though she was clearly outmatched. She never gave up, her dark braids bouncing up and down as she ran.

A glance at her watch and Lindsay sighed at the time. She reluctantly got to her feet, stretched her five-foot six-inch frame, and ran her fingers through her windblown hair. Her lunch break almost over, she gathered up her canvas lunch bag and started across the park.

A child's voice yelled, "Stop the ball!" and Lindsay turned to see a large rubber ball heading right for her, the two little girls in hot pursuit. Smiling, she reached down and scooped up the ball.

As soon as her hands touched it, her senses were overwhelmed with a horrific vision. She saw the smaller girl lying nude in a shallow hole. Lindsay watched in horror as a shovel methodically piled dirt on the girl's tortured little body. Bile rising in her throat, she swallowed in a desperate attempt to keep the contents of her stomach where they belonged. She shuddered and took a few deep breaths, trying to calm her racing heart. It took a moment before she was able to toss the ball back to the running children.

"Thank you," the smaller girl called out.

Lindsay forced herself to smile. "You're welcome," she called back as the girls dashed off to continue their game. "Please, God...no," she whispered, the reality of the vision sinking into her consciousness. *It can't happen. I have to do something.*

These girls were often at the park when Lindsay ate her lunch, and her gaze swept the area in search of the woman who always accompanied them. She spotted the blonde woman sitting on a bench with her nose in a book and walked toward her. Somehow, she had to make the woman believe that her little girl was in grave danger. The fact that the woman's eyes seldom left the book she was reading caused Lindsay great concern. The child needed to be watched with diligence, and Lindsay knew she had to make the woman understand that she could not take her eyes off the girl for even a moment.

Throughout her life, Lindsay's visions had been intrusive, inconvenient, and inconsistent, but Lindsay had never been able to call one up at will and, thus, had never done well in tests that were supposed to measure such abilities. Skeptics looked down their noses at her, and even believers went away disillusioned when she could not perform on cue. Perhaps it was not a gift, but rather a curse. Indeed, the unpredictability of her visions and people's lack of understanding of her intentions were two of the reasons she had moved to a new town, where no one knew of her and her supposed gift, to start over. She had promised herself that it would be different here. She would keep these things to herself.

But how could she do that when she'd never had a vision so horrific before? An innocent life was at stake, and she had no choice but to tell. Some unthinkable evil was waiting to claim that child, and she could not live with herself if she didn't try to prevent her vision from becoming a reality.

"Excuse me." Lindsay watched the woman lift her eyes from her book, an annoyed expression on her face. "I'm, um, sorry to bother you." She wondered how she could possibly tell this woman the future she saw for her beautiful little girl. Dropping her eyes to her hands, she shifted from foot to foot, her heart pounding in her chest.

"Are you all right, dear?" The woman's expression changed to concern, and she reached out to touch Lindsay's hand.

"No, I'm not," Lindsay answered, lifting her eyes, then quickly glancing down at her hands again. *This is so hard.* "I'm not really sure how to explain this so you'll believe me, but I—I swear it's true."

"Why don't you sit down and tell me what this is about?" The woman patted the bench next to her. "My name is Alice. I'm sure when we talk it out, you'll see that whatever the problem is, it's not half as bad as you thought."

"I wish that were true," Lindsay said, taking a seat next to Alice. "I'm Lindsay Ryan." She extended her hand. "I work as a customer service rep at Harpers Unlimited, and I spend most of my lunch breaks here at the park." After taking a deep breath, she continued. "Sometimes I see things that other people can't. I don't know why. Most often, it happens when I touch an object. I get a picture in my mind of an event in the life of the person the object belongs to. I'm not always clear whether the event is in the past, present, or future."

"And...?" Alice's expression changed to skepticism.

"And I intercepted the ball your little girl was playing with." Lindsay turned, pointing to the smaller girl, and the vision washed over her again. She closed her eyes, her body betraying her emotions with a violent shudder. "I..." She took another deep breath, willing her voice to stop trembling. "I saw your little girl's body lying in a shallow grave, and someone was shoveling dirt on her." Lindsay couldn't bring herself to describe the condition of the body. It was bad enough to have to tell the woman that her little girl had been murdered in her vision.

"I'm not sure when it happens." She thought a moment. "As fast as kids grow and change, I think it's in the near future, because she looked the same as she does right now." Lindsay recognized the look of disbelief in Alice's eyes, but she continued anyway. A little girl's life was at stake. "Please, I'm trying to help. You've got to believe me. I'm not the sort of person who gets my kicks out of scaring people." She grasped Alice's hands. "Just give me the benefit of the doubt and don't take your eyes off her." Without waiting for an answer, she got up and strode quickly away, hoping that she had scared Alice enough to make her watch the girls more closely.

Lindsay managed to make it back to work and into the restroom before she lost the battle to keep her food down. She couldn't get the picture of that little girl out of her mind. How could someone prey on one so young and innocent? Yet she knew he was out there—waiting. She dried her face on a paper towel and tried not to think about it anymore. She had done all she could do, hadn't she?

Michael Thompson watched Lindsay emerge from the ladies' restroom. He had been a little concerned when she had rushed by a few minutes ago, looking pale and distressed. She had been working for him for almost four months and seemed to be a loner, keeping to herself most of the time. She was a good, dependable employee, though, and great with the customers.

"Are you okay, Lindsay?"

"Just a little upset stomach," Lindsay answered. "I'm sure a couple of Tums will fix me right up."

"Good." He smiled. "I don't want one of my best people getting sick on me."

"Alice, Daddy's home!" Mandy's face lit up as she shouted. He'd had to work late almost every night that week, and she had been afraid she would have to go to bed without seeing him again. The little girl ran across the room and threw herself into his waiting arms. She hugged him tightly and smothered him with kisses. Soon, another shouted greeting of "Daddy" rang out, and Mandy's sister, Tracy, joined the hugfest.

Alice smiled as she watched the man carry his babies up the stairs. Greg Carpenter was a large man with straw-colored hair and sky blue eyes. Neither of the girls had taken after him, though, and the little dark heads pressed against his shoulders stood out in contrast. Tracy, the seven-year-old, had eyes of the softest brown like her mother's, and he called her his little doe-eyed girl. Mandy was five, and although she more closely resembled her mother, her eyes were hazel dappled with soft flecks of yellow and green.

As they disappeared up the stairs, Alice wondered again whether she should mention the strange woman at the park. It was a difficult decision. She was fairly certain that the woman was delusional, but these were not her children. She supposed she should tell Greg, let him decide if he wanted to take the warning seriously. Tomorrow morning would be soon enough, she decided. She flipped off the lights and headed to bed.

Alice heard the sound of the shower and pushed the switch on the coffeemaker. Greg would be down soon for his morning cup of coffee. She wanted to talk to him about the woman in the park before the girls got up. Holding her steaming cup of tea, she sat down at the table to wait.

She had just finished her tea when she heard his footsteps on the stairs. As was her routine, she deposited her cup in the sink, grabbed his mug, filled it, and handed it to Greg as he entered the kitchen.

"Morning, Alice."

"Good morning," she replied, sitting back down in her chair. "Something happened yesterday at the park that I need to talk to you about."

Greg sat across from her, his brow wrinkling in question. "A problem with the girls?" His long fingers wrapped around his mug. It was hard being both mother and father to them, and he had been putting more and more of the responsibility on his housekeeper's shoulders recently. When his team at work finished implementing the new system, things would get back to normal. But for at least the next few weeks, Alice would be stuck with extra work.

"A woman approached me yesterday at the park. She said that she'd had a vision about Mandy."

"A vision?"

"Yes. She said that in this vision, Mandy had been...murdered, and someone was burying her."

Greg slammed his mug down on the table, spilling coffee everywhere. "Good God! I can't believe you would even listen to such garbage, Alice." He stood, walked to the sink, and grabbed the dishtowel to wipe up the mess. "She's probably a scam artist, trying to get money out of me."

A hand went to Alice's mouth to stifle the gasp that threatened to escape. She had never expected this reaction from her employer. *It's the stress from all those hours at work. This was the last straw.*

He wiped furiously at the spill. "Next thing you know, she'll be here trying to sell me some magic spell she has that will prevent it, and when nothing happens to Mandy, she'll take credit for it." Greg tossed the towel in the sink, his eyes shining with anger. "People like that should be tarred and feathered." Somewhat calmer after his outburst, Greg refilled his mug and sat down again. "I'm sorry if I seemed angry at you, Alice, because I'm not. It's just..." He took a sip of his coffee.

"I understand." Alice decided it probably wouldn't do any good to tell him that she believed the woman was not out to defraud him. She was just some sick, deluded soul. *He probably wouldn't believe me anyway, and it would just make him angry again.* In fact, she regretted telling him about the woman at all.

Greg nodded and took another sip of coffee. "Keep the girls away from the park. I don't want them around that woman again."

Lindsay sat under her usual tree, but was not engaged in her usual casual people watching. It had been a week since she had warned Alice of what she had seen, and neither she nor the girls had been back. It was unusual not to see them, and Lindsay could only hope that nothing had happened to the child. *She could be trying to avoid running into me again*, she thought, sadly. Hopefully, the reason was that Alice had taken the threat to the girl seriously and was keeping both children home to protect them.

The exhaustion of the past week settled in around Lindsay, and she yawned. Sleep had been almost impossible, and when she did manage to drift off, she was awakened by nightmares of her horrific vision.

Lindsay was so disturbed that she had considered going to the police with the information but realized they would probably laugh her out of the station. After all, what could she tell them? "Well, Officer, I had this vision that a little girl, whose name I don't know, was killed by a man I couldn't see."

The fact that she was still having visions of the child's grave led her to believe that telling the woman in the park had not changed anything. If the warning had been taken seriously and the family was keeping close tabs on the little girl, why was Lindsay seeing the image over and over?

Lindsay closed her eyes. *If only I could see more, I might be able to do some good.*

Every day that this went on made her more certain her instincts were right—that the danger was growing more imminent with each passing hour. She had to do something. But what?

There was only one sure thing. She couldn't let this go until she found the little girl and saw for herself that she was okay. *Not this time.* She would tell her boss that she needed to take some personal time off and hope that her job was still waiting for her when she returned.

Determined, Lindsay folded her lunch bag, stood, and brushed off her pants. She knew she had seen the trio walk into the park from the side opposite the parking lot. The fact that Alice didn't park in the lot suggested they lived in the neighborhood. Lindsay resolved to drive slowly through the streets on that side of the park until she found them. *Perhaps not the best plan, but I'm doing something.*

In the midafternoon warmth, Lindsay sat in her car in front of the large Tudor-style house and watched the two little girls play in the yard. *Alone. She's left them alone. Doesn't she realize how easy it would be for someone to snatch the little one up and be gone before she even knew what had happened?* It was clear Alice had not taken her warning seriously.

Lindsay sighed. Somehow, she had to make Alice believe her. Gritting her teeth, she forced herself out of the car, wiped her sweaty palms on her slacks, and started up the driveway.

The girls stopped their game and watched Lindsay approach. "I remember you," the younger girl said. "You're the lady from the park."

"That's right." Lindsay smiled. "Is your mother home?"

"We don't have a mom," the older girl said. "Alice takes care of us."

"Then I guess I need to see Alice."

The girl ran to the front door and slipped inside.

"You have to wait here," the younger girl said. "We're not supposed to bring strangers in the house."

Lindsay noticed again how easily she could have taken the trusting little girl and run away with her. She knelt down in front of her. "That's right, honey, but you also need to remember not to talk with strangers or go with anyone, no matter how nice they seem." She put her hand on the girl's shoulder to keep her attention, and the image of the brutalized body washed over her again. She pulled her hand away as if it had been scalded. The vision of the child was much clearer this time, and Lindsay was afraid she was going to be sick again. She knew she had to pull herself together. She couldn't let this little girl see how upset she really was; it would frighten her, and that was the last thing she wanted to do.

The door opened and Alice stepped out on the front porch with the older girl at her side. She frowned when she saw Lindsay talking to the younger girl.

"Mandy, you and Tracy go on inside and wait for me. I'll be there in a minute. I need to talk to this lady."

The girls scrambled inside, leaving the two women alone to talk.

Lindsay stood and turned to face Alice. "I'm truly sorry to bother you."

"Then why did you?"

Lindsay shrugged off the animosity, then stepped closer to Alice. She lowered her voice, not wanting her words to carry to the girls on the other side of the door. "I just can't stand by and do nothing when I know that little girl is in danger." Indicating the yard with her hand, she said, "They were out here alone."

Alice turned and started for the door. "Mr. Carpenter doesn't want me to talk to you, and he doesn't want you around the girls. They're his children; I have to respect his wishes. Please don't come here anymore."

"But they were out here alone!" Lindsay grabbed her arm. "Can't you see how dangerous that is?"

Alice pulled her arm from Lindsay's grasp. "Children need to be able to play, and besides, I can't be with them every moment."

"It would only take a moment for someone to snatch her. I could have easily taken her."

Without another word, Alice went back inside and closed the door. It was clear to Lindsay that these people were not going to watch the little girl. She would have to do it herself.

Lindsay sat in her car, sipping on a bottle of water as she watched the house across the street. The children had not been out to play in the front yard at all in the three days she had been on her stakeout. At least her presence was doing something. The girls were being kept inside and away from danger. But sitting in the car day after day was taking its toll on her. Not only was she missing work, but also she was tired and miserable.

She wondered again at the advisability of jeopardizing her job when she had no idea at all how long it would be until the danger to the child was over. She couldn't sit out here forever. Could she? And what would happen if the stalker did show up? Would she be able to stop him? There were so many questions that didn't seem likely to be answered any time soon.

The summer weather was hot and sticky, and sitting in a car was definitely not high on her list of fun things to do. Movement at the front door caught her eye. She sat up straight and watched Alice usher Mandy and Tracy out of the house and into a blue Saturn parked at the curb. Lindsay started her car, then flipped a U-turn and followed the Saturn down the block, relieved to be doing something.

Alice pulled into the parking lot of the Value Plus Market, and Lindsay breathed a sigh of relief. It was air-conditioned inside, and she would finally be able to get out of the heat. She parked her car and waited for Alice to get the girls out and go inside.

Lindsay grabbed a cart and followed at a distance as Alice walked through the store. She picked up a few snacks and another case of water that she would need if she was to keep up her surveillance. She was really in a quandary. After all, this was not her child. Why did she feel so compelled to keep watch when the girl's own family didn't seem to be at all concerned with her safety?

When Alice took her cart to the checkout stand, Lindsay quickly stepped into the express line and was checked out and waiting in her car before Alice and the girls emerged from the store. Alice drove straight home, and Lindsay parked across the street again and settled in again to watch.

Just as she opened a granola bar, a car pulled up in the driveway and a dark-haired man jumped out and ran to help Alice carry in her groceries. The man was not in the house long before the door opened and he walked down the driveway. He didn't stop at his car, though, and continued down the drive and across the street. Lindsay noted that he was a nice-looking man with curly dark hair and a disarming smile. And the smile never left his face as he approached her car.

"Hi." He bent over and looked in her open window. "My name's Eddie Dellacroix. Mandy is my niece."

"I'm Lindsay Ryan."

He squatted down so that he would not have to keep bending over to talk to Lindsay. "Alice told me what you've been doing, and I think it's commendable, but my brother-in-law doesn't quite see it that way." He crossed his arms and leaned them against the car door. "As a matter of fact, he's getting really pissed off and considering a restraining order."

"I'm sorry he feels that way. I'm only trying to protect his little girl. I just don't know how to make him believe me."

"I think that's a lost cause, but I believe you."

Lindsay smiled at the charming young man. It was nice to hear that at least someone in the family believed her. "Could you talk to him? Perhaps get him to at least give me the benefit of the doubt?"

Eddie nodded. "I'll try, but I think you and I need to get together and talk. When I have a better understanding of what's going on, I'll have a better chance of convincing Greg. Could you meet me at Mo's Steakhouse tonight at seven?"

"Sure. I know the place."

Eddie stood up and flashed that smile again. "Good, I'll see you then."

Lindsay leaned back and watched him go. She returned his wave as he drove away, then reached for her bottle of water. *Finally, someone believes me.*

Lindsay arrived at Mo's just before seven. She could hardly believe her good luck to have an ally, finally, in the little girl's family. Perhaps now she could get them to take the threat seriously.

A young man greeted her as she walked in. "How many in your party, ma'am?"

"Two, but I'm meeting him here and I'm not sure if he's arrived yet. May I take a quick look around?"

"Sure. If you don't find him, just come on back and I'll seat you."

"Thank you." Lindsay stepped past him and entered the dining room. She spotted Eddie, and he stood up and waved her over.

"I'm glad you could make it."

Lindsay sat across from him as a waiter arrived at their table.

"Can I get you something to drink?" The waiter handed her a menu.

"Just water, please, and I don't need a menu. I'm going to have your chef salad."

"What kind of dressing would you like on that?"

"Ranch, please."

Eddie handed the waiter his menu. "I'll have the New York steak, rare, with baked potato."

"Sour cream and chives?"

"No, just butter."

"Thank you," the waiter said. "I'll be right back with your water, ma'am."

Lindsay smiled. "Thank you."

Eddie placed both elbows on the table and leaned forward. "Why don't you start at the beginning and fill me in on everything that's happened."

Just then, the waiter arrived with Lindsay's water. "Thanks." She took a sip, then looked at Eddie. "I was eating lunch at the park one day when Mandy and Tracy were playing kickball. The ball got away from them, and I caught it to toss it back. As soon as I touched it, I had a vision of Mandy. It was horrible. I'd rather not describe what she looked like, but she was dead, and someone was shoveling dirt on her."

Eddie's dark eyebrows rose, but he kept silent. He encouraged Lindsay to continue with a nod of his head. She took another swallow of water.

"I went to Alice in the park and told her what I saw. When I continued to have visions, I felt compelled to find out what, if any, precautions had been taken. I guess Alice didn't believe me because when I found their house, I saw the girls playing in the front yard all by themselves. No one was even watching them. That's when I decided that I'd watch them."

"How do you know that the vision was real? Has this happened before? I mean, couldn't it have been a hallucination?"

"I don't do drugs, and I wasn't hallucinating." Her glare was defensive and frosty.

"I'm sorry. I didn't mean to imply that you do drugs."

"Didn't you?"

"Okay. Maybe I did. Look, I'm just trying to figure out what happened, and I'm trying to rule out all the possibilities so it's clear in my mind. I don't want to take up your cause with Greg only to find out later that you're a druggie and all this was just a bad trip."

Lindsay nodded. What he said made sense. "Sometimes I see things or events when I touch something. Things that have happened, or will happen, to the person who owns it. It's even stronger when I touch the person themselves."

"Why don't you go to the police?"

"They wouldn't believe me."

"But if you tell them what the man looked like—"

"I don't know what he looks like."

Eddie looked puzzled. "I thought you said you saw him shoveling dirt on Mandy?"

"No, I just saw her body and dirt slowly covering her. I could see the end of the shovel as it dumped the dirt, but nothing else." She ran her fingers through her hair. "God, I wish I could see more of him." She looked up at Eddie, a tear starting down her face. "And no one believes me."

"I believe you."

Lindsay smiled. "Thanks."

Lieutenant Rowers opened the door to his office, and his gaze fell on the attractive woman sitting across the room at a large desk. Her light brown skin, almond-shaped brown eyes, and well-defined cheekbones gave her an exotic look. She appeared to be deep in thought as she examined the contents of a large box that sat on a chair at her side. Detective Rachel Todd was a striking woman, but at forty-one years old, she had made her job the only love in her life. She radiated an air of confidence, and indeed, she'd earned it. Nineteen years on the job and she was damn good at what she did.

"Todd, in my office, now." The lieutenant turned, not waiting for his detective, and returned to sit behind his desk.

"What's up?" she asked as she dropped into the chair in front of his desk.

"This one's personal, Todd." He handed her a folder. "My wife's cousin thinks this woman is trying to pull a psychic scam on him, and from what I could dig up on her, he might be right. She has a history of this type of thing. It's all in that folder."

Rachel opened the folder and glanced through it as he continued.

"She hasn't asked for any money yet, so there's nothing we can do, but she's been hanging around in front of their place and shadowing them whenever they leave the house."

"So if she hasn't done anything yet, what is it you want me to do?"

"I want you to go talk to her. Scare her off. Tell her if she doesn't back off, we'll go after her as a stalker."

Rachel nodded. "I'll talk to her first thing tomorrow."

"Tonight. I want you to talk to her tonight. I'd do it myself, but I don't want to be accused of harassing her because someone in my family doesn't like her."

Rachel sat in her car in front of Lindsay Ryan's home and looked through her file again. No one had been home when she got to the residence, and she decided it was best to sit and wait. It would not do to go into work in the morning and tell the lieutenant that she hadn't talked to the woman. She glanced at her watch again just as an SUV pulled into the driveway. *Finally.*

She watched a man, a woman, and three small children get out of the SUV. "Excuse me," she said as she got out of her car.

"You take the kids in the house, hon, I'll see what she wants." The woman nodded and ushered her children up the walk and into the house.

Rachel pulled her shield and ID out of her pocket and held it up for the man to see. "My name is Detective Todd, and I'm looking for Lindsay Ryan. Does she live here?"

The man nodded and pointed to a tiny little place, perched atop a two-car garage. "She lives in the apartment above our garage."

"Thanks," Rachel said as she turned and started for the staircase leading up to the apartment. *Damn. If I'd had the correct information in the first place, I could have finished this and been home by now.* Before she got to the door of the apartment, it opened and a young woman with red hair started down the stairs. Rachel met the woman at the bottom step and held up her identification.

"Lindsay Ryan?"

"Yes."

"I'm Detective Todd. We've had a report that you've been stalking a five-year-old girl. Stalking is a crime we take very seriously, Ms. Ryan, especially when the victim is a small child."

"I'm not stalking her."

"Her father says you are."

"This is ludicrous. I'm just trying to keep her safe." Lindsay looked over and saw that her landlord was listening with interest to what was going on. *Oh, great. He's going to think I'm a pedophile.*

"Talk to the girl's uncle Eddie. He'll tell you."

"He'll tell me what? Oh, yeah, I forgot. You're just a misunderstood humanitarian who's just trying to protect a complete stranger. Now try telling me one I believe."

"Isn't that what you do, Detective Todd? Protect complete strangers?"

"The difference is it's my job. I get paid to protect complete strangers from people like you."

Lindsay was outraged but said nothing.

"Look, Ms. Ryan, I don't know what you're trying to pull here, but it's not going to work. We know you've done this sort of thing before with this psychic scam of yours."

"That was my father. If you'd done a little more checking, you'd know that. I was just as upset as the people he cheated. He used me too. The police picked up both of us, but they only charged him."

"What I see is a father who wanted to protect his daughter and took the rap for the both of you, and I've got to tell you that I have no patience with people who prey on the weaknesses of others."

Lindsay crossed her arms over her chest and glared at Detective Todd. "That's not what happened, but I guess you'll believe what you want to believe."

"I guess I will."

"Look. I haven't done anything wrong," Lindsay said, "so if you'll excuse me, I've got things to do." She brushed by the detective on the narrow stairs, and as their shoulders touched, another vision flashed in her mind. In this one, she saw bloody hands gripping a shovel. They were digging. Digging a grave. On the back of the left hand, she could see a tattoo that appeared to be the astrological symbol for Scorpio. The vision unnerved her, but at least it had given her an identifying feature of the little girl's murderer. It was a start.

"Stay away from Mandy Carpenter, Ms. Ryan."

Lindsay glanced back at the detective, and she saw it. A tattoo. Detective Todd had a tattoo on her left hand. The same tattoo. The hands in the vision were dirty and covered in blood, but the tattoo was clear. How could she have been so stupid? All this time, she had been thinking the murderer was a man. But there was no doubt in her mind that those were the hands, and that was the tattoo. She had succeeded in doing just the opposite of what she had intended to do. Instead of keeping Mandy safe, Lindsay was the cause of Detective Todd making contact with her.

CHAPTER TWO

The visit from Detective Todd had shaken Lindsay. Seeing that tattoo up close and personal had really scared her senseless, and she couldn't get over the fact that it was all her fault. *What the hell use is it to have visions if I keep interfering and can't help?* It made her more determined than ever to keep Mandy safe from that woman. But how could she keep the girl safe when the people around her didn't want her to?

Lindsay pulled from her purse the napkin that Eddie had written his number on and picked up the phone. She was glad she had thought to ask for his number.

"Hello?"

"Eddie?"

"Speaking."

"I know who the would-be murderer is."

"Lindsay?"

"Yes, it's me."

"You had another vision?"

"Yes, just a little while ago."

"You saw his face this time?"

"No, she just paid me a visit."

"The murderer?" He paused for a moment. "Hey, wait a minute. Who paid you a visit? I thought you said the murderer was a man?"

"I thought so, really, but in this vision I saw hands digging a grave. The left hand had a tattoo. She had the exact same tattoo. It was her. I know it." Lindsay's voice broke and she started to cry. "What am I going to do, Eddie? It's all my fault."

"It's not your fault."

"It is. Don't you see? If I hadn't been so obstinate in trying to keep Mandy safe, her father would never have called the police. I'm the reason that woman's involved in all this."

"A policewoman? Are you joking? You're telling me the murderer is a policewoman?"

"Yes," Lindsay said with a sob. "Hold on a minute." She put down the phone and headed for the bathroom. Taking a deep breath, she ran some cold water in the sink and then splashed it on her face.

Feeling a little more in control, she returned to the couch and dropped down on it dejectedly. "I'm back. Sorry."

"You okay?"

"Eddie, you've got to get me in to see your brother-in-law." Lindsay said, ignoring his question. "We have to convince him I'm telling the truth. Get him to call off the cops." She ran her fingers through her hair. "Maybe there's still time. Maybe she hasn't seen Mandy yet."

She thought a moment. "Wait a minute. If it's not Mandy, she'll just go after someone else." She got up and began to pace back and forth. "Oh, God, Eddie, how can we stop her?"

Lindsay parked her car across the street from the Carpenter house and turned off the engine. Eddie had said he would meet her there, but she didn't see his car yet. Perhaps he had run into heavy traffic. She sat back to wait and glanced at her watch. Nine o'clock. The girls should be in bed.

The porch light came on and the front door opened. A man she assumed was Greg Carpenter came out and stood a moment facing her car. Then suddenly he walked rapidly across the street.

"What the fuck do I have to do to get you to leave my family alone?"

Lindsay got out of her car. "Please, if you could just listen to me—"

"I already called the cops on you, lady, so get the hell out of here or they'll be hauling your ass off to jail!"

"A police detective came to see me about an hour ago. That's why I'm here. Eddie's supposed to meet me here so we can talk to you."

"Eddie? What's Eddie got to do with any of this?"

"I told him about the detective who came to see me. She's the one from my visions. She's the one who will hurt Mandy if we don't stop her. Eddie will help me convince you that I'm telling the truth."

"Ha! If you think I'll listen to anything my wife's idiot brother has to say, you're stupider than you look. Now get the fuck out of here." With that, he turned and stormed back across the street into his house.

Lindsay got back in her car and sat a moment, wondering if she should wait for Eddie or leave before the police came. This time, they might actually do what Greg Carpenter said and haul her off to jail. It was clear that the irate man was not in the mood to listen to anything she had to say. Perhaps it was best if she left. Eddie could talk to him alone, if he ever came. Maybe Greg would listen if she were not there to make him mad.

The decision made, Lindsay started her car and drove home.

"She what!" Rachel slammed the door to Lieutenant Rowers's office.

"Calm down, Todd." Lieutenant Rowers pulled out his guest chair and motioned for her to sit.

"It's kind of hard to be calm when someone accuses you of being a murderer." Rachel dropped down in the chair and crossed her arms over her chest. "Try it sometime, Ben, and see if you like it."

"Consider the source and chill. You know we're not taking anything she says seriously."

"It still pisses me off. I'd love nothing more than to wring her pretty little neck."

The lieutenant laughed. "You and me both. Greg was hopping mad when he called me last night." Rowers sipped his coffee and frowned. It was cold. "I had to laugh, though, when he told me what she said about you. I mean, where does she come up with this stuff?" He got up, walked to the microwave, and placed his cup inside. "This broad's crazy as a loon if she thinks we're gonna believe her." He punched the timer, emphasizing his point.

Rachel shook her head. "That's what I can't figure out. She knows no one will believe her, so why say it?" She leaned forward and rested her arms on the desk. "I just don't get it." She pursed her lips in thought. "What if she's trying to build a reputation as a genuine psychic? What better way than to predict something like this and name the perp. Perhaps she believes she's clever enough to do it and set me up to take the fall. The lesson in the press would be that if they had listened to her, the disaster could have been averted. Probably figures with all the publicity, people would be beating down her door, offering her money to prevent whatever catastrophe she may see in their future."

"Sounds far-fetched, but you may just have something there, Todd."

"Let me go pick her up." Rachel stood up. "I'd like to talk to her again. Maybe she'll break. We may not have enough to hold her more than forty-eight hours, but we can keep her away from the Carpenters for a while."

Rowers nodded. "Do it."

A loud banging on her door awakened Lindsay.

"Police, Ms. Ryan, open the door."

"Just a minute, I'm not dressed." Lindsay jumped out of bed and grabbed the clothes she had taken off the night before. The knocking came again. "I'm coming, I'm coming." She opened the door, and a scowling Detective Todd greeted her.

"I need you to come with me, Ms. Ryan." She put her hand on Lindsay's shoulder and turned her around. "Spread your legs." Lindsay complied and the detective patted her down. "You're under arrest for stalking Mandy Carpenter." She placed a handcuff on Lindsay's left hand and reached for the other. "You have the right to remain silent—"

"Please," Lindsay interrupted. "You got me out of bed and I really need to pee." She looked over her shoulder at the detective. "Can't you at least let me go to the bathroom first? I need to brush my teeth too."

Detective Todd removed the cuff. “Okay, but leave the door open. We wouldn’t want you climbing out a window, now, would we?”

Tears started down Lindsay’s cheeks again as she headed to the bathroom. She wiped them away. This situation was going from bad to worse. If she went to jail, there would be no one to watch Mandy.

Lindsay used the toilet, then washed her hands and splashed water on her face. God, she was tired. Her hair was mussed and tangled, her eyes puffy and swollen. She had spent half the night pacing and crying. She hadn’t been able to get in touch with Eddie, and she was just plain scared of what was going to happen.

“Hurry up. I don’t have all day.”

“I just need to brush my teeth,” Lindsay said as she picked up her toothbrush and squeezed toothpaste on it. *I wonder if they told her what I said about her last night.* She looked over at the woman standing in the doorway, shooting daggers at her. *Yep, they told her.* She rinsed out her mouth, placed her toothbrush in the holder on the back of the sink, and turned toward the door. *Well, can’t put this off any longer.*

At the police station, Detective Todd opened a door to a small room and ushered Lindsay inside. The room was empty except for a lone table with four chairs around it. A large mirror hung on one wall, and all the other walls were bare.

“Sit down, Ms. Ryan, and make yourself comfortable. You’re going to be here a while.” The detective reached over and unlocked the cuffs, then sat on the table edge opposite Lindsay. “Okay, let’s try this again. You say you received a premonition that Mandy was in danger.”

Lindsay nodded. “I’ve told you all this before.”

“Well, I guess you’re going to have to tell it again.”

“Okay, when I touched the ball in the park, I saw Mandy’s nude body lying in a grave. It was covered with cuts and bruises, and someone was shoveling dirt on her.”

“And you could see the person shoveling the dirt?”

“No. I could not see the person.” Lindsay ran a hand through her hair. *Why do we have to go over all this again?*

The detective nodded. “Then what happened?”

"I went to the woman who I thought was her mother, and I told her about what I saw."

"Okay, Ms. Ryan, now we get to the stalking part. You relayed your warning to the family. It should have ended there, but it didn't. You started stalking them. Why is that?"

"Because the visions intensified. When they wouldn't stop, I knew the family didn't believe me. That they weren't going to keep the little girl safe." Lindsay leaned forward. "I couldn't just leave her to that fate. Someone had to protect her."

"So you appointed yourself as her guardian?"

Lindsay sat back in her chair and crossed her arms over her chest. "Something like that, yeah."

"Okay..." Detective Todd stood up and walked around to stand beside Lindsay. "And where do I come into this fantasy of yours?"

Lindsay looked her right in the eye. "It was your hands I saw in the vision. You were digging Mandy's grave."

"And you know this how?"

"I recognized that tattoo." Lindsay's gaze dropped to the detective's hand.

"I don't appreciate being labeled a murderer, Ms. Ryan."

With defiance, Lindsay brought her eyes back up to look the detective in the eye. "I saw your hands."

"Very slick, Ms. Ryan." Detective Todd pulled up a chair and sat down. "Now, how about the truth."

"I told you the truth, Detective Todd. Now I think I want a lawyer."

The detective got to her feet without saying a word and walked to the door. She motioned at Lindsay to follow. "Come on."

They walked down the hall until they reached a door with a keypad on the wall next to it. Rachel punched in some numbers and the door opened. They walked another twenty feet and came to a second door, which the detective opened the same way.

On the other side of the door was a desk. "Hey, Frank," Detective Todd said to the man behind the desk. "This is Lindsay Ryan. Stick her in lockup until we can get a PD down here to talk to her." She looked at Lindsay. "Have fun, Ms. Ryan." And with that, she was gone.

Frank handed Lindsay a large envelope. “Print your name and address here, and sign here. Remove any jewelry, belts, and shoelaces, and put them, along with any other personal possessions on your person, in the envelope.”

Lindsay placed her purse in the envelope, then unlaced her shoes and took off her watch and dropped those items in as well.

Frank sealed it and stuck it in a slot marked *R*. Then he picked up the phone and punched in a number. “Deb, I’ve got a female for lockup who needs to be processed. Could you come get her? Thanks.”

Within moments, a woman officer rounded the corner and approached them. Frank handed her some paperwork and she nodded at him, then turned to Lindsay.

“Okay, follow me.” She led Lindsay to a small vacant room and closed the door. “Take your clothes off.”

Lindsay complied and submitted to the humiliation of a strip search. Then she was led to a holding cell, with stops along the way to pick up a sheet and blanket and a sack lunch.

“Hold on to these, you’ll need ’em.” Deb unlocked the cell door and stepped aside.

Clutching the bedding, Lindsay walked into the cell and looked around. Everything was either cement or steel. Two bunks were bolted to the wall, and a stainless steel sink and toilet were bolted to the wall and the floor.

Lindsay’s stomach growled and she remembered that she hadn’t eaten that morning. She picked up the brown bag, looked inside, and found a bologna sandwich and an apple. After she finished eating, she looked at her wrist, only then remembering that they had taken her watch. Pulling her legs up to her chest, she wrapped her arms around them and rested her head on her knees. This was going to be a long day.

The guards were just passing out the dinner trays on the second day when Lindsay was pulled out of the cell and taken back to the same small room that she had been in the previous day with Detective Todd. A young man sat at the table in the same seat that she had used. When she walked in, he stood and extended his hand.

"Miss Ryan, I'm Paul Richards, your public defender." She shook his hand, and he pulled out a chair for her. "Please sit down, Miss Ryan."

Lindsay sat and the young man walked around the table and sat across from her. *He looks so young. Is he really a lawyer?*

"I was just looking over your paperwork while I waited for them to bring you out, Miss Ryan, and I've got a few questions for you." He glanced down at the folder on the table. "Did you ever touch or threaten Mandy Carpenter?"

Lindsay shook her head. "No, I never threatened Mandy. I was trying to keep her safe." She thought a moment. "Wait, I did touch her shoulder once. That was the first day I visited the Carpenter house. Alice asked me not to come back to the house, so after that, I sat across the street in my car. I never went on their property again and never spoke to any of the Carpenter children, only the girl's uncle Eddie and Greg Carpenter. And *they* came to me. I didn't approach *them*."

"I'll have you out of here today, Miss Ryan. I'm just sorry you had to spend the night in jail. They don't have enough here to make a stalking charge stick. You've made no threat, implied or otherwise. Unless they've got more than they've shown me, we've got no problems here."

"Rachel, why do you have to be so distrusting? Perhaps this woman does have the gift of vision."

"You wouldn't trust either, if you saw what I see every day. The world is full of predators, Mother, and it's my job to get them off the street."

"There are genuine seers; you've seen them yourself. When you—"

"No," Rachel interrupted. "When I was a kid, I believed in that stuff. I also believed in Santa Claus. Does that make him real? Besides, now her story has changed. Now she's trying to convince everyone that I'm the murderer." She held up her hand. "Claims she saw my tattoo in her visions."

"Perhaps she just misinterpreted what she saw. Visions are always subject to interpretation, and the person receiving them may not always be able to decipher the riddle correctly. I've seen it happen."

Waheya walked to her daughter and placed a hand on each cheek. "Oh, sweetheart, what has this job done to you?" She looked deeply into her daughter's eyes. "The world is full of people, some bad, some good. I don't deny that there are bad people out there, but don't let your job turn you away from the fact that the good far outnumber the bad."

"Yes, and they need to be protected. Mother, this woman is a scam artist and a stalker. She's a predator, and her target's an innocent little girl. This psychic vision bullshit is just the ploy she's using to make herself famous, and she's using a little girl to do it. I have to stop her."

Abruptly, Rachel turned and strolled to the couch. She picked up her glass of tea from the coffee table before sitting down. She knew she wasn't going to convince her mother; in fact, she didn't want her mother's faith in people to change. That was one of the things she loved so about her. Leaning back, Rachel closed her eyes and brought the chilled glass to her aching head. *Why did I have to mention this case to her*? "I'm tired and I have a headache. Could we please talk about something pleasant?"

Waheya sat next to her and squeezed her free hand. "Just one more thing and I'm done."

Rachel groaned, but she opened her eyes and smiled. She realized that she came by her stubborn streak honestly. "Okay, just one more thing."

"Let's say that the odds are 80 percent against this being a genuine vision—"

"Try 99 percent."

"Okay, 99. That still leaves a chance—"

"Mother..." Rachel sighed.

"A slight chance," Waheya continued, "that this child is in danger." She squeezed her daughter's hand again. "If it were Trish, would you leave even 1 percent to chance?"

"But we're not talking about Trish." Rachel felt her heart clench at the sound of her daughter's name.

"She's someone's daughter," Waheya continued. "Could you live with yourself if something happened to that child and you did nothing to try to prevent it?"

"I am doing something." Rachel closed her eyes again as memories of a daughter lost to her washed over her. She kept that part of her life locked away. It hurt too much. Trish had made a choice, and there was nothing Rachel could do about it. She opened her eyes and revealed the longing that she was usually so good at hiding. "You know I hate it when you bring up Trish."

"She needs her mother."

Rachel pulled her hand away, anger rising quickly in her face. "Trish made a choice. She picked the woman she wanted to call Mother, and it sure as hell wasn't me!" Rachel stood and strode quickly across the room.

"She was fifteen years old when she made that decision. She was having a hard time accepting that her mother was a lesbian. You know what it's like for girls that age."

"Of course I do. I let her go live with them, didn't I?" Rachel gripped the glass in her hand tightly, her knuckles turning white. "What about when she was twenty and announced she was getting married? She wasn't a child anymore, but she still wouldn't introduce me to her fiancé as her mother." Rachel's hand shook, tea spilling over the edge of the glass. "How do you think that made me feel? It was a life sentence. She married the man, for God's sake." There was a cracking sound as the glass shattered, and she just stood, staring at the mess of spilled tea and broken glass on the floor.

Waheya gently took Rachel's arm. "Come on, hon, let's get this cleaned up."

Rachel nodded mutely and pulled herself back together. The mask she used to hide her emotions, even from her mother, fell back into place. She let her mother lead her into the kitchen, surprised when she saw blood running down the sink as Waheya rinsed off her bleeding hand. She could see bits of broken glass and held still as her mother carefully picked them out of her hand.

Rachel had been hurt and angry that her daughter was embarrassed to introduce her to her fiancé and his holier-than-thou family. But when Trish had said she could come to the wedding, with the stipulation that she exclude Lisa, it was the last straw. That was the last time she had seen Trish, and she had never seen the baby. Well, she had seen pictures of David; her own mother had kept her well supplied with those. And the videos Waheya had given her were nearly worn out from so many viewings.

Eddie parked in front of Lindsay's apartment.

"Thanks for picking me up and bringing me home, Eddie. I really appreciate it," Lindsay said as she got out of the car. "That bitch was happy to drag me down there, but apparently the taxi service only runs one way."

"No problem. I'm just sorry you had to spend all that time in jail." He followed her up the narrow stairs to her apartment and waited for her to open the door.

Lindsay tried her key and it wouldn't fit in the lock. Puzzled, she turned it the other way and tried it again with no luck.

"Something wrong?" Eddie peered over her shoulder.

"My key doesn't work." She looked over her shoulder at him. "My landlord must have changed the lock."

"He can't do that."

Lindsay held up the key. "Well, he apparently did." Her expression changed to anger and she marched down the stairs with purpose. At the front door of her landlord's house, she knocked loudly. When he opened the door, Lindsay's anger was full blown. "Why did you change my lock?" she asked, as Eddie stepped up on the porch behind her.

"Just check your mailbox and beat it. We don't want your kind here." He started to close the door in her face.

Eddie reached out and stopped the door from closing. "You can't just lock her out like that. There are procedures to follow when you want to evict a tenant. Haven't you ever heard of a little thing called the law?"

"And what are you, a cop?" The landlord's voice was full of sarcasm.

Eddie reached into his pocket and pulled out a shield. "As a matter of fact, I am." He held it up for the man to see. "Now give her the new key so she can get into her apartment."

The landlord's attitude changed somewhat at the sight of Eddie's ID. "You have to understand...we have children here. We can't keep someone under our roof who might hurt them."

Eddie started to speak, but Lindsay stopped him. “It’s okay, Mr. Mills. I don’t blame you for being concerned after the way I was hauled out of here. Just give me a week or so to find another place, and I’ll get my stuff out of here.”

“Your belongings are already gone.” Mills nodded toward the mailbox in the front yard. “I left a letter with the name of the place and the key to the storage unit in your mailbox. It’s paid up for a month. After that, it’s your problem. Like I said before, this is our home and we don’t want you here.”

Lindsay turned around without a word and walked to the mailbox. Those people going through all her personal belongings felt like such a violation. She was used to people thinking she was weird, but the disgust in her landlord’s voice when he’d said, “We don’t want your kind here,” was hard to take. She reached into the box and collected her mail, then turned to find Eddie leaning against his car.

“Eddie, thanks for your help. I seem to be losing all sense of myself, and you’re the only one on my side.” Tears were ready to escape, but she held on to her last shred of dignity...almost. “Okay, I have to regroup. I have to...”

Eddie reached over and brushed the tears off her face with his thumb. “Hey, it’ll be okay. You can stay at my place till you figure out where you’re going to go. Come on, we’ll go in my car. You can come back for yours later.”

“Thanks.” Lindsay gave him a half-hearted smile. At least she had some place to stay the night. “I didn’t know you were a cop,” she said, suddenly remembering the badge he had flashed to Mr. Mills.

“I’m on leave of absence from the Spokane Police Department. I was involved in a shooting incident, and I took some time off to get my head together. Decide if I really want to be a cop. I’ve never had to kill anyone before, and it really shook me up. I needed to get away for a while.” He turned the key in the ignition. The motor started and he pulled away from the curb. “They made me see a shrink, but when they okayed me to go back to work, I asked for a few more weeks. I wasn’t sure they’d give ’em to me, but they did.”

Lindsay’s smile grew broader. “I’m glad they did. I really need a friend right now.”

Eddie returned the smile. "I hope you don't mind staying a bit out of town. I'm staying at my grandfather's cabin. It's not too far out, though."

Lindsay suddenly doubted the advisability of going out to the boondocks with someone who was not much more than a stranger. But he was a cop, after all, and he had been nothing but kind to her.

"How about this, since I'm starving. Let's get something to eat. Give you a chance to pull yourself together. Then we'll come back for your car, and you can follow me to the cabin. How's that sound?"

Lindsay wiped her face again and nodded. "Sounds great."

Lindsay awoke to the smell of coffee brewing. She sat up and stretched, feeling fairly well rested for the first time in two weeks. Perhaps it was because she felt safe knowing that Eddie was in the front room, sleeping on the couch. Whatever the reason, it felt good.

She shrugged into the robe Eddie had given her to wear while she washed out her clothes and headed for the bathroom. "Boy, that coffee sure smells good," she called out before entering the bathroom for her morning routine.

"You ready for some breakfast?" Eddie called back. "I've got some pancake batter ready to go here."

"Sounds wonderful. I'd love some. I'll only be a minute."

When she arrived in the kitchen, the table was set and Eddie was at the stove flipping the pancakes. "That's what I call service."

Eddie turned around and flashed a smile. He waved his spatula toward the coffeepot. "Help yourself to some coffee. These are almost ready."

"Where do you keep the cups?"

"They're in the cupboard to the left of the sink."

Lindsay grabbed a cup and poured the coffee. "Anything I can do to help?"

"Nope, I think I've got everything covered." He put the last pancake on the plate and carried it to the table. "Dig in."

"You don't have to tell me twice," Lindsay said as she picked up her fork and stabbed it through two of the cakes and slid them onto her plate.

Eddie put a stack of pancakes on his plate and reached for the syrup. "I'm glad to see you look so much better this morning. I was worried about you."

"I feel better. Last night was the first good sleep I've had in a while."

Eddie smiled. "I'll only be here two more weeks, but you're welcome to stay until I close up the place and go home."

Lindsay shook her head. "I couldn't impose on you like that."

"Don't be silly. It's because of my family that you're homeless. The least I can do is provide you with a place to stay while you look for a new apartment."

"I don't know how to thank you."

"No thanks necessary." Eddie smiled. "It's my pleasure. I hate to eat and run, Lindsay, but I need to get my ass in gear and get out of here."

Lindsay glanced at her watch. "Darn, it's later than I thought. I've got to get out of here too."

"Oh, no, you don't." Eddie shook his fork at her. "You're staying here and taking it easy today. That's an order."

"But Mandy—"

"You don't need to worry about Mandy. I'll watch over her today. She'll be fine." He grinned. "You just relax and stay out of trouble." He stuffed the last bite in his mouth. "Well, gotta go."

"Miss Ryan doesn't live here anymore," the landlord called out as the police detective knocked on the door of the garage apartment.

Rachel turned and walked down the stairs. "When did she move out?"

"Yesterday."

"Did she happen to leave a forwarding address?"

"No, but she and that cop she left with looked pretty chummy. Maybe you should ask him."

"A cop? Did you catch his name?"

"Nah, he showed me his ID, but I wasn't paying attention. I think his name might have been Edward. He was a big fellow with curly brown hair. Drove a Ford with Washington plates."

The description sounded like Greg Carpenter's brother-in-law, Eddie, but Carpenter had never mentioned that Eddie was a cop.

Rachel pulled one of her cards out of her pocket and handed it to the man. "If she gets back to you with a forwarding address, please give me a call."

"I sure will," he said, taking the card and shoving it in his pocket.

Rachel turned and walked back to her car. None of this made any sense. Would Greg Carpenter's brother-in-law take in the woman who had been stalking his niece? This just kept getting stranger and stranger. Then again, Ms. Ryan was damn attractive. *Perhaps he has the hots for her.*

She pulled out her Palm Pilot and looked up Carpenter's work number. *I bet that if I can find Eddie, I'll also find Ms. Ryan.* She punched in the number on her cell phone.

"Greg Carpenter speaking."

"Mr. Carpenter, this is Detective Todd. I've got a couple of questions I'd like to ask about your brother-in-law, Eddie Dellacroix."

"Why the questions about Eddie?"

"To tell you the truth, I think he's attracted to Ms. Ryan, and I hoped he could help me locate her. I need to know where he lives."

"He's been staying at his grandfather's old place."

"Do you have that address?"

"Sure, hold on a minute."

Rachel waited while he looked up the address and gave it to her. Her mother's words kept playing in her head. If it were Trish, would she leave even 1 percent to chance? *No, I couldn't,* she thought. *I've got to talk to Ms. Ryan one more time.*

"Thanks, Mr. Carpenter. There's just one more thing I need to know. Is your brother-in-law, Eddie, a police officer?"

"Eddie, a cop? Hell, no. Where'd you ever get an idea like that?"

"Ms. Ryan's landlord told me that she went away with a cop, and the description he gave sounded as if it might have been Eddie. Guess he was wrong." She thanked him again for the information.

Lindsay Ryan's history still bothered Rachel, but she might have told the truth. And what if these visions about Mandy were real and she'd been telling the truth about that too? *The woman didn't even blink when she looked me in the eye and told me she saw my hands digging a grave.* Could it be, as Waheya had suggested, that Lindsay had simply misinterpreted what the vision meant? Rachel shook her head and started the car. She really needed to talk to Lindsay Ryan again. There were just too many questions and not enough answers.

The drive out to the cabin took about thirty minutes. As Rachel turned onto the dirt access road, her cell phone rang.

"Todd."

"The girl's gone missing!" Lieutenant Rowers's voice boomed into her ear.

"What?" Rachel stopped the car. "When?"

"They're not sure. They've been looking for her for about half an hour. Wanted to make sure she was really missing before they called us. We've got to find that Ryan woman and bring her in for questioning."

"I'm on it. I'll get back to you as soon as I pick her up."

Rachel started the car moving again, but the washboard surface of the dirt road made driving with any speed impossible. *Damn, I was hoping I was wrong about her.* Slowly, she made her way to a clear spot where she could pull over and park. She walked up the hill and onto the wooden porch, then paused in front of the door.

Hearing footsteps on the porch, Lindsay smiled. Eddie was home. She hurried to the door to greet him and then backed away from what she saw. The late afternoon created a striking silhouette in the doorway. It was Detective Todd.

One look at the woman and Lindsay knew, without having to be told, that something had happened to Mandy. She felt it in her bones. *Has she killed her already? Is she here now to get rid of me too?* She was so scared she could taste it. How had the detective found her? Lindsay's heart was pounding so loudly that she could hardly hear herself think. *This is it. This is where she kills me.*

"Why are you doing this?" She backed away from the detective in the doorway.

"Look, let's just cut to the chase. The little girl is missing, just as you predicted. I don't know if I believe you, but I'm not going to discount any possibility." The detective watched Lindsay's face. "If you're involved, it'll go easier on you if you cooperate and tell me where the girl is." Rachel advanced and Lindsay fought down her panic. "I need you to come to the station with me. We need to ask you some questions."

Lindsay looked around furtively for a way to escape. Though she had had no vision, she was certain that the detective was going to take her to some out-of-the-way place to kill her. There was no way to escape the cabin except the door that Detective Todd was blocking.

Pretending to cooperate, she nodded and started for the door. As soon as she cleared the doorway, she bolted, knowing her very life depended on staying ahead of the detective. To her left was a hill with a few scrub weeds and bushes along one edge. Not wanting to run uphill when she could see no place to conceal herself, she swung around and headed for a stand of trees not far in the distance. If she could just make it to the tree line, there might be a chance to hide. Adrenaline pumped through her body, giving her feet wings.

Damn! Why do they always have to do it the hard way? Rachel started after the woman at an even pace, her longer legs eating up the distance between them.

Lindsay thought her lungs were going to burst. She would have given anything to be able to stop running. She could hear the steady pounding of the detective's feet and knew she was almost on her. Suddenly, she felt arms around her, and they were both falling. If she hadn't been so scared, it would have been a relief to stop running. She lay on the ground gasping for breath. This was it. It was over.

Instead, Detective Todd stood up and pulled Lindsay to her feet. They were both breathing hard, but the policewoman held tight to her arm and started walking her back toward the cabin.

It took a moment for Lindsay to notice that Eddie's car was parked at the bottom of the hill. Eddie knew about the tattoo, and Lindsay knew he would help her if he could. *Please don't let her notice his car...please!*

They reached the cabin, but Detective Todd kept them moving past it toward her car.

"Can I please go to the bathroom before we go?"

The detective rolled her eyes. "You've got to be kidding."

"I really need to go. Please. I don't think I can make it down the hill without wetting myself if I don't go first."

"Okay, but I'm going in with you. I'm too tired to chase you down again."

"I won't try to run away again."

"You'll forgive me, Ms. Ryan, if I don't believe you."

Lindsay saw the door to the cabin open behind the detective, and Eddie stepped quietly onto the porch. When Lindsay saw the gun in his hand, she breathed a sigh of relief.

Eddie fired and she watched in horror as Detective Todd dropped to the ground. She had wanted him to subdue her, not shoot her.

While Eddie was disarming the detective, Lindsay ran inside and returned a moment later with the cordless phone. She had just started to dial 911 when Eddie knocked the phone out of her hand.

"What do you think you're doing?"

"Calling the police," Lindsay replied, trying to control her rising panic.

"Are you crazy? You think I want to get arrested for shooting a cop?"

"They'll understand when we explain to them what happened. She took Mandy. They'll have to believe me now."

Eddie shook his head. "What makes you think they're gonna believe you this time? They think you're a crazy woman as it is."

Tears started down Lindsay's face, and she reached up and scrubbed them away. "They have to believe me this time. You'll back up my story. I'm sure they'll believe another cop."

"He's...not...a cop."

Lindsay's gaze tracked to Detective Todd, who was clutching her thigh in apparent agony. She could see blood seeping through the detective's fingers and soaking into the dirt. "Why would I believe anything you have to say? You kidnapped Mandy."

"No." Rachel shook her head. "He's been...lying to you."

"You're wrong. I saw his ID."

Dirt sticking to her bloody hands, Rachel tried to push herself into a sitting position. "Anyone can get...one of those for the right...price."

"You're losing a lot of blood." Lindsay turned back to Eddie. "We've got to get her some help."

Eddie shook his head. "I have no intention of letting her go."

"What do you mean?"

"He means...he's going to finish what he started...and kill me."

"No. He wouldn't do that." Lindsay looked over to the big man. "Tell her, Eddie."

Eddie shook his head and pointed his gun at her. "Go help the cop up. We've got work to do."

CHAPTER THREE

Lindsay helped the detective up and supported her with an arm around her waist. Eddie made them walk around to the back of the cabin where a padlocked shed stood off to the side. He reached into his pocket and pulled out a set of keys.

"Open the door," he said, tossing the keys to Lindsay. "You'll find a shovel inside. Get it."

She caught the keys and stepped up to door. The lock gave way easily and she grabbed the shovel as ordered.

"We only have one shovel, so you two will have to take turns digging." Eddie pointed to a clear spot about fifty feet away. "Over there." He gave Lindsay a shove. "Get going."

Lindsay again wrapped her arm around the injured detective and helped her walk toward the site where Eddie wanted them to dig. It was slow going, and she winced every time she heard the detective groan in pain. "I'm so sorry, Detective Todd. This is all my fault. I really thought you were the one."

"It's not your...fault."

Lindsay felt the detective falter and dropped the shovel to keep her from falling. Once she had her steady again, she picked up the shovel and gave it to the detective to use as a support on the other side. "If only I'd understood what I was seeing, we wouldn't be in this mess. I'm sorry."

When they arrived at the spot, Rachel was surprised to see that a hole had already been dug. *Mandy's grave.* She looked around for the body of the child. "Where is she?"

"She's waiting for me in the cabin. I haven't had a chance to have my fun with her yet." Eddie sneered at her. "My, my, you don't look very well, Detective Todd. I think you'd better take the first shift. Wouldn't want you to pass out before you get to take your turn."

Lindsay took the shovel from Rachel. "She's in no condition to dig."

"Give her the shovel." Eddie raised his gun and pointed it at Lindsay. "She digs her grave, you dig yours." He raised his eyebrows and feigned concern. "Nothin' wrong with your arms now, is there, Detective Todd?"

Rachel fought to keep her head clear as she reached to take the shovel back from Lindsay.

"I can do it." Lindsay stubbornly shook her head and hung on to it. "You're hurt, Detective Todd."

Eddie grabbed the shovel and backhanded Lindsay, causing her to stagger a few steps. He turned and thrust the shovel at Rachel, then backed away so he was close enough to keep both women in sight but out of reach if they decided to try to use the shovel as a weapon.

Keeping most of her weight on her uninjured leg, Rachel took the shovel and jabbed it into the ground. She was breathing hard and having difficulty staying on her feet. The pain was excruciating, but she kept at it. A wave of dizziness came over her, and she clutched the shovel for support.

Lindsay saw her sway unsteadily and came to her side instantly. "Are you okay, Detective Todd?"

"I...think," she gasped, glancing at Lindsay's tear-stained face, "if we're going...to die together...we should at least be on a...first-name basis. Call me Rachel."

Lindsay swallowed hard, the realization that they were indeed going to die together apparently starting to sink in.

"Stop the chatting," Eddie said. "Dig."

Rachel felt Lindsay's eyes on her watching her dig. As she watched her own hands scoop the dirt out of the growing hole, she wondered exactly how they had looked in Lindsay's vision.

Her good leg beginning to tire, Rachel struggled to maintain her balance. Blood streamed steadily down her thigh, and she was beginning to feel cold, even though she was sweating. She felt a shiver go through her body as another wave of light-headedness swept over her. Dropping to her knees, she took a few shallow breaths. She felt shaky and weak and it took effort to hold her head upright. Lindsay immediately squatted down beside her.

Eddie came close and nudged Rachel rudely with his foot. "Get back on your feet and keep digging."

As quickly as she could, Rachel scooped up some loose dirt and tossed it into his eyes. "Run, Lindsay!" She used the last of her strength to tackle Eddie, and they both went down, but he was on his feet again in a matter of moments.

"Fucking bitch!" He kicked Rachel hard in her injured leg, then wiped frantically at the dirt in his eyes. "God damn it!" He stumbled toward the water spigot beside the tool shed.

God, what I'd give for a cell phone, Lindsay thought as she rounded the corner of the cabin. She glanced at the open door and wondered if she should take the time to go in and call for help. She had no idea how long the dirt would delay Eddie, but she turned and ran toward the porch anyway. Hopefully, he would run on by in his search, giving her a precious bit of time. Grabbing the phone off the porch, she ran into the cabin, ducked down behind the couch, and quickly dialed 911.

"Nine-one-one, what is your emergency?"

"Police, I need the police! There's a man trying to kill us. He already shot a police detective and kidnapped a little girl. We need the police and an ambulance."

"What is your name, ma'am, and where are you calling from?"

"My name is Lindsay Ryan, and the woman Eddie shot is Detective Rachel Todd. I don't know the address here, and I can't stay on the phone. He'll find me. I'll leave the phone off the hook so you can trace the number. Please hurry."

Lindsay set the phone down and crawled to the window. She saw Eddie drop a water hose and scan the surrounding area. Then he started up the hill, away from the cabin. *Please let him keep going that way...please.*

She crawled to the bedroom door, opened it, and slipped inside. She found Mandy lying on the bed, her feet and hands bound by duct tape. Her mouth was also covered, and tears ran down her cheeks.

"Shh, it's okay, sweetie, I'm gonna get you out of here." Precious moments passed as she crawled to her purse, grabbed her nail kit, and pulled out a pair of cuticle scissors. They weren't very big, but they would have to do. When she finally got all the tape off, the little girl clutched on to her and sobbed.

"We've got to be really quiet so he won't find us, Mandy. Do you think you can do that?" The little girl nodded. "Good girl. Come on, we're getting out of here."

Lindsay opened the bedroom window and motioned for Mandy to come to her. She helped the little girl out and then followed her. Once they were both safely outside, she grabbed Mandy's hand and ran to where Rachel still lay in the freshly dug dirt. She had to get her up and moving before Eddie came to see if she had doubled back. Dusk would give way to nightfall soon, and if they could just stay ahead of him until then, the darkness would make them that much harder to find.

"Rachel," she called, tapping the unconscious woman on the cheek. "Rachel, wake up."

Nothing.

She slapped her harder, and Rachel moaned. "Detective Todd, you have to get up."

Rachel heard a voice calling from a great distance, and she tried to focus on it. Blackness threatened to engulf her again, and she felt a hard slap to her face. Moaning, she opened her eyes to slits and tried to focus on the face above her.

"Lindsay?"

"Yes, it's me. We don't have much time. You have to get up. I can't carry you."

"I can't," Rachel whispered. "Just...get out of here."

"Yes, you can, I know you can. We don't have time to argue about it...please, get up." Lindsay sounded very anxious and almost frantic. She grabbed Rachel's hand.

Rachel pushed Lindsay's hand away and glanced at Mandy. In that one heartbeat of crystal-clear thought, she realized how wrong she, too, had been. "Just take the girl and leave. I'll only slow you down."

"I have no intention of leaving you here. Now get up!" Lindsay slapped her again. "That's an order, Detective Todd!"

At the command, Rachel's years of training kicked in, and she struggled to get to her feet. With Lindsay's help, she managed the feat. Standing as straight as she could, she raised her hand to her brow in salute, a somewhat pained smile on her face. "Yes, ma'am." Lindsay's arm wrapped around her waist, then Lindsay pulled her arm over her shoulder. Together, they staggered toward the closest bushes that might provide cover, as Rachel prayed she could stay on her feet.

They had traveled only about thirty yards when Lindsay felt Rachel go limp in her arms. Try as she might, she couldn't stop the wounded woman from slipping to the ground. All Lindsay managed to do was break her fall. She didn't know if she could wake her and get her on her feet again. Even if she could, she was running out of time. She grabbed Rachel's hands and unceremoniously dragged the unconscious woman with her eye on a good-sized row of bushes about twenty feet away.

Using all her strength and some reserve she didn't know she had, she managed to drag Rachel to the far side of the bushes and pushed her under as far as she could. "You get under there too," she said to Mandy, and the child crawled under the shrubbery. Lindsay took Mandy's hand and placed it over the wound on Rachel's thigh, but Mandy pulled it away.

"Blood," she said as fresh tears streamed down her face.

"Yes, it's blood, sweetie. Rachel's hurt, and her blood is leaking out. We need to try to make her better. You want her to get better, don't you?"

Mandy nodded, but her tears continued to fall.

"Good girl." Lindsay took both of Mandy's hands and placed them on the wound. "I need you to push here to keep the blood from leaking out. Can you do that for me?"

"I can do it."

Lindsay smiled. "I'm going to go see if I can find someone to help us. You stay here and take care of Rachel, and remember," she placed her finger up to her lips, "not a sound."

Mandy immediately left Rachel and wrapped her bloody hands around Lindsay's arm. "Don't leave me," she sobbed. "Take me with you. I'm afraid. Uncle Eddie hurt me."

"Oh, sweetie, I know you're afraid, but you'll be safe if you stay under here and be quiet. Eddie won't find you." Lindsay stroked Mandy's cheek. "I wouldn't leave you if I didn't have to, and Rachel needs someone to take care of her."

Mandy just clutched her tighter. "I want my daddy."

"I'll go call your daddy and tell him to come get you, but you need to stay here."

"No, I want to come with you."

Lindsay didn't know what to do. She couldn't take Mandy with her, but it was clear the girl was not about to be left behind. Suddenly she remembered that Rachel had a cell phone. *Idiot*, she chastised herself. *Why didn't I remember that sooner?* Checking the detective's pockets, she found the phone and pulled it out.

"Do you know your phone number, Mandy?"

The little girl nodded. "555-3457."

Lindsay dialed the number and waited for an answer.

"Hello?"

"Mr. Carpenter, this is Lindsay Ryan."

"Where's my daughter? What have you done with Mandy? If you've hurt her, I swear I'll—"

"Mandy's okay, she's here with me now. I'm going to put her on the phone." Lindsay took the phone away from her ear. "Your daddy wants to talk to you." She took Mandy's left hand and placed it back over Rachel's wound. "Keep pushing while you talk to your daddy, okay?"

"Okay."

"It's really important that you keep pushing real hard on Rachel's hurt. Don't take your hand away for anything, and remember you need to be quiet, so talk softly, okay?" Mandy nodded and Lindsay handed her the phone.

Lindsay was confident that with full darkness, Rachel and Mandy would be almost invisible under the bushes. If she could just draw Eddie away from them until darkness set in, they would be safe. *Just stay ahead of him until the police arrive; that's the game.*

Carefully, she peered over the top of the bush and spotted Eddie. He was back at the grave site, and from what she could see in the fading light, he looked like the predator he was. She saw him kick the pile of dirt repeatedly, then stop and put his hands on his hips and slowly turn around, searching in all directions. It wouldn't be long before he spotted the drag marks and followed them to Rachel and Mandy. She ducked back down and crawled away from them, making sure to keep the bushes between them.

It felt as if she had been crawling forever when she sat back on her heels and took stock of her tortured hands. They were starting to blister, and she breathed a sigh of relief that she wouldn't have to crawl anymore. Thank goodness she was wearing her jeans, which at least protected her knees.

"Here goes nothing," Lindsay said aloud as she stood and looked to see where Eddie was. Luck was with her, and she could see in the dim light that he was walking in the opposite direction. She ran full-out for the trees, making no effort to stay out of sight. "Here, fishy, fishy," she muttered under her breath.

Eddie saw Lindsay running and fired at her, but at that distance and with the light almost gone, he didn't even come close. "Damn," he said, and started after her. He knew he couldn't let the women get away or his plan would go up in smoke.

He had thought that taking the squirrelly redhead out to the cabin was a stroke of genius, but now he wasn't so sure. It was a perfect plan. She would have no alibi. He could kill her and Mandy, and the police would think Lindsay had taken the child and run. They already suspected her, and if she disappeared too, that would be the icing on the cake. He, on the other hand, had made sure to have an alibi. In fact, he had stopped several times after he had taken Mandy and stashed her in the trunk of his car.

The more people who saw him around the time Mandy disappeared, the better.

He still couldn't figure out why the police detective had shown up. Just one more problem he didn't need. Anger built up in him as he ran. *Damn! She made it to the trees. Now she'll be that much harder to find.* He stopped a moment and bent over to catch his breath. *That bitch will pay for this. She's gonna be praying for death before I get done with her.*

Lieutenant Ben Rowers turned on the dirt road leading to the cabin with three police cars, an ambulance, and a paramedic unit following close behind him. He hadn't been able to get Rachel on the phone, which gave credence to the Ryan woman's statement that the detective had been shot. He still wasn't sure what Ryan was trying to pull, but he intended to find out.

Spotting a couple of cars ahead, he stopped and got of the car. It was dark there, with no streetlights, but his headlights illuminated Rachel's car. She was at the cabin. Rowers turned and waited for his men to close ranks around him. "Okay, listen up. Todd's car is over there, so I can only assume that the message we received may be true." He looked toward the paramedics, who had just arrived. "We'll let you know when it's safe to go in."

The squad of police officers fanned out slightly behind Lieutenant Rowers. They would take their cues from him on tactics. He had signaled for a silent approach.

"This doesn't look good," Rowers said as they neared the cabin's porch. All the lights were out, and the door stood open. "Stephens and Kelly, circle around the house to the right. Trevor and White, you go the other way. The rest of you come with me in the front."

They rushed inside and turned on the lights. After verifying that the small cabin was indeed empty, Rowers took a better look around. He found the phone on the floor behind the couch and put it to his ear. The connection to the 911 dispatcher was still open. "Lieutenant Rowers here. We've secured the cabin and I'm terminating the call. Thanks for your help."

"Lieutenant, out here!"

"What have you got?" Rowers hung up the phone and sprinted for the door.

"A shell casing, sir," Stephens said, his flashlight illuminating the object in question. "And blood over there."

"Kelley, I want you to call CSU, then set up a perimeter around the crime scene. I don't want the evidence compromised any more than it already is. The rest of you, hear this. We've got a little girl and a cop out there. We know at least one of them has been shot. Let's go find 'em."

Just then, Officer White rounded the corner of the cabin. "I found a site out back where someone's been digging. And there's more blood."

"Lead the way," Rowers said. They moved around to the back of the house. Using flashlights, they could see Officer Trevor kneeling about fifty yards beyond the back of the cabin.

"Looks like they were digging graves, Lieutenant," White said, "and someone was bleeding pretty bad. There's an awful lot of blood."

"Too much blood." Rowers pulled out his cell phone and punched in some numbers. "I need a medevac chopper out here as fast as I can get it!" He paused a moment to listen. "I don't care what it takes. Do it! We've got an officer down and she's running out of time." He disconnected the call and had just turned to his men when a shot rang out. Rowers started for the sound at a dead run. "Come on, boys, we've got work to do."

Lindsay heard movement and held her breath, knowing the slightest sound might give her away. Eddie was almost to the tree she was hiding behind, and she strained to hear from which side he was approaching. Slowly, she crept around the tree, keeping it between them, hoping against hope that he wouldn't hear her.

Suddenly, a twig snapped and her heart stopped. Now she had no choice but to run again. She heard the loud boom of gunfire, but thankfully, he missed, and she kept on running. Then she saw the lights. Lights that bobbed up and down, as if whoever was holding them was running. *The police have finally arrived!*

Another shot rang out as Lindsay ran into the open, and she felt the sting as a bullet ripped through the flesh of her arm. The lights were almost to her now, and she ran desperately to meet them.

"Stop where you are and hold your hands out where I can see them," a male voice called out, and Lindsay came to a halt and raised her arms away from her body, palms facing out. Her lungs burned and her legs shook from exhaustion. It had taken everything she had, but she'd made it.

"I'm unarmed," she said as she dropped to her knees.

"Who shot at you?" the police officer asked.

"Mandy's uncle Eddie. Eddie took Mandy and he was going to kill us all."

"Kelly, take Trevor and White and search the tree line. The perp's Eddie Dellacroix, and he's armed and dangerous. Be alert." The policeman knelt down in front of Lindsay. "Miss Ryan, I'm Lieutenant Rowers. Where are they? Where are Mandy and Detective Todd?"

"I hid them under some bushes, then led Eddie off in another direction."

"Are they injured?"

"Mandy's okay, but Rachel's bad off. She was shot in the leg and has lost a lot of blood."

When Lindsay's breathing had evened out some, Rowers helped her to her feet. "Stephens, call down and get those medics up here. And you, Miss Ryan, I need you to show us exactly where they are."

"This way," Lindsay said and started off at a slow jog. The police officers fell in behind her, and even in the dark, she moved directly to Rachel's hiding place. "Under there." Once again, she dropped to her knees.

Rowers shone his light under the shrubs, and two frightened little eyes stared back at him.

"Daddy!" Mandy shrieked into the phone as she shrank down and closed her eyes.

At her reaction, Rowers turned the flashlight around and lit up his face. "It's okay, Mandy, it's me, Uncle Ben. It's okay to come out now, sweetheart."

"I can't," Mandy said. "Lindsay told me I couldn't stop pushing on the lady's cut. It's important. Her blood's leaking out."

"You did a good job, Mandy, but you can stop now. We're going to take her to the doctor so he can fix her up."

Mandy took her hand away from the wound and crawled out from under the bushes. She spied Lindsay on the ground and ran to her. "I did it, Lindsay. I pushed real hard, and I didn't stop for anything."

"You did good. You're a brave girl," Lindsay said as the girl flew into her arms. "I'm proud of you."

"Oh, no! Your blood's leaking out too. Did you cut yourself?" Mandy immediately covered the wound with her hand and started to push. She still clutched Rachel's phone in her other hand, her daddy momentarily forgotten in her excitement of being rescued.

"It's just a little cut, sweetie. I'm okay. Is your daddy still on the phone?"

Mandy looked at the phone, nodded, and brought it back up to her ear. "Daddy, Uncle Ben's here to take the lady to the doctor so he can fix her up. Lindsay says I did good!" The little girl listened for a moment and then handed the phone to Lindsay. "My daddy wants to talk to you."

Lindsay took the phone and put it to her ear. "Mandy's fine, Mr. Carpenter."

"Thanks to you, Miss Ryan."

"Please, you don't have to thank me."

"I need to do a lot more than thank you. I need to apologize." He paused for a moment and continued. "I'm so sorry for the way I treated you when you were just trying to protect my baby."

"I can't talk right now, Mr. Carpenter. I'm going to give the phone back to Mandy." She handed the little girl the phone and crawled to where Lieutenant Rowers and Detective Stephens had just pulled Rachel free of the bushes.

"Damn, I can't find a pulse!" Rowers sat back on his heels. "Where's that fucking chopper!"

Lindsay squeezed between the officers hovering over Rachel. "Is she breathing?" She couldn't see Rachel's chest moving, so she resorted to holding her hand above the detective's nose and mouth. It took a moment, but she felt it. Rachel was still breathing. "There it is," she said. "I feel it. She's breathing."

Detective Stephens knelt by Rachel's side. He had taken off his shirt and folded it to use as a bandage. He held it against her thigh with a firm pressure. Rowers knelt on her other side, and Lindsay was up by her head.

At that moment, an out-of-breath Officer Kelly arrived and reported that the perp had slipped away in the dark. The other two officers were right on Kelly's heels.

Rowers grunted an acknowledgement. "Figures," he said. "Eddie grew up with his grandfather in these woods. He knows them like the back of his hand."

Lindsay stroked Rachel's face. The normally warm, brown skin was unnaturally pale. "She's cold." Lindsay looked up at the officers standing around the wounded detective. "Take off your shirts." The response was immediate as police officers stripped off their clothing and handed the items to her.

Working gently but surely, Lindsay wrapped one shirt tightly around Rachel's upper body, then folded up the rest and used them to elevate her legs. As she attended the unconscious woman, an overwhelming sense of sadness washed over her, in part caused by the guilt she felt over being responsible for the detective's injury. But it was more than that. There was a profound sadness in Rachel, and it seemed to roll over Lindsay in waves when she touched her.

"Here they come," Stephens said.

Everyone looked over to see the flashlights of the medics bob up and down as they ran over the rough ground. They had come as far as they could by truck and took to foot when the terrain made driving impossible.

The medics arrived with their equipment and started to work on Rachel. They checked her vital signs and cut her pants off to assess the wound. Lindsay was vaguely aware of the lieutenant's phone ringing behind her.

"That was the chopper. ETA five minutes."

The medics put a pressure bandage on Rachel's wound and started two IVs of normal saline, wide open. They placed an oxygen mask over her mouth and nose and elevated her legs even higher than Lindsay had them. At the sound of a helicopter, the police waved their flashlights to help guide it in to land in the nearby clearing.

"Can I take a look at that arm?" one of the medics asked, and Lindsay remembered, for the first time since they had pulled Rachel out from under the bush, that she also was injured. She nodded and held out her arm, noticing that it had almost stopped bleeding.

"Doesn't look too bad," the medic said, and cleaned away the blood so he could see exactly what the damage was. "You're lucky, miss." He smiled. "A few stitches and you'll be good as new."

The helicopter landed about twenty yards away. More medics arrived with a gurney and additional medical equipment. When they moved Rachel onto the gurney, Lindsay noticed that her shirt was open and wires had been attached from the wounded woman to an EKG machine. Unable to push the gurney over the uneven ground, four men picked it up and carried Rachel to the chopper.

The medic helped Lindsay to her feet. She wavered a little, and he held her arm to steady her. "Do you need help getting to the helicopter?"

"Thanks, but I think I just stood up too fast," Lindsay said. "I'm okay."

When she started walking toward the chopper, Mandy ran up and wrapped her arms around her. "Don't leave me!"

"I won't leave you." Lindsay took her hand. "Come on, we're going to ride in a helicopter."

"No!" Mandy dug her feet into the ground and stopped. "I'm scared."

Lindsay knelt down in front of her. "It's okay, Mandy. I'll be right there with you."

Mandy shook her head. "No."

"Okay, then." Lindsay stood up. "I'll say good-bye to you here. You be a good girl, now." She started toward the helicopter again, and before she had walked the twenty feet, Mandy ran after her. Lindsay smiled and held out her hand. "It'll be fun. You'll see."

One of the medics helped them into the helicopter seats. "We're just about to lift off, ma'am, please buckle up."

"Thanks," Lindsay said and reached over to buckle Mandy into her seat. "I'm Lindsay, and this is Mandy."

He smiled. "Mike."

Lindsay looked over at Rachel. "Is she going to die, Mike?"

"Not if we can help it, but I'm not going to lie to you, ma'am."

"Lindsay."

"This is a very serious situation, Lindsay. I don't want to give you false hope. At this point, it could go either way." Lindsay felt the blood drain from her face and he speedily added, "She's in good hands, and if she's strong, she's got a chance."

Lindsay nodded, and Mike went to his seat and buckled himself in. Her eyes returned to Rachel, and she watched the activity around the gurney. "She's strong. She'll make it."

"This is tango-bravo-seven-one-zero on our way in. Code three. Patient is female, late thirties–early forties, GSW to the thigh. We've got her on O2 and started two lines of normal saline. Pressure is sixty over forty; pulse one-thirty, respiration's thirty. ETA approximately fifteen minutes."

The helicopter landed and the medics rushed to get their patient out of the chopper and into the hands of the waiting trauma team. Lindsay and Mandy followed them onto the elevator and down to the emergency room. Rachel was taken into one of the trauma rooms, and an older woman rushed to the glass partition to watch what was going on in the room.

Greg Carpenter was sitting in the waiting area and stood up when he saw they had arrived. His daughter spotted him immediately.

"Daddy!" Mandy shrieked, and let go of Lindsay's hand. She fairly flew across the room and into his waiting arms. She had been upset on the flight to the hospital when she wasn't able to talk with him and had remained sullen and quiet. "I want to go home." She wrapped her arms around his neck.

"We'll go home as soon as the doctor checks you over."

Tears started down Mandy's face and she clutched him tighter. "I don't want to go to the doctor. I want to go home."

"It won't take long, sweetheart. Daddy needs to make sure you're okay." He looked over at Lindsay. "Thank you," he said, then turned and walked away.

Lindsay watched them go. Her sense of relief was enormous. *Now to see to Rachel.* The older woman was still standing at the window, and Lindsay walked over to join her. There was a frenzy of activity inside the small room as the trauma team worked to save the detective.

The lead doctor's voice was loud and clear as he barked out orders. "Fuck! Her pressure's bottoming out. Hang more blood. Give her a cc of epi—now! Start compressions."

A young doctor placed one hand over the other and started pumping rhythmically on Rachel's chest.

"No good," the doctor in charge said. "Run the IVs wide open. Pump the goddamned blood. Come on, come on!" He looked up at the monitor again. "She's in V-fib. Charge the paddles to two hundred." A high-pitched whine filled the room as the machine charged. "Clear," he said and placed the paddles on Rachel's chest. Her body jerked upward.

The woman standing next to Lindsay covered her face with her hands and backed away from the glass. "I can't watch her like that anymore." She turned and walked to the chairs against the wall and sat down. "Please, God, don't take my baby."

Tears flowed down the woman's face, and Lindsay found tears trickling down her own cheeks as well. "She's strong." Lindsay approached where the woman sat and knelt in front of her. She covered the woman's hands with her own and squeezed. "She'll pull through."

The woman looked into Lindsay's tear-stained face. "Are you a friend of Rachel's?"

"No, not really."

"You were with her, weren't you?"

Lindsay nodded. "I'm Lindsay Ryan."

"Waheya Todd. I'm Rachel's mother. Can you tell me what happened?"

Lindsay got to her feet and sat in the chair next to Waheya. "I'm afraid it was my fault, Mrs. Todd. I'm responsible for Rachel getting shot. If I hadn't attempted to escape and run, she would have been gone by the time he got there." She shook her head. "I thought she was the killer, and I almost got her killed."

"You're the one with the gift of sight—the seer."

"More like the curse of sight. It's not a gift if you don't understand what you're seeing." Lindsay leaned over, put her elbows on her knees, and buried her face in her hands. "I'll never forgive myself if she dies."

The doctor's approach interrupted their conversation. Waheya was on her feet in an instant to meet him.

"Is she going to be all right?"

"What we're dealing with here is a gunshot wound with severe blood loss and possible vascular damage. As soon as we get her pressure and other vital signs stabilized, we'll send her to surgery. We'll explore the wound and bring in a vascular surgeon to repair any injured vessels. The big problem is that the diminished blood flow from the sustained hemorrhage and low blood pressure may have caused major organ system damage. Her heart, kidney, lungs, and even brain may have been damaged. She's not likely to wake up for twenty-four hours, and then her systems will have to be evaluated."

"Can I go in and see her?"

The doctor nodded. "You can stay with her until we're ready to take her up."

Waheya turned to Lindsay and reached for her hand. "Good-bye, my dear. And don't be so hard on yourself. I'm sure Rachel doesn't blame you for this, and I know I don't."

"Thank you," Lindsay said as she watched Waheya walk away with the doctor.

At that moment, a young doctor arrived. "If you'll come with me, Miss Ryan, I'll get that arm sewn up for you."

She followed him into a small room and sat to wait.

"When was the last time you had a tetanus shot, Miss Ryan?" He brought over a suture kit and sat across from her.

Lindsay shrugged. "I have no idea."

The young doctor laughed. "If it's been that long, I think you're due." He cut the bandage off her arm and swabbed the area with Betadine.

Lindsay looked away as he injected a local anesthetic around the wound, then sutured it closed.

"You can look now," he said as he bandaged her arm. "All done." He stood and crossed to the sink to wash his hands. "Keep it dry for the next twenty-four hours, then wash it daily with a mild antibacterial soap."

"Thank you." Lindsay stood to leave.

"Oh, Miss Ryan. I almost forgot to tell you that there are a couple of police detectives waiting to talk to you. They're out at the front reception area."

"Okay, thanks." She hurried out of the room. Perhaps they could tell her what happened with Eddie.

CHAPTER FOUR

Lindsay stepped out of the elevator and headed toward the nurses' station. She was exhausted. She'd had no idea it would take so long to give a statement to the police, but it seemed when one officer was through with her, another would take his place and ask the same questions all over again. And to find out that Eddie had evaded capture was quite a blow.

She would have liked nothing more than to go home, take a shower, and go to bed, but she had to check in on Rachel first. She wasn't sure she could live with herself if the detective died. Her clothes were still coated in Rachel's blood, and she shuddered. Then it suddenly dawned on her that she had no home now, and no transportation to get there even if she had a place to go. Her car was still up at the cabin, along with her money and everything else she owned that was not in storage.

"Can I help you?" a nurse asked as Lindsay approached the station.

"Yes, please. They told me downstairs that Rachel Todd would be brought up here when she gets out of surgery. Is there a place I can wait?"

"Oh, sure. The waiting room's right down the hall, third door on the left."

"Thank you."

As Lindsay approached the room, she could see Waheya and a woman with long hair plaited into a single braid down her back.

Waheya appeared to be comforting the other woman. As Lindsay got closer, she could hear the younger woman sobbing.

"I love her so much, I can't lose her."

Lindsay pivoted around and walked back the way she had come. She didn't know why it bothered her so much to hear the woman professing her love for Rachel, but it did. It was ridiculous, really. She and Rachel weren't even friends. She retraced her steps and got back on the elevator. With no place else to go, she ended up back in the waiting area for the emergency room. *I guess this is as good a place as any to spend the rest of the night.* She looked for a spot that had a few empty chairs so she would be able to lie down. *At least I'll have a roof over my head tonight.*

Waheya held on tightly to the young woman in her arms. "She's going to make it through this, Trish. We have to believe that."

"But the doctor said—"

"I know what the doctor said." Waheya pushed her granddaughter away and took her face in her hands. "He said there's a chance we could lose her. A chance, Trish. Your mother's a strong woman. Don't give up on her."

"I don't want to give up on her. I'm just so scared I'll lose her without ever getting to tell her that I'm sorry and that I love her."

"Deep down in her heart, she knows you love her."

"Does she?" Trish tore away from Waheya to pace back and forth. "She probably hates me."

Waheya grabbed her by the shoulders. "I don't want to hear talk like that. Rachel doesn't hate you. How could you even think such a thing?"

"She chose Lisa over me."

"You put her in an impossible situation, Trish. She loved Lisa very much, but not more than she loved you—just in a different way. And Lisa was dying; she couldn't just walk away."

Trish's expression became contrite, and she bowed her head. "I know that now. I just wish I could have seen it then. I guess it was all about me in those days. When David was born, it changed everything, but it was too late. She already hated me. It breaks my heart to think about what I put her through."

"Didn't I tell you I don't want to hear any talk like that? Your mother was hurt and angry, but she never hated you."

A man entered the waiting room carrying two cups of coffee. "Any word yet about your friend?" He handed one cup to Trish and the other to Waheya.

"No." Trish shook her head. "She's still in surgery."

He looked at his watch, then back at Trish. "It's getting late, sweetheart, we really should be leaving."

"I'm sorry, Doug, but I can't leave until I know she's going to be all right."

"I'm sure Waheya will call you as soon as she knows anything. It doesn't do your friend any good to sit out here. She doesn't even know you're in the building."

"I don't care. I'm not leaving."

Doug eyed his wife's tear-stained face. "You've never even mentioned this woman before. Why is she suddenly so important that you can't leave her?"

Trish took a sip of her coffee, then looked Doug square in the eye. "Because she's my mother."

Doug's mouth dropped open. "But I thought Betty—"

"Betty's my stepmother. She married my dad when I was twelve." Trish walked over and took Waheya's hand. "Waheya is my grandmother."

"But..." Doug slowly sank onto the nearest chair. "You let me believe all this time that Waheya was an old family friend and that Betty was your mother. Why?"

"I was afraid."

"Of what? Me?"

"Of your family." Trish took another sip of her coffee, then placed the cup on the floor. "I was ashamed to let anyone know that my mom was...is...a lesbian. I almost told you when I realized I was falling in love with you. But then you invited me to join your church, and I listened to your father preach about the sin of homosexuality. I couldn't take the chance that if you and your family found out, they would talk you out of seeing me." Tears started down her face. "I abandoned my mother once. I won't do it again. If she comes through this, I'm going to do my best to get her to forgive me. I want her in my life. I want my son to know his grandmother."

"But I'm not just anyone," Doug said. "I'm your husband. You should've told me."

"Yes, I should have told you, but by the time I met you, I'd had lots of practice letting people believe in my fictitious life. I went to live with Dad and Betty when I was fifteen because I was a coward. The kids at school gave me a hard time when they found out my mom was a lesbian. They made dyke jokes and I was embarrassed. I didn't even want to go to school. Living with Dad gave me a chance to start over. No one knew me at the new school, and I never told anyone about my mom. The really sad part is that I love my mom, and I knew I was hurting her, but I still let my new friends think that Betty was my mother. I never actually lied and told anyone she was my mother, but I called her Mom and everyone assumed."

"You could've told me. Your mother is the one guilty of the sin, not you. My father also preaches not to visit the sin of the parent on the child."

"If loving is a sin, then we're all sinners," Waheya said. "My daughter is guilty of nothing more than loving someone with all her heart."

Doug turned to Waheya and nodded. "I'm sorry I said that, Waheya. It's not for me to judge her. That's between her and God." He turned back to his wife. "I'm sorry you didn't feel you could share this with me, Trish. I love you, and as far as I'm concerned, your mother will always be welcome in our home."

Lindsay awoke to the sound of shouting. She sat up and rubbed her eyes, then looked in the direction of the commotion and saw a man kicking one of the vending machines on the other side of the room. She was stiff and sore from sleeping across the uncomfortable chairs and groaned as she stood up and stretched out her aching muscles.

She yawned and made her way to the restroom, glancing at her watch to find that it was only six in the morning. Even at that early hour, half the chairs in the area were filled with people waiting to see a doctor.

The quiet of the restroom offered a respite from the constant drone in the waiting area. Her nerves were all but shattered.

After locking herself into one of the stalls, she sat on the toilet and cried. It was more than just a few tears. This was the first time since this nightmare had begun that she was truly alone. Her chest heaved as sobs wracked her body, and she did not attempt to hold it back. Minutes passed, and still she cried.

A knock on the stall door brought Lindsay back to awareness.

"Are you okay in there?"

"Yes, I'm all right." She pulled off a wad of toilet paper and blew her nose as she waited for the woman to finish and leave. When she heard the restroom door close, she exited the stall, then went out to the sink to clean up.

"Okay, Lindsay girl, it's time to stop feeling sorry for yourself," she told her reflection in the mirror.

Once again, Lindsay stepped off the elevator on the fourth floor and walked to the nurses' station. "What room is Rachel Todd in, please?"

"She's in 415," the nurse behind the counter answered.

"Thanks." With that, Lindsay set off resolutely down the hall and stopped in front of 415. She took a deep breath, pushed the door open, and walked inside.

The doctor she had seen the night before finished writing something on Rachel's chart, then hung it back at the foot of her bed. When he noticed her, he smiled. "Good morning." He glanced at her bloodstained clothing. "Looks like you've been here all night."

Lindsay nodded. She noticed he picked up something from Rachel's bed and placed it on top of some type of medical machinery. "How's she doing?"

"Everything looks good. Vitals are all strong and I just extubated her. Didn't want her to wake up with a tube down her throat. That can be pretty scary." He pushed the wheeled apparatus toward the door. "I don't expect her to wake up for at least six or eight hours, perhaps more." Deftly maneuvering the machine, he pushed the door open and was gone.

Lindsay walked over to Rachel's bed and stood looking down at her. The detective appeared so peaceful. Lindsay reached out, picked up the detective's limp hand, and held it a moment. "I never meant for anything like this to happen to you. I'm so sorry."

The door across the room opened, and Lieutenant Rowers walked in. He joined Lindsay at Rachel's bedside, and they both just stood for a moment watching Rachel sleep. "We haven't found that bastard who did this to you, Todd, but we will. I swear it." He looked over at Lindsay. "I know I just missed the doc. I saw him down the hall. Is she going to be okay?"

"He said everything looks good, but she probably won't wake up till tonight."

Rowers nodded, then took in Lindsay's disheveled hair and bloodstained clothing. "You been here all night?"

"Yeah." Lindsay nodded. "I didn't have anywhere else to go. My car is still up at Eddie's cabin, and I didn't have any money on me to take a cab up there to pick it up."

"How long's it been since you've eaten?"

"Yesterday at lunch, I think."

"Come on. I'm taking you out to eat, then we'll go pick up your car."

Lindsay got out of Lieutenant Rowers's car and walked toward the cabin. There were four uniformed police officers stationed on the property: two up at the cabin, the other two down the hill at Eddie's car. He would find a fine reception if he tried to come back for his belongings.

They passed the spot where Rachel had been shot, and Lindsay had to look away, as the blood was still visible. Lieutenant Rowers lifted the yellow crime scene tape for Lindsay and then ducked under behind her. Lindsay walked directly to the bedroom and collected her purse and keys.

"Got 'em," she said, holding the items out for Rowers to see.

He nodded and escorted her back outside. "What will you do now?" he asked as they walked back down the hill to her car.

"The first thing I'm going to do is get my clothes and find a motel room so I can get cleaned up. I can't stand wearing these clothes a minute longer than absolutely necessary." She huffed out a breath. "Then I guess I need to go check and see if I still have a job. The way my luck's been going, they'll have given me the boot too."

Rowers pulled out his business card and handed it to Lindsay. "You have any problems with the job, give me a call. I'll be glad to explain things and put in a good word for you."

"Thanks." Lindsay accepted the card and smiled. With a small wave, she opened the car door and slid inside. It felt good to be back in familiar territory again. She pushed the key into the ignition.

Suddenly, a vision came unbidden, and she saw Eddie pull a woman out of a car. The woman fell to the ground and screamed as he put his gun to her head and pulled the trigger.

Lindsay felt sick, but she managed to get out of her car and run toward the lieutenant. "Wait!" She waved frantically for him to stop as he backed up to turn around.

Rowers opened the door just as Lindsay got there. "What's wrong?"

"I saw Eddie!"

"Where?" Rowers was out of his car in an instant, service revolver in his hand, his eyes scanning the area.

"Not here," Lindsay said. "In my head."

"What did you see?" Rowers relaxed and put his gun back in its holster. "Every thing you've seen so far has been right on."

"He killed a woman and took her car."

"Is that something that's going to happen?"

Lindsay shook her head, frustration showing clearly on her face. "I don't know for sure, but I got the feeling that it had already happened."

Rowers nodded. "Did you get a good look at the car?"

"It was green."

"What make?"

"I'm not sure." Lindsay ran her fingers through her hair. "Maybe it was a Toyota."

"You can't give me any more than that?"

"I'm sorry. I've just never been into cars. They all look pretty much the same to me. I know it had a Mickey Mouse head on the antenna and tape over a crack in the left taillight."

"That's enough description for an APB. This tip may just help us find him. Thanks."

"I hope so," Lindsay said, then turned and walked back to her car.

Lindsay stepped out of the shower and reached for a towel. God, it felt good to be clean again. She dried off, patting carefully around the stitches on her arm, then tossed the damp towel over the shower door. She was exhausted, but there was just so much to do. As she ran her comb through her tangled hair, she contemplated her list.

The first thing was to talk to Michael Thompson and see if she still had a job. When she had called him before, she purposefully did so when she knew he would be gone for the day. She hadn't wanted to have to explain anything, just tell him she was taking some time off. And she knew that talking to his machine would ensure that no questions were asked. Of course, not talking to him live and in person, she had no idea if he had fired her or not. And if he had tried to call to find out what was going on, there would have been no one to take the call.

Lindsay had retrieved her clothes from storage, but she had to rummage through the boxes to find anything. From the open box on the bed, she pulled out a rust-colored pair of cotton pants. She searched through the box for a shirt to go with them and found none. Another box seemed likely, and she placed it on the bed. "Ah, here it is," she said as she picked up a cream-colored pullover top with rust and gold designs haphazardly scattered across it. If she was still employed, the next thing on her list would be to find herself a new apartment. The sooner, the better. She didn't want to keep living out of boxes in a motel room any longer than necessary.

After dressing quickly, she ran her fingers through her damp curls and sighed. "It's showtime," she said as she walked out the door. "Please let me still have a job."

The drive to Harpers Unlimited was a short one, but Lindsay's stomach had tied itself in knots by the time she got there. She liked her job, and more importantly, she needed it. The prospect of starting over again did not sit well, and wondering what would happen was driving her nuts.

"Come on in," Michael Thompson said when Lindsay knocked on his office door. When he saw her, his face lit up. "Well, well, the prodigal daughter returneth." He got up, walked around his desk, and pulled out his guest chair for her.

"Thank you." Lindsay sat in the proffered chair.

Michael returned to his seat and sat down too, leaning his arms on the desk. "I was wondering when, or if, I was going to see you again."

"I'm sorry I left you hanging like that," Lindsay said. "I need this job, and I hope I haven't messed that up."

"Don't worry, Lindsay, you've still got your job. In fact, you're kind of a hero around here. Everyone's been talking about how you saved that little girl. It was all over the news last night and this morning."

This was the first time she had gotten such a positive reaction to her gift, and Lindsay smiled. Perhaps things were going to be okay after all.

Brown eyes fluttered open and then closed again. Rachel attempted to swallow. Her mouth was dry, her lips sticking together. She tried to lick her lips to wet them, but her tongue was dry too. *Where the hell am I?* She opened her eyes and tried to roll over again, causing a sharp pain to shoot up her leg and into her groin. She felt someone take her hand, and she looked over to see the worried face of her mother looking down at her. *A hospital. I'm in a hospital.*

"Wa...water...could I...have some water?" she whispered.

"Sure, sweetheart, just let me put your bed up a little first."

Rachel nodded and waited as the bed slowly lifted her into a sitting position. Memory was coming back now, and she remembered Lindsay helping her get away from that psycho, Eddie.

"Here you go, baby." Waheya lifted a glass of water to Rachel's mouth and bent the straw so she could drink.

Rachel lifted her head and took a few swallows, then relaxed back onto her pillow. "Thanks...needed that. How long have I been here?"

"Since last night."

"Miss Kitty..."

"Miss Kitty's just fine. I fed her this morning, and I'll make sure she's taken care of until you get home." Waheya put the water back on the bedside table and picked up Rachel's hand. "How are you feeling, hon?"

"I feel like hell." Rachel moved her legs slightly and grimaced. "Damn, that hurts."

Waheya patted her daughter's cheek. "I'm sorry, baby. Let me run out to the nurses' station and let them know you're awake and that you need some pain medication. I'll be right back."

Rachel nodded and closed her eyes. *Pain medication would be good right about now.* The sound of approaching footsteps prompted her to open them again, but she was not prepared for the sight that greeted her.

"You gave us quite a scare last night," Trish said. "We thought we might lose you."

"I would think that would be a relief for you."

Tears slid down Trish's face. "I would never wish you dead, Mom. I love you."

Rachel turned her face away. "You sure had me fooled."

"Oh, Mom, I know I've given you every reason to hate me, and I don't blame you if you do. But I do love you." She drew nearer the bed. "I'd like us to start over, if you'll give me another chance."

Rachel remained silent and kept her face turned away.

"I understand." Trish wiped the tears from her face. "I won't bother you again." She walked to the door, then stopped and turned back. "We're having David's third birthday party next month. I'd love for you to come and meet your grandson. No matter what's happened between the two of us, he deserves to know his grandmother." With that, she was gone.

Rachel turned to see her disappear through the doorway. She almost called out for Trish to come back, but she couldn't do it. Tears started down her face and she angrily wiped them away.

Her tear-stained face greeted Waheya when she walked back into the room. She rushed over and picked up Rachel's hand, squeezing it. "Oh, baby, I'm sorry you're in so much pain, but they'll be here soon with the medication. I promise."

As if on cue, a nurse appeared and injected something into Rachel's IV. "This won't take long."

"Thank you."

The nurse went on to take Rachel's pulse and blood pressure and then made notes on the chart at the end of the bed. "The doctor will be in to check on you within the hour." She turned and started for the door. "He'll answer any questions you have."

"Are you feeling any better?" Waheya squeezed Rachel's hand.

"Mmm," Rachel said, as the medication took hold. "Much better."

Waheya reached over and stroked her brow. "That's good, baby. You just relax now." She glanced at her watch. "I think I should tell you that Trish will be here soon."

"She was already here."

"Trish was here? Why did she leave?"

"I couldn't..." Tears trickled down Rachel's face again, and she turned away.

"What happened?"

"She said she wanted to start over." Rachel wiped the tears from her damp cheeks suffused a dull pink. "Said she wanted me to come to David's birthday party, but I've no intention of playing her game. I'm her mother, God damn it! I won't go over there and pretend to be a friend of the family. That may work for you, Mom, but I just can't do it." Full indignation flamed her cheeks and neck.

"No, baby, you're wrong," Waheya said gently. "I was there last night when she told Doug that you're her mother."

Rachel turned back, her eyes wide with surprise. "She told him?"

Waheya nodded. "She said she was wrong before and doesn't care anymore what people think. She wants you back in her life."

"I don't know what to say." Rachel was dumbstruck by this new information. "I'm not sure I can just pretend the last few years never happened. It hurt too much."

"I know, sweetheart, but isn't she worth the effort? No matter what's happened, she's still your daughter, and she wants to make it up to you. Can't you please try? Just one day at a time."

Rachel sighed. "Will you tell her something for me?"

"Of course I will."

"Tell her that I can't guarantee anything, but if she still wants to put our relationship back together, yes, I'm willing to try."

Lindsay sighed as she opened the door to her motel room and flipped on the light. She tossed her purse and keys on the table, then headed to the bed. Exhausted, she flopped down, rolled onto her back, and crossed one ankle over the other. She had looked at five apartments that afternoon and had submitted an application for only one of them. The one she'd really liked was a one-bedroom quite a bit larger than that little over-the-garage place, and the cost was almost the same. Hopefully, her application would not take long to be processed and approved, and she could get out of this motel room.

The phone rang, and Lindsay jumped. She was not expecting a call. In fact, no one even knew she was there except Lieutenant Rowers and the manager of the apartment complex. *Could she have processed the application that quickly?* Lindsay shook her head. *No, she told me it would probably take a few days.* Suddenly, her heart beat wildly. *Something's happened to Rachel.* She quickly sat up and snatched the phone.

"Hello?"

"Miss Ryan?"

"Speaking."

"This is Linda Marshal from Hillcrest Apartments. I've completed your credit and employment checks, and if you still want the apartment, it's yours."

Lindsay's heart slowed down, and she couldn't stop the grin that spread across her face. "Wow, that was fast," she said. "I didn't expect to hear from you this soon."

"It didn't take long to run your credit check and send it to the owner for approval. Turns out he was sitting at his computer when I sent it over, and he answered right away. Doesn't always work out that way. Sometimes it takes him a couple of days to get back to me. That's why I told you it would take a few days."

"Thanks for getting back to me so quickly. I really appreciate it. When can I move in?"

"Tomorrow, if you like. Bring me a check for the rent and security deposit, and I'll give you a key."

"Thanks, Linda. I'll be by in the morning to pick up my key. See you then." Lindsay hung up the phone, the smile still on her face. "Yes! I really wanted that place."

Michael had suggested she take a few more days off work. It was an offer she couldn't pass up. That gave her four full days to get herself situated in the new place.

Her stomach rumbled, and she realized she was starved. "Idiot, why didn't you pick something up when you were out?" She got up, grabbed her purse and keys, and started for the door. It sure was going to be nice to have a place where she could cook again. This going out for every meal was getting old real fast.

Rachel awoke to find a tall woman with sandy-colored hair standing beside her bed.

"Hi," the woman said. "I'm Claire, and I'm your physical therapist."

"I suppose this is going to hurt?"

Claire nodded. "Afraid so."

"Okay." Rachel sighed. "When do we start?"

Claire grabbed the chair by the bedside and pushed it away. "Right now."

Rachel grimaced. "Okay, I'm ready. What do I have to do?"

"Nothing this time. We're going to start with passive exercises."

"Which means?"

"It means that I'm going to be doing all the work. Later on, you'll be lifting and moving the leg on your own." Claire pulled the covers back and lifted Rachel's right leg, bending it at the knee, then lowered it back to the bed.

Rachel's hands gripped the sheets, and she gritted her teeth to stifle a gasp as the therapist repeated the simple movement several more times.

"I know this hurts like hell, but it really is necessary." Claire put the leg down and pulled the covers back up.

When the pain eased a bit, Rachel's clenched muscles began to relax a little. "Gosh, that was fun," she said. "I can't wait to do it again." She watched Claire walk to the end of her bed and make a note on her chart. “You look too happy. I think you get your kicks out of torturing people.”

Claire grinned. “Darn, you’ve figured me out, and I thought I was being so subtle.” She winked at Rachel. “I’ll be back later and we’ll do this again.”

“Oh goodie, I can’t wait.” Rachel crossed her arms over her chest. “How long will it take to get my leg back in good working order?”

“Somewhere between four and six weeks you should be walking about pretty well,” Claire said. “You’ll need a cane for a while, but for how long, I don’t know. It really depends on you. We’ll do as many exercises as you can tolerate. Some people can tolerate a lot of pain, others can’t. It’s as simple as that.” She leaned against the door frame. “The more you can manage to do, the quicker your progress will be. You’ll leave the hospital with crutches, but I want you to use them to help you walk as soon as the pain allows. That means putting that foot on the ground occasionally and putting some weight on it. When the stitches are removed, we’ll move your therapy to the pool. The water will help support some of your weight and allow you to work on range-of-movement exercises with more ease and less pain.”

Rachel grimaced. “And the fun just goes on and on.”

Rachel took a bite of green beans, then pushed her tray away. She was ready to get out of this damn place and the sooner, the better. She leaned her head back, placed her forearm over her eyes, and heaved a big sigh.

“You need to eat if you expect to get your strength back, Ms. Todd.”

Rachel took her arm away from her face and looked at the frowning woman who had arrived at her bedside. She glanced at the nurse’s badge. “If anyone had bothered to check the paperwork I filled out this morning, Ms. Tyler, you’d know that I’m a vegetarian.” She glanced at the discarded tray. “They sent me turkey with bread and potatoes, all covered in turkey gravy. And most of the beans had gravy too. Don’t you people know what vegetarian means?”

"I'm sorry," the nurse said. "But some people who call themselves vegetarians eat fish and poultry."

"Okay," Rachel shook her head, "let me put it this way. I don't care if it walked, swam, or took flight. If it's a creature that someone had to kill, I don't eat it."

Nurse Tyler picked up Rachel's tray and started for the door. "I'll see if I can find something more to your liking."

"Thank you," Rachel said to the nurse's back as she left the room. She reached for the remote and turned on the television. Almost stir-crazy, she flipped from channel to channel in an effort to find something to stave off boredom for a while. She caught a bit of movement out of the corner of her eye and turned back to the door.

"Is it okay if I come in?" Trish stood hesitantly in the doorway. She seemed caught between coming and going.

Rachel nodded, turned off the television, and placed the remote on the bedside table. She watched Trish walk over and sit on the edge of her bed. "Mom told me that you finally told Doug the truth."

"I wish I'd done it a long time ago."

Rachel looked down at her hands. "So do I."

Trish covered one of Rachel's hands and squeezed gently. "I'm so sorry I hurt you."

Rachel glanced down at their hands and then back to Trish's face. "I'm not ready to forgive and forget yet, Trish. I'm not sure I ever will be."

"But Waheya said—"

"I said I would try...and I will. One step at a time. We're talking, and that's the first step."

"Yes, all right. One step at a time. What's the next step?"

"I hate that you referred to your grandmother as Waheya, and I just want to let you know that I won't put up with being called Rachel instead of Mom. I've spent too many years as a nonentity in your life. If you want a relationship, I will be acknowledged as your mother totally, or we go back to the way we were and never see each other again."

"I'm sorry," Trish said. "I didn't mean to call her Waheya. It was just a slip of the tongue. A habit that I need to work on breaking." She rubbed her hands nervously on her legs. "I know you're going to find this hard to believe, but I've missed you so much, Mom. I really have. I know I hurt you, but I was hurting too."

"You have no idea what hurting is until you have your own child throw you away as if you were a piece of trash."

"I know I have no right to complain that I was hurt, because I did it to myself. But I do have an idea what I did to you."

Rachel shook her head but remained silent.

"When I held David in my arms for the first time, I couldn't believe how much I loved him. I don't know what I'd do if he did to me what I did to you. That's when I really understood what I'd done."

"That was almost three years ago, Trish. Why did it take you so long to tell me?"

"I was afraid." Trish brought both hands up and covered her face as tears streamed down her cheeks. "I didn't think you'd want to hear anything I had to say by then. I thought you hated me." Tears turned into full-fledged sobs and her whole body shook. "I'm sorry. I'm so sorry." Trish collapsed onto her mother's chest, gripping her tightly. "Then you were shot, and I was so scared I would lose you forever and never get to tell you how much I love you. Please don't hate me, Mom. Don't hate me."

Rachel wrapped her arms around Trish. She cried as well. No matter what had happened, this was her little girl, and she was hurting. Suddenly, nothing else mattered but the need to comfort her child. "I don't hate you," she said as she pressed a kiss on top of her daughter's head. "I never could."

CHAPTER FIVE

When Waheya pushed through the door to room 415, the welcome sight of her daughter and granddaughter almost overwhelmed her. Trish was lying across Rachel, and Rachel had her arms around her. They both appeared to be asleep, and Waheya walked silently over to the bed so as not to startle them. With a closer look, she realized that Trish was the only one asleep.

Rachel's eyes were half-closed, but she smiled. She looked down at Trish and brushed a lock of hair out of her face. Trish made a little snoring sound and nuzzled into her chest.

"I see you and Trish have worked things out." Waheya pulled over a chair.

Rachel looked over at her, and a single tear made its way down her face. "I had no intention of forgiving her this easily, but it broke my heart to see her hurting so badly." She leaned over and pressed her cheek to the top of Trish's head. "I couldn't help it. She's my baby."

"Well, it does my heart good to see the two of you together again. I'd almost given up hope that it would ever happen."

Rachel lifted her head and nodded. "I'd given up too." She gently stroked her daughter's hair. "I still can't believe she's here."

Just then, the door to the room opened again, and Lieutenant Rowers walked in. "You look like something the cat dragged in." He walked over and stood beside Waheya's chair.

"Gee, thanks." Rachel smiled and looked toward Waheya. "Mom, this is Ben, my boss. Ben, Waheya, my mother." Then she gestured down at the woman sleeping in her arms. "And sleeping beauty here is my daughter, Trish."

Ben reached out and took Waheya's hand. "Nice to meet you, ma'am." He looked back at Rachel. "I didn't know you had a daughter, Todd."

"Yeah, well, we had a bit of a falling out a long time ago. Last night was the first time I'd seen her in years."

"Well, I'm glad to see that something good came out of all of this."

"Me too, Ben," Rachel said, "me too. So tell me, what's been happening with the case while I've been flat on my back in this damn hospital?"

"Bad news. Eddie's still at large, and according to Ms. Ryan, he's killed someone." Ben pulled another chair up to the bed and sat. "Our little psychic friend had another vision yesterday morning. She told me that he'd carjacked a woman. Said he shot her in the head and took her car." He shifted uneasily in the chair. "We found the car abandoned this morning, but we still haven't found Mrs. Warren's body. I think I'll give Ms. Ryan a call and see if she can give us any more help."

"I liked that girl," Waheya said.

Rachel cocked her head in question. "You met Lindsay?"

"Yes." Waheya nodded. "She sat with me while we waited outside the trauma room the other night. The doctors weren't sure you were going to make it, and she felt pretty guilty. She blames herself for you getting shot."

"It wasn't her fault."

"Well, she thinks it was. She said that if she hadn't run, you wouldn't have been shot."

"If it was anyone's fault, it was mine. If I'd just believed her in the first place—"

"Okay, okay." Ben lifted up a hand to shush her. "I've heard about all of this I can take. Yes, we all made some mistakes, but it was Eddie's fault, not hers and not yours. Don't place the blame where it doesn't belong."

"I suppose you're right," Rachel sighed and caressed Trish's hair, "but I can't help wondering how things would have turned out if I'd just given her the benefit of the doubt. Maybe I could have gotten her to talk to me, and together, we could have figured it out."

"Nah," Ben said. "She wouldn't have talked to you. She was sure you were the killer. I still can't figure out what she saw in that vision of hers that would make her think it was you."

"It's easy. She saw me digging a grave and thought it was Mandy's." Rachel cleared her throat. "And I did dig a grave, just like she said I would, but it was for me, not Mandy." She reached for her water pitcher but couldn't quite reach it. "Mom, could you pour me some water?"

"Sure." Waheya picked up the glass and pitcher. "This is almost empty, hon, and there's no ice. I'll go get you a fresh one."

"Thanks, Mom."

Trish started snoring again, but this time it was louder, and she woke herself up. She sat up and yawned. "I'm sorry I went to sleep on you like that, Mom. I don't think I've slept more than two or three hours since you were shot. I guess it just caught up with me." She noticed a damp spot on her mother's chest, where she'd been lying. "I drooled all over you." An embarrassed smile crept onto her face.

Rachel smiled back. "That's okay. It's not the first time, and besides, a little drool never hurt anyone."

"Are we gonna be okay, Mom?"

"Yes." Rachel squeezed her hand. "I think we are."

Waheya smiled as she walked out the door.

"Thanks for coming this morning, Miss Ryan," Lieutenant Rowers said. "I really appreciate it."

"You're welcome, but I'm not sure how much help I'll be. I've never been able to perform on command."

"I understand, but we've got a grieving family on our hands, and I'd sure like to find her for them."

"I'll do the best I can."

Rowers took her arm and escorted her across the police impound yard toward a green car. "You were right, you know. It was a Toyota."

"Believe me, that was just a lucky guess." Lindsay stopped short of the car and regarded the lieutenant. "I've been wondering about Detective Todd. Could you tell me how she's doing?"

Rowers smiled. "Pretty damn good, considering how close we came to losing her. It'll take a bit of time and a lot of physical therapy, but she'll be okay."

Lindsay wanted to jump for joy, but she tried to sound casual. "That's good to hear."

Clear-minded now, she walked up to the car and placed her hands on the hood. It was warm to the touch, but that was the only thing that came to her. She closed her eyes and waited, but nothing happened. She opened her eyes and looked over at the lieutenant. "I'm not getting anything."

"Maybe if you get inside and sit where she usually sat?"

Lindsay nodded, opened the door, and slid inside. She leaned back in the seat and sat a moment. Nothing. She placed her hands on the steering wheel. Nothing. Frustration welled up inside her, and she beat her hands on the wheel. "Damn it! I'm not getting anything."

"It's okay, Miss Ryan," Rowers said. "We knew it was a long shot."

"It's not okay." Lindsay leaned back and closed her eyes, trying to regain her composure. She took a few deep breaths, then opened her eyes and looked again around the car interior. A coffee cup perched in the cup holder, and she reached to pick it up, but again felt nothing. Then her eyes fell on a small medallion hanging from a chain around the rearview mirror. She lifted it off and gasped as the scene she had seen before played out in front of her.

As if she were watching a movie, she saw Eddie pull the woman out of her car and toss her to the ground. Saw him put the gun to her head and pull the trigger. She forced herself to look away from the woman this time and look around. Across the road, she could see a sign. In front of her, Eddie dragged the woman into the bushes at the side of the road, then drove away. Just as suddenly as it began, the vision ended, and she was sitting back in the car again.

Lindsay's stomach twisted into knots from the scene she had just witnessed, and she took a few calming breaths before trying to speak. "The victim—Mrs. Warren—is hidden in some bushes across the road from a sign that reads, Caution, Deer Crossing." She scrubbed her face with her knuckles. "That's all I got. I hope it's enough."

Rowers nodded. "It's enough. It shouldn't be too hard to track down all the deer crossing signs." He opened the door, and Lindsay climbed out of the car. "Everything go okay with your job? Do you need my assistance with anything?"

"Oh." Lindsay's face brightened a bit. "I still have a job. And not only that, I found an apartment. I'm going over there now to pick up my key."

"You need any help? I'm sure I can round up some friends who would be happy to lend a little time and few muscles."

"I wouldn't want to impose."

"Don't be silly. It's the least I can do, after what you've done for us. You tell me where and when, and I'll have 'em there."

"Thanks a lot, guys," Lindsay said to the two burly men who had moved her, lock, stock and barrel, into her new apartment. "I don't know what I would have done without you. I could have handled the boxes, but the furniture would have been impossible by myself."

"It was our pleasure," the taller man said. "If you need anything else, just give us a holler." He climbed into his truck and started up the motor. "You take care, now."

"I will," Lindsay said as she watched them drive away. With their help, moving in had been quick and painless. Now all that remained was to unpack the boxes, and she headed back to tackle that job. One of her new neighbors was on the walkway, and Lindsay couldn't help but wonder if the rather masculine-looking woman was a lesbian. The woman's eyes swept over her body and Lindsay smiled. *Oh, yeah, she is.*

"Hi, I'm Pat," the woman said. "Welcome to Hillcrest."

Lindsay extended her hand. "It's nice to meet you, Pat. I'm Lindsay."

"One of those big, strong men your boyfriend?" Pat asked.

Lindsay shook her head. "I don't have a boyfriend."

Pat's face brightened. "Why is it that a pretty woman like you isn't attached?"

"I guess the right person hasn't come along." Lindsay could feel her face flush at the unexpected compliment, and she grinned. She had always felt awkward and uneasy when she received a compliment from a man, but it was totally different coming from a woman. In fact, she realized, she rather liked it.

"You look like you could use a break," Pat said. "Why don't you come over to my place for a drink?"

"Sounds great. I'd love to. All that moving can make a body mighty thirsty."

Pat led the way to her apartment and unlocked the door, then stepped aside so Lindsay could enter. "I've got beer or white wine. Which would you prefer?"

"Wine would be great."

"Coming right up." Pat turned toward the kitchen. "Make yourself comfortable on the couch, and I'll be right back with the drinks."

Lindsay looked around the room on the way to the couch. She wasn't much of a drinker, but she had the distinct impression that Pat was interested in her, and she decided to use a little wine to help her relax and go with it. She'd had two unsuccessful relationships with men when she was in her early twenties. But with her mother's failing health, she'd devoted all her time to taking care of her. There had simply been no time to explore her attraction to woman.

Pat returned with a bottle of wine and two glasses. "I meant it when I said you were pretty," she said as she filled the glasses. "In fact, I find myself quite attracted to you. Does that shock you?"

"No," Lindsay replied. "I'm not shocked. But I have to say that this is the first time I've ever had a woman tell me she was attracted to me." She drained her glass and reached for the bottle to refill it.

"Now I'm shocked. Have you been hiding in a cave somewhere?"

Lindsay laughed, and it felt good. "No, just hiding in a very small town. I've only lived in Asheville for a few months." She could feel a buzz starting from the wine and took another sip.

"Asheville's not exactly a big city." Pat laughed and leaned closer. "I'm not one to beat around the bush, Lindsay, so I'll just come right out and say it. I find you very sexy, and I'd love to have sex with you." Lindsay's mouth dropped open and Pat laughed again. "Now I know I shocked you."

When Lindsay quickly emptied her second glass of wine and reached for the bottle again, Pat removed it. "Oh no. I don't want you so drunk you don't know what's going on." She whispered into Lindsay's ear, "I want you."

Lindsay leaned back and closed her eyes as she felt a hand cover her breast. She moaned and pushed her breast harder into the contact.

Nimble fingers unbuttoned her blouse, and her bra was unhooked and pushed out of the way. A soft, wet tongue caressed her breast, then hungrily pulled her nipple into a warm mouth to feast on it. Then hands were moving down her body, pushing her shorts and panties down, then pulling them off.

"Oh, Rachel, yes," she said as she pushed herself into the fingers that entered her. Too soon the orgasm swept her away, and she collapsed, her breath coming in soft gasps.

Lindsay opened her eyes and was shocked to see Pat looking at her, a puzzled expression on her face.

"Where did you just go?" Pat asked. "And who the hell is Rachel?"

What happened? Lindsay looked down to see that her clothes were still intact. *It was so real.* "I'm sorry." She didn't know what to say, or how to explain to Pat what had just happened. Hell, she didn't really know what just happened. *Was it the wine that caused the hallucination?* It couldn't have been a vision, because she knew for a fact that Rachel didn't have much use for her. It had to be the wine.

"Rachel's a police detective, and I just had this wild hallucination that she was making love to me." She shook her head to clear it. "I didn't think I was that drunk."

Pat picked up her glass, downing the contents in one gulp. "If you're so hung up on this Rachel person, what are you doing here with me?"

"I'm not hung up on her," Lindsay retorted. "At least, I didn't think I was." She sat up straight and ran her fingers through her hair. "I hardly know her. And I'm here with you because I was curious about what it would be like to be with a woman and you're the first one that's ever tried to seduce me."

Pat grabbed the wine bottle and refilled her glass. "Lucky me." She raised her glass and took a sip.

"I really am sorry," Lindsay said. "That vision was as much a surprise to me as it was to you."

"You know," Pat set her drink down and leaned forward, placing a gentle kiss on Lindsay's lips, "I can still take you into the bedroom and you can experience the real thing."

"I...I can't."

"Well, you can't blame a girl for trying." Pat sat back and picked up her drink again. "Since you're so hung up on her, why don't you do something about it?"

Lindsay huffed out an exasperated breath. "I told you I'm not hung up on her."

"Try telling that to someone who believes it. I was here, remember? I saw what happened."

"Rachel didn't much like me before I almost got her killed." Lindsay looked down and fidgeted with her hands. "I'm sure if she never sees me again, it'll be too soon."

"You almost got her killed?" Pat's eyes grew round, the dawning of understanding. "You're the Lindsay from the paper. The psychic."

Lindsay nodded. "It's a long story."

Waheya pushed the button on the garage-door opener and waited for the large door to open. "I don't know why I did that. I'm not parking in the garage. As soon as I get you settled, I'll run to the market. I cleaned out your refrigerator, but I haven't restocked it yet."

"You didn't have to do that, Mom."

"I beg to differ with you, my dear," Waheya said as she turned off the ignition. "As long as I'm taking care of you, the kitchen is my domain. What I say goes." She got out of the car and pulled a pair of crutches out of the backseat.

"I don't need a caretaker." Rachel crossed her arms over her chest. "I'm perfectly capable of taking care of myself." She watched her mother walk around the car and stand, waiting for her to get out. Stubbornly, she pushed open the door but flinched as she tried to get her injured leg out of the car. "Okay," she said with a sheepish grin. "Maybe I do need a little help."

With aplomb, Waheya carefully lifted Rachel's leg so she could turn in the seat. Then she took Rachel's hands to steady her as Rachel pulled herself into a standing position, balancing on her good leg. After handing Rachel the crutches, Waheya then let go but carefully watched her hobble to the door and into the house.

Inside, a huge calico cat bounded toward Rachel and wound around her legs. Walking with the crutches was difficult, but Rachel made it to the couch.

"Hey there, Miss Kitty. Did you miss me?"

Miss Kitty jumped up onto her lap, her motor turned up full blast. She then stood on her hind legs and pushed her head into Rachel's face.

"Yeah, I missed you too."

Exhausted from the short trip from the garage to the house, she leaned back and closed her eyes. Moments later, she drifted off to sleep, Miss Kitty purring contentedly on her lap.

Waheya opened the door to find Trish and David standing on the porch.

"Mom only came home yesterday," Trish said. "I hope it's not too soon to bring David over to meet her. He can be pretty rambunctious. I don't want to tire her out."

"He's the best medicine she could have." Waheya looked down at David. "How's my big boy?" She scooped the toddler up in her arms. He had a SpongeBob doll clutched in one hand, and he wrapped his other arm around her and grinned from ear to ear.

"I have a new gramma!"

"You do?"

David nodded. "I have this many," he said, tucking SpongeBob under his arm and holding up both hands. Trish reached over and closed one hand. He looked at his remaining hand and repeated, "I have this many grammas."

"Oh my, that's a lot," Waheya said as she turned and carried him into the house. "What a lucky boy you are."

Trish followed them in and looked around the living room. It really hadn't changed that much. In fact, the only change she could see was the addition of pictures of David. "Can you remember all their names, David?"

"Uh-huh. Gramma Betty, Gramma Nanny—"

"No, we just call her Nanny, not Gramma Nanny."

David looked puzzled. "But you said she's my gramma too?"

"She is," Trish said. "But she likes to be called Nanny."

The toddler shrugged and went on with his list. "Gramma Ruth." He stopped a moment and looked at Waheya. "Did you know that you're my gramma?"

Waheya put David on the couch and sat down beside him. "I'm not just your gramma, I'm your great-gramma."

At that moment, David noticed a picture of himself that he'd never seen before. It was on the coffee table, and he dropped his doll to crawl closer to it. "Look, Mama, it's me," he said, pointing. He climbed off the couch and picked up the photo.

Trish took the picture away from him and set it back on the table. "You can look, but don't touch. You wouldn't want to break Gramma Rachel's picture, would you?"

"I won't break it."

"I know you won't because you're going to leave it right there." Trish picked him up and sat him back on the couch.

David frowned and looked around the room. "Where's my new gramma?"

"She's taking a nap." Waheya stood up and held out her hand. "Would you like to go with me to see if she's awake yet?"

David grinned and slid off the couch to take her hand. Then he remembered his doll and grabbed it. "SpongeBob says he wants to see my new gramma too."

Rachel heard voices in the other room and yawned. *Mom's got that TV up kind of loud.* She heard the unmistakable sound of a very young child's voice. After she listened a moment, she realized that it was not the television. "David?" Quickly, she sat up and reached for her crutches. She'd been waiting for this meeting for three years. Her heart raced as she slowly walked to the door. *What if he doesn't like me?*

She opened the door and there he was. Her breath caught. He was beautiful. She watched him reach up to take her mother's outstretched hand, then stop when his big brown eyes fell on her.

David cocked his head to the side and studied her. "Are you my new gramma?"

Rachel tried to speak, but no words came out. She cleared her throat and tried again. "Yes, I am." She slowly crossed the room and stopped in front of him.

David reached out and touched one of Rachel's crutches. "What's this?"

"It's a crutch. It helps me walk."

"Why?"

"Because I had an accident and hurt my leg." Rachel crutched to the couch and eased herself down. She wanted to just grab David up and hug him, but she didn't want to push herself on him until he'd had a chance to get to know her a little better.

David examined the bandage on her leg. "Is this your boo-boo?" Rachel nodded. "Does it hurt?"

"Just a little."

David leaned over and kissed the bandage. "Is it better now?"

"Much better," Rachel said, "but you know what would really help would be a big hug. Do you think I could have a hug?"

David grinned and scrambled up onto the couch and wrapped his arms around Rachel's neck. She wrapped her arms around him and sighed. She finally had her grandson in her arms, and it felt wonderful.

"You've only been out of the hospital for a week, baby," Waheya said. "Don't push yourself so hard. You're going to overdo."

"My therapist said to do as much as I could tolerate."

"Yes, but I bet she didn't realize what an overachiever she was talking to. If you keep this up, you'll cause more harm than good."

Rachel slowly lowered her leg to the floor. "Don't be such a worrywart, Mom. I won't hurt myself."

Miss Kitty picked that moment to climb up on her stomach and turn daintily in a circle before flopping down to make herself comfortable, her paws kneading happily into Rachel's midsection.

Rachel grinned and scratched her under the chin. "You think I'm down here for your convenience, don't you?"

She rested a moment then lifted the leg again and began to count off the seconds. It hurt like hell, but if that was what it took to get back on her feet, so be it.

Waheya watched as Rachel strained to hold the leg up for the full count. Her face was red and her leg was beginning to tremble. "Rachel Lynn Todd, I do believe you're the stubbornest woman I've ever seen."

"I come by it naturally," Rachel said as she lowered her leg to the floor. "But you'll be happy to know that I've reached my limit." She picked up Miss Kitty and set her gently on the floor. "Give me a hand up, will ya?"

Waheya reached down, took both of Rachel's hands, and helped her to her feet. "If you're hungry, I'll go start lunch."

"Oh, I forgot to tell you. Ben's coming over and he's bringing lunch." As if on cue, the doorbell rang. Rachel shook her head and smiled. "Is that timing or what?" She let her mother get the door.

"Nice to see you again, Ben," Waheya said. "Come on in."

Ben stepped inside and closed the door. "How's our patient this afternoon?"

"Hungry. It's about damn well time you got here." Rachel limped to the kitchen table and propped her crutches against the wall before she sat down. "And since I'm a cripple, you get to wait on me." She couldn't hold her feigned irritability and broke out in a grin.

Ben placed the pizza on the table while Waheya went to the cupboard to get the plates.

"Can I interest you in a cup of coffee, Ben?" she asked. "It's a fresh pot."

The lieutenant took off his coat and hung it on the back of his chair. "I'd love some. Just point me in the direction of the cups, and I'll help myself."

"They're in the cupboard right above the coffeepot." Waheya placed three plates on the table. "How about you, hon?"

"Water for me, Mom," Rachel said as she peeked inside the box. "Mmm. Onions, tomatoes, mushrooms, and peppers. Yummy." Ben joined her at the table and helped himself to a slice and picked all the vegetables off. "You're taking all the good stuff off, Ben."

"Hey, you eat it the way you like it, and I'll eat it the way I like it." He lifted his plate and scooped everything he had just removed onto Rachel's plate. "Oh, by the way, I forgot to tell you that we found Mrs. Warren. She was right where Lindsay said she'd be." He took a bite, then reached for his cup. "In fact, the only vision she's had that didn't turn out to be true was the one about you."

Rachel grabbed a slice of pizza for herself and heaped all of Ben's discarded vegetables on top of it. "Oh, it was true all right. I already told you that she saw me digging a grave in the vision, and I did dig a grave. She just misunderstood why I was digging." She managed a big bite without losing the loose veggies. "You know, I really can't blame her for thinking I was the murderer. Under the same circumstances, I probably would have come to the same conclusion."

"She's a nice kid," Ben said.

Rachel nodded, her mouth full of pizza.

"Who?" Waheya asked as she joined them at the table.

"Lindsay Ryan," Ben said. He looked over at Rachel. "She got kicked out of her apartment because of us, you know."

Rachel swallowed her bite of pizza, then frowned. "No, I didn't. I knew she'd moved, but I had no idea we were the cause."

"Her landlord was afraid to have her living so close to his kids; thought she might have been a dangerous stalker. So he moved all her stuff out the day we hauled her in. That's why she was staying with Eddie at the cabin."

Rachel threw down her slice of pizza, loose vegetables flying off all over the table. "He can't legally do that. I've a good mind to pay him a visit when I get back on my feet."

"Back off, Todd," Ben said. "People don't always think clearly when they're scared for their kids. Lindsay was upset about being kicked out, but she told me she didn't blame him."

"Well, it still pisses me off."

"Yeah, well, she found a larger apartment that she likes better, and I had a couple of the guys help her move into the new place."

"You know what, Ben?" Rachel smiled and picked up her pizza again. "You're just an old softie."

Claire climbed out of the pool and grabbed her towel. "Okay, one more time across and back, and we're done." She monitored the action as Rachel propelled herself through the water using only her legs. "I wish all my patients worked as hard as you do. It's amazing what you've accomplished in just over three weeks."

"I have to work hard," Rachel said. "I have a slave driver for a physical therapist." She kicked back to the edge of the pool, tossed her flotation board onto the deck, then walked to the steps and held on to the rail as she climbed out of the pool. She shook her head, sending water flying in all directions.

"Speaking of slave drivers," Claire said. "From now on, we're only going to do the pool every other day. I need to get you started at the gym on the leg machines. Your leg is doing great as far as range of motion goes. It's time we concentrate on strengthening it."

Rachel stood up straight and saluted. "You're the boss." She dried off, grabbed her cane, and headed for the showers. "I'll see you tomorrow. I'm looking forward to getting back into the gym again. I've missed it."

As she walked to the shower room, Rachel's mind wandered. She found herself thinking about Lindsay Ryan. She imagined herself running her hands through Lindsay's soft red hair and kissing those oh-so-lovely lips. Her thoughts often wandered in that direction, and she chastised herself for thinking that way about a woman who probably hated her guts. *Why this woman, you idiot?* It was the first time she'd been remotely interested in anyone since Lisa died, and it had to be a woman she'd basically put through hell by accusing her of being a stalker, arresting her, and getting her thrown out of her apartment. *Well, Rachel, old girl, you've got to face her and apologize.* With a sigh, she nodded to herself. "Yep. Gotta do it."

Lindsay set a plate filled with fresh-out-of-the-oven sweet rolls on the table. "My mom used to make these every Sunday when I was growing up." She smiled a wistful smile. "Boy, did I love Sundays."

"Wow! These are great." Pat nearly swooned as she took a bite.

"You act surprised," Lindsay said. "Didn't you think they'd be good?"

"Of course I did, but these are better than good." Pat smacked her lips. "They're wonderful. In fact, they're so good that if you weren't so hung up on that cop, I'd ask you to marry me."

Lindsay rolled her eyes. "How many times do I have to tell you—"

"I know, I know. You're not hung up on her."

"Besides, it wouldn't matter even if I did have a thing for her. She's in a relationship, and I've gotta tell ya, Pat, there's no competition. The other woman's drop-dead gorgeous."

"Oh, I don't know." Pat couldn't suppress a big, appreciative grin as she let her eyes sweep Lindsay's body. "You're not so bad to look at yourself." Then she leaned back, closed her eyes, and took another bite. "I really am in heaven."

Lindsay laughed. "It sure doesn't take much to please you."

Pat put down her roll and licked her fingers. "The old saying—the quickest way to a dyke's heart is through her stomach—is true." She placed both hands over her heart and grinned. "It's yours."

"I thought it was a man's heart they were talking about in that old saying."

"Whatever." Pat shrugged, picked up her sweet roll, and took another bite. "It works either way."

Lindsay was delighted. "I wish I'd had a friend like you back home. It sure would have brightened up the last few years. I felt so lonely and isolated in that little close-minded town."

"If you hated it so much, why did you stay?"

"I couldn't leave my mom. She was in a serious car accident when I was eighteen. It caused a brain injury that prevented her from processing short-term memory into long-term." Lindsay leaned back in her chair and sighed. "It was awful while she was in the hospital. Every time she woke up, she didn't know where she was or what had happened. I'd have to calm her down and explain to her all over again. It was better when we could take her home. At least she woke up in familiar surroundings and didn't panic. My dad couldn't deal with it and moved out, but she never really understood that he was gone. Every day she'd forget and ask me where he was."

"Your dad sounds like a real piece of work."

"You have no idea. I kept asking him to come see her, but he wouldn't do it." Lindsay picked up one of the sweet rolls and took a bite. "Oh, I forgot the coffee." She got up, grabbed the coffeepot, and filled two mugs. "Next Sunday will make eight months since I lost my mom." She sat back down and took a sip of her coffee. "I really miss her."

Pat covered Lindsay's hand with her own. "I'm sorry you've had to go through the last eight months alone, but you've got a friend now."

"Thanks." Lindsay grinned. "And I'd like to know more about your life. Are you close to your folks?"

"We get along, I guess." Pat shrugged. "They'd prefer that I wasn't so butch. Kinda makes it hard for them to pretend that I'm Little Miss Normal." She picked up her cup and took a sip. "But it's my life. They've accepted that I'm not about to change."

"I don't know how my mom would have taken the news that I'm a lesbian," Lindsay said. "I suspected that I was gay, but I never told her. Didn't seem to be worth putting her through the shock of finding out, when she wouldn't even remember anyway."

"Mmm." Pat nodded. "Makes sense."

"Dad doesn't even know where I am. I couldn't have told him even if I'd wanted to, which I didn't."

"What do you mean, you couldn't have told him? I don't understand."

"I didn't know where I was going. My mom had a small life insurance policy that she left me, and I decided to use it to start a new life. I packed up everything I owned and put it in storage. Then I just got in my car and drove. No destination in mind. I just wanted to get away. When I drove into Asheville, I knew it was where I wanted to stay. It was comfortable. Not a teeming metropolis and not a hick town like the one I ran from. Once I was settled here, I had my stuff shipped. End of story."

Pat smiled. "I'm glad you chose our fair city to settle in."

Lindsay grinned back. "So am I."

Rachel parked her car in front of Lindsay's apartment building and shut off the motor. This was the first time she had been behind the wheel of a car since the shooting, and it felt good to be able to go somewhere on her own. She loved her mother, but the constant hovering over the last few weeks had taken its toll on her nerves and disposition. Waheya had made it clear that she would do all the driving until the doctor gave the okay. She even kept Rachel's keys hidden, just in case.

Rachel slid out of the car and grabbed her cane, then stood looking at the building, unable to force her legs to move. *Come on, you coward. How hard can it be to apologize? She's a nice person. She's not going to bite your head off.*

Finally willing her legs to move, Rachel started up the walkway. "Excuse me," she said to a rather butch-looking blonde woman who was uncoiling a water hose. "Do you know which apartment Lindsay Ryan lives in?"

"Sure," the woman said. "Lindsay's door is the last one on the right."

"Thanks." Rachel turned right and continued down the walkway. Once in front of Lindsay's door, she rang the doorbell. Shock was evident on the redhead's face when she opened it and found Rachel standing there.

"Detective Todd, what a surprise." She stepped back and opened the door all the way. "Please, come in."

"Thanks," Rachel said as she walked into the room.

"It's good to see you up and around. I have to tell you, the last time I saw you, you didn't look very good."

Rachel nodded. "That wasn't one of my better days."

"I've been calling Lieutenant Rowers to keep up on how you're doing," Lindsay said. "He tells me that Monday you start back to work on light duty."

"True." Rachel nodded again. "The doctor wanted to keep me off work for six weeks, but I badgered him into letting me go back a week early. I was going stir-crazy at home."

"Can I get you something to drink, Detective Todd?"

"Sure," Rachel said. "Anything cold would be nice. And please, we worked this out before. Call me Rachel."

"Okay...Rachel. Something cold coming up. Make yourself comfortable, and I'll be right back."

Rachel sat on the couch and looked around the small room. She had to admit that this place was a lot nicer than the postage-stamp-sized apartment above that garage. She looked up and smiled when Lindsay returned with a glass in her hand.

"I hope you like Pepsi," Lindsay said as she handed her the glass. "It's all I have that's cold."

"Pepsi's fine," Rachel said and took a swallow.

Lindsay sat at the other end of the couch, and the room fell into an awkward silence. "So, what brings you to my door?" she finally asked.

"Well, I know I could use the excuse that I was just doing my job." Rachel placed her glass on the table, then laced her fingers together in her lap. "But I still wanted to come by and tell you I'm sorry I treated you so badly." She looked down at her hands. "You didn't deserve that."

"Thanks," Lindsay said, and then she laughed. "I must confess that when I first met you, I thought you were a first-class bitch that only a mother could love."

"I guess I deserved that."

"Perception can be very subjective. I'm sure your lover has never thought of you that way. It was clear to me, when I saw her there in the hospital, that she loves you very much."

Lover? Who the hell...She has to be referring to Trish. No one came to the hospital to see me that night except Mom and Trish, and Lindsay met Mom. "For someone who's supposed to be psychic, you sure get things mixed up a lot, but I guess I should be flattered that you think a beautiful young woman like Trish would be attracted to an old broad like me."

"You're not old, and she was more than attracted to you. She said she was in love with you." Lindsay could still hear the words the sobbing woman had uttered in the waiting room that night.

"I'm old enough to be her mother," Rachel said coyly. "In fact, I'm old enough to be a grandmother."

"No, you're not."

"Oh, but I am, Lindsay. In fact, that was my daughter Trish."

"Oh." Lindsay smiled. "Wow, that's great."

"Is it now?" Rachel cocked her head and grinned. "Let me get this straight. Did you mean great that I don't look old enough to be Trish's mother? Or were you relieved that we aren't lovers?" She wiggled her eyebrows. "I hope it's the latter."

Rachel's smile broadened as she watched the blush creep up Lindsay's neck and blaze in her cheeks. "My, my. I haven't caused a woman to blush like that in a very long time. I think I quite like it."

Lindsay fanned her face and grinned. "Okay, I admit it. I was a little jealous when I thought she was your partner. I know I had no reason to be. I mean, you and I aren't even friends."

"For the record, I'm not in a relationship, and I haven't been in one for a very long time. How about you?"

Lindsay shook her head. "No, there's no one in my life." She moved a little closer on the couch, but her face turned serious. "As long as we're apologizing, I'm sorry I almost got you killed."

"Not your fault. Eddie's the one who pulled the trigger," Rachel said. "Let's keep the blame where it belongs."

Lindsay looked down and worried a loose thread in the hem of her shirt. "I can't help feeling guilty."

"I wish you wouldn't. I'm going to be okay, and more importantly, you saved Mandy's life. You've got nothing to feel guilty about."

Lindsay looked up, the smile returning to her face. "Thank you."

"I really admire you, Lindsay. No matter how much we all tried to stop you, you stuck to your guns. Most people would have backed off and left Mandy to her fate. You're really very special."

"No, really I'm not."

"Oh, but you are," Rachel insisted. "And I'd love to get to know you better."

Lindsay blushed again. "I'd like to get to know you better too."

"Good." Rachel's face lit up with a radiant smile. "Since we've both agreed that we'd like to get to know each other better, how would you like to spend Saturday together?"

Lindsay grinned. "That sounds great. What did you have in mind?"

"Well, you'll have to trust me, because I'm not going to tell you. You'll just have to wait till Saturday."

"This is going to make me crazy, you know."

Rachel smiled again. "A good kind of crazy, I hope."

"You're really not going to tell me, are you?"

"Nope." Rachel looked at her watch and frowned. "Listen, I've got to get home or my mother will send the force out looking for me." She took a last swallow of Pepsi, then stood and grabbed her cane.

Lindsay walked with Rachel to her car. "I'm sorry you couldn't stay longer, but I'm glad you stopped by, and I'm really looking forward to Saturday."

"Me too," Rachel answered as she opened the door. She stuck her cane in the backseat, then slid behind the wheel. "What say I come by around ten Saturday morning? Oh, I almost forgot; dress casually and wear comfortable walking shoes." She winked at Lindsay and started the car.

"Comfortable walking shoes, got it," Lindsay said. "I'll see you Saturday." She waved as Rachel drove away, then wrapped her arms around herself as she watched long after the car was out of sight.

"Earth to Lindsay," Pat said as she joined her on the sidewalk. "Are you planted there?"

Lindsay turned and threw her arms around her friend. "She likes me, Pat!"

"Of course, she likes you. How could anyone not like you?"

"I mean she really likes me." Lindsay let go and stepped back. "She asked me out on a date for Saturday. Well, she didn't actually call it a date, but she asked me to spend Saturday with her."

"And what about Miss Drop-Dead Gorgeous you told me about?"

Lindsay grinned. "Turns out I was wrong about that. It was her daughter I saw that night at the hospital."

"I need to hear more," Pat said. "Let's order a pizza and you can tell me all about her visit. For starters, how did you find out it was her daughter?"

"Oh, that." They turned and walked toward Pat's apartment. "I kind of mentioned that I saw her lover at the hospital that night, and she told me she was not in a relationship and that it was her daughter, Trish, that I saw."

Pat opened her door and stepped aside for Lindsay to enter. "You actually came right out and just asked her? Boy, you don't mess around; you cut right to the chase."

"Well, it wasn't quite like that." Lindsay sat at the kitchen table and waited for Pat to join her. "What did you think of her?" She grinned at Pat. "Isn't she about the sexiest thing you've ever seen?"

Pat smiled back. "Well, I will admit she's pretty easy on the eyes." She sat down across from Lindsay and pulled the phone over. "What do you like on your pizza?"

"Anything you like is fine," Lindsay answered. "I'm not picky." She watched as Pat punched in the number and placed their order. "Wow, you didn't even look up the number. Either you eat a lot of pizza or you've got a great memory for numbers."

"None of the above," she said. "My ex-girlfriend used to manage the place. For some reason, I still remember the number."

CHAPTER SIX

When Rachel arrived home, she found Waheya unpacking groceries and putting them away. "You know, Mom, it's not like I'm trying to get rid of you or anything like that, but you don't really need to do all my grocery shopping anymore. You gave me my car keys back, remember?"

"Of course, I remember," Waheya said. "I'm not quite senile yet." She put the last item in the pantry, and then turned to Rachel. "It's just that I know how hard it is to carry things with just one hand, and I figured I'd help out until you get rid of that cane."

Rachel walked over and wrapped her arms around Waheya. "Have I told you lately how much I love you?"

Waheya squeezed back. "I love you too, sweetie, and it's always nice to hear." She released her grip and sat down at the kitchen table. "Let me get off my feet for a few minutes and then I'll start some dinner."

"You know you're spoiling me, Mom." Rachel followed Waheya to the table and sat down across from her. "A gal could get used to being waited on hand and foot. You may just be creating a monster." When Waheya laughed, Rachel joined in. "You think I'm kidding, but I'm not."

"I've had years of practice dealing with my spoiled children," Waheya said. "I think I can deal with it."

"By the way, I got my release from the doctor today. I start back to work on Monday."

"So soon?"

"I need to get back to work, Mom. All this idle time is driving me nuts."

Waheya sighed. "I know, but I can't help but worry. I don't want you to overdo."

"No, ma'am, I won't overdo. The doctor released me for light duty only, and Ben says he'll hold me to it. I'll just be hanging around the department, catching up on paperwork and helping out with research on open cases. No street work, so you don't need to worry."

Waheya nodded in approval. "Good."

"I did an impulsive thing today, Mom," Rachel confided, "and now I'm not so sure I should have."

"What did you do?"

"I asked Lindsay to spend Saturday with me. I thought I'd take her to the powwow."

Waheya's face lit up. "Is that all? From the look on your face, I thought it was something bad."

"It seemed so right and natural to ask her when I was over there a little while ago, but now I'm having second thoughts. I'm not sure I'm ready to get involved with anyone, Mom."

"Honey, it's just an afternoon out with a friend. I wouldn't call that getting involved." Waheya reached over and squeezed Rachel's hand. "And besides, even if it was more, it's been almost four years since Lisa died. If you're not ready by now, you never will be."

"I know you're right, Mom," Rachel said. "It's just when I come home to our house, and I look around at our things...I don't know, it almost feels disloyal to be attracted to someone else, and I am attracted to Lindsay."

"Well, it's not disloyal, sweetheart. And Lisa would be the first one to tell you that."

Rachel laced her fingers together and smiled. "Yeah, I think she would."

"I know she would."

"When I was with Lindsay this afternoon, I enjoyed flirting with her. She got so flustered, and it was cute." Rachel started to laugh. "Do you know that she thought Trish and I were lovers? Can you believe it?"

"Where did she get an idea like that?"

"Apparently, she saw her at the hospital that first night." Rachel grinned. "She told me she was jealous."

"You really like her, don't you?"

"Yeah, I do," Rachel said. "And it's not just that she risked her life to save me, although I can't deny that may be part of it."

"Then don't be afraid to go for it, baby. You deserve to be happy, and I know you haven't been for a long time."

"I will," Rachel said. "Thanks, Mom."

Lindsay grabbed her towel and stepped out of the shower. She dried her hair, then rubbed the fabric briskly over her body. That task complete, she tossed the towel over the shower door and picked up her comb, ready to run it through her damp hair. She jumped at the sound of the doorbell, grabbed her robe, and rushed to the door.

Please don't let that be her, I'm not ready yet. She opened the door and breathed a sigh of relief. "Oh, it's only you," she said when she saw Pat standing on her doorstep.

"Gee, thanks. I'm glad to see you too."

Lindsay laughed. "I didn't mean it like that." She opened the door wide and stepped aside. "I'm glad you're here. I need your advice on something. Come on back." She led the way to her small bedroom and picked up some clothing from the bed. "Do you think this is casual enough?" She held up a pair of nice slacks and a jacket for her friend to see.

Pat shook her head. "You told me she said to wear comfortable walking shoes. That strongly suggests you're going to be doing some walking, probably outside. If I were you, I'd wear some shorts. It's supposed to be pretty warm today."

"Hmm, you could be right about that," Lindsay said. "Darn, I wish I knew where we were going. That'd help a lot." She pulled open a drawer and rummaged through it. "How about these?" She held up a pair of dark blue walking shorts.

"Perfect."

Lindsay tossed the shorts on the bed, then pulled open another drawer. Now that she was wearing shorts, she would have to rethink the rest of her ensemble. A nice jacket and blouse simply would not do. She found a sky blue T-shirt with Winnie the

Pooh and Piglet on the front and smiled. "This will do." She turned back to Pat. "Go ahead and help yourself to something cold to drink while I get dressed, and I'll be out in a minute."

"I don't get to watch?"

"No, you don't get to watch." Smiling, Lindsay grabbed Pat by the shoulders and shooed her toward the door. "Now scoot."

"Ya can't blame a gal for trying," Pat said as she sauntered out of the room.

"You're incorrigible, you know that?"

"I know. It's part of my irresistible charm that somehow you seem to be able to resist." Pat shrugged. "Go figure."

Lindsay closed the door and returned to the bed. *I wonder if she'll try to kiss me*? She pulled a bra and panties out of a drawer. *Am I making too much of today? What if she only wants to be friends?* She took off her robe and tossed it on her nightstand. The image of Rachel making love to her resurfaced, and she couldn't stop the involuntary shiver that swept over her body. *No, that was real. Just be patient, Lindsay girl. It'll happen.*

Her thoughts were interrupted when Pat said, "Better hurry up, Lindsay, lovergirl's here."

Lindsay threw open her bedroom door and rushed to the window, one of her shoes still in her hand. She saw Rachel get out of her car and start for the apartment, and her breath caught in her throat. Rachel was dressed in a pair of faded cutoff jeans and a red tank top. "Damn, she looks good in red." Lindsay sat on the couch and hurriedly put on her other shoe.

The doorbell sounded and Pat reached for the doorknob.

"Do I look okay?" Lindsay stood and tucked her shirt into her shorts.

Pat gave her a thumbs-up and opened the door. "Hi, I'm Pat," she said, extending her hand. "We sort of met the other day when you were here."

Rachel smiled and took her hand. "Nice to see you again, Pat. I'm Rachel." She looked past Pat at Lindsay, and her smile broadened. "You ready?"

Lindsay grinned and nodded. "I was worried this might be too casual," she said, indicating her shorts. "But I see we're on the same wavelength."

"Better bring something a little warmer for this evening. It'll get cold as soon as the sun goes down."

"Right," Lindsay said, then turned and ran back into the bedroom. She returned a moment later with a bag clutched in her hand. "Okay, I'm ready."

The three women walked to Rachel's car. "I'll see you tomorrow," Pat said as she closed the passenger door for Lindsay.

Lindsay flashed Pat a grin. "See you tomorrow." She grabbed her seat belt and buckled herself in. "Okay," she said, turning to Rachel. "It's Saturday, so you can tell me where we're going."

Rachel started the car and buckled her seat belt. "You'll see when we get there," she said and pulled the car away from the curb.

"That is so not fair. You said I only had to wait till Saturday."

"Trust me, it'll still be Saturday when we get there."

"But I want to know now. I've waited two whole days. You have to tell me."

Rachel shook her head.

"Please?"

"Nope."

"You're mean." Lindsay crossed her arms over her chest and stuck out her lower lip.

"Guilty as charged." Rachel glanced over at her companion and gently laughed. "And you're cute when you pout."

Lindsay tried to hold on to her pout, but when Rachel started laughing, she couldn't help joining in. "No fair," she said. "I can't stay mad at you when you make me laugh. Can you at least tell me how long it's going to take to get there?"

"A little over an hour." Rachel looked over and smiled when Lindsay groaned. "Don't worry, the time will fly by. You'll see." She motioned with her thumb toward the backseat. "I've got a cooler in the back if you need anything to drink."

Lindsay unbuckled her seat belt and turned so she could reach the cooler. She peeked in and saw that it contained at least a dozen bottles of water and a six-pack of Pepsi. She grabbed one and turned back around. "You remembered," she said, popping the top and taking a sip.

"I'm a cop. I get paid to remember little details."

"You want anything?"

"Nope. I'm good."

Lindsay took another sip, then set the can in the drink holder. She cocked her head and studied Rachel's profile. With her exotic features and lovely brown skin, she really was striking. "What made you decide to become a cop?"

"Well, my father was a police officer and I worshiped him," Rachel replied. "He tried his best to discourage me. He didn't think being a cop was very ladylike." She looked at Lindsay and grinned. "As you can see, it didn't work. I can't remember ever wanting to be anything but a cop."

"Did he come around?" Lindsay was intrigued. "About you being a cop, I mean."

Rachel checked her mirror and passed a slow-moving truck. "He never knew. He was killed when I was ten." She stole a glance at Lindsay. "The guy who did it got off on a technicality. I think that made me even more determined to be a cop."

"I'm so sorry," Lindsay said. "I lost my mom a few months ago, and I know what it's like to lose someone like that."

"Damn. You'd just lost your mom when we put you through hell. I'm sorry."

"You already apologized for that. It's over."

"I know, but just the same, I feel guilty about it."

Lindsay put her hand on Rachel's arm. "Well, don't. And besides, I'm the one who got you shot."

"What happened to me happened, and I wouldn't change it even if I could."

"I don't understand."

"If I hadn't been shot, my life would have kept on the way it was."

"And that's a bad thing?"

Rachel nodded. "A very bad thing. No matter how bad getting shot seemed at the time, it was a blessing to me in disguise. It brought my daughter and grandson back into my life. That alone was worth it all."

"You have a grandson?"

"I told you I was a grandmother, Lindsay."

"No, you told me you were old enough to be a grandmother. There's a difference."

"Okay, okay." Rachel laughed. "My daughter is almost twenty-five, and I have a three-year-old grandson."

"You must have been a child bride."

"Trish was born when I was seventeen," Rachel said, "but her father and I were never married."

"Did you love him?"

"He was my best friend in school, and everyone thought he was my boyfriend. By senior year, he thought so too. I was pretty sure I was gay by then, but I wasn't ready to admit it to myself, let alone anyone else. Instead, I was sixteen, and stupid, and wanted to prove to myself that I was straight." Rachel rolled her eyes at the memory. "Needless to say, the only thing I proved was that you can get pregnant with only one try. I was seven months pregnant when I graduated."

"They let you graduate with your class?"

Rachel nodded. "Richard and his father tried to pressure me into getting married, and I might have done it if it wasn't for my mom. She's really something. She stood toe to toe with Mr. Morton and told him that no one was pushing her daughter into doing something that wasn't right for her."

"See, we've got something in common. My mom was pretty cool too."

Lindsay glanced at her watch. They had been on the road for over an hour when they pulled up in front of a stone wall with a sign atop it constructed of large wooden planks. The sign read, Welcome. Cherokee Indian Reservation.

"We're going to the Cherokee Indian reservation?" Lindsay couldn't hide her delight.

"Yep, they're having a powwow here this weekend, and I thought you might enjoy coming. Have you ever been to a powwow?"

"No, I haven't. You sure we're allowed to attend? I though a powwow was where all the head guys from different tribes got together in the old days and discussed war strategies, or treaties, or political stuff. No squaws allowed. I didn't realize they still had them."

Rachel laughed. "I'm afraid you've been watching too many old western movies. A powwow is a celebration, and the Cherokee Nation has always been a matriarchal society. Many tribal leaders and warriors were women. In fact, our women didn't lose the right to vote until the white man forced them to embrace the white man's laws. And 'squaw' is another thing popularized by westerns." She dropped her light tone. "Indian women are not called squaws. That's actually a derogatory term. It's like calling a woman a cunt or a whore."

"I guess I just put my foot in it," Lindsay said. "I didn't realize I was using a Cherokee curse word. I'm sorry."

"Nothing to be sorry about; you didn't know. Besides, the Cherokee language has no curse words or obscenities. 'Squaw' is not a Cherokee word. I can't remember what tribe it originated with, but it was not a curse word, it was just the word for the female genitalia. It was the white man who twisted the word to mean what they wanted from Indian women. Now most people don't have any idea that it's offensive to us."

"You're Cherokee?"

"I'm biracial. My mother is Cherokee and my father is black." Rachel drove into the fairground parking area. "Come on. Let's go see if we can get a good spot."

"Have you been to many powwows?" Lindsay got out of the car and stretched.

"More than I can count." Rachel walked around to the back of the car and opened the trunk. "I grew up here, and my grandmother has been one of the food vendors for as long as I can remember. My mom and Aunt Sanaqua do most of the work now, but Elisi's still in charge of the fry bread."

"Were you born on the reservation?"

Rachel shook her head and pulled two folding chairs out of the trunk. "I was born in New Orleans, but when Dad died, my mom packed us up and moved back home. She was born here."

"Your dad wasn't?"

"No. He was a big-city boy, born and bred. He came out here on vacation and met my mom." A smile came to Rachel's face. "For him, it was love at first sight, but it took a couple of years of writing back and forth before my mom was convinced it wasn't just a summer fling for him and that it was really going to last." Rachel handed the chairs and a blanket to Lindsay. "Hold on to these and I'll get the cooler."

"Maybe I better take the cooler. I don't want you to hurt yourself."

"Oh, ye of little faith. You're just like my mom; always worrying." Grinning, Rachel reached into the trunk and pulled out a handcart. "Not to worry. This little baby will carry all the weight. I wouldn't have tried to lug that cooler any distance even before I was shot." She closed the trunk and walked to the side of the car. With a faint grunt, she pulled the cooler out and settled it onto the handcart.

"These will fit on that thing too," Lindsay said, stacking the chairs on top of the cooler. She handed Rachel the blanket, then stepped behind the handcart. "I'll drive, you lead the way."

Rachel raised her eyebrows. "Anyone ever tell you you're a pushy broad?" She reached into the car, grabbed her cane, then started off across the grass.

"Once or twice." Lindsay fell into step beside her, guiding the cart, and they walked down the hill toward a grouping of vendors' stands that formed a large circle. Once inside the circle, she could see another smaller circle, this one made out of bales of hay. Spaced behind the bales were several large drums. There was a large expanse of grass between the vendors' tents and the hay bales, and Rachel found a spot she liked on the grass and spread out the blanket.

After positioning the handcart in a corner, Lindsay took off the chairs, then wrestled the cooler off as well. "There. All set," she said.

Rachel reached into her pocket and pulled out a small bottle of sunscreen. She squeezed some into her palm and rubbed it on her face and arms, then poured out more for her legs. "Here," she tossed the bottle to Lindsay, "put some of this on. We're going to be outside most of the day, and I wouldn't want that pale skin of yours to burn."

"Thanks. I didn't even think about bringing sunscreen. Of course, I didn't know it was going to be an outdoor day." Lindsay squeezed out some of the lotion and rubbed it on her arms. "I'm surprised you need sunscreen."

"I may be darker than you are, but I can still burn, or worse yet, get skin cancer. I don't believe in taking any chances. My mom's bringing a large umbrella for us to use. That'll help too."

"Your mom's going to be here?" Lindsay hoped the disappointment didn't show on her face. She had thought it was going to be just her and Rachel on this outing.

"All my family on my mother's side will be here," Rachel said. "Aunts, uncles, cousins. And my grandmother makes the best fry bread you've ever tasted."

"I've never tasted fry bread."

"Do you like tacos?" Lindsay nodded. "Then you've got to try an Indian taco made with my grandmother's fry bread. You'll love it."

Lindsay smiled at Rachel's enthusiasm. "I can't wait to try one."

"Come on. We have two or three hours before the dancing starts. Plenty of time to make the rounds."

The first stand they came to was filled with everything leather. There were belts, tunics, dresses, moccasins, and jewelry. Lindsay stopped to admire them and picked up a beaded leather necklace. "These are beautiful."

The vendor turned around. "Thanks. I'll have more stuff out in a little while. I'm a little late getting set up." His eyes tracked to the woman standing beside her. "Rachel!" He rushed over and pulled her in for a big hug. When he released her, he took a step back and looked her up and down. "I heard what happened, but you look good." He noted the cane. "Guess you won't be dancing today."

Rachel shook her head. "Maybe next time." She turned to her companion. "Lindsay, this is my cousin, Brian. Brian, this is my friend, Lindsay."

Brian shook Lindsay's hand. "It's very nice to meet you, Lindsay. I don't know how you got her here, but thanks. It's been years since she's graced us with her presence."

"Believe me, I didn't do anything," Lindsay said. "Coming here today was her idea."

Brian reached over and grabbed Rachel's hand. "C'mere, I've got something for you."

Lindsay stayed where she was and looked at the jewelry on display while Rachel followed her cousin. When Rachel returned, Lindsay noticed she was wearing a pair of leather moccasins. "Why are your shoes wet?"

"You walk them dry," Rachel said. "That way the leather forms to your foot." She turned to Brian. "Thanks, *gusdi idadadv*, I'll pick up my other shoes later."

He pulled her in for another hug. "I still can't believe you're here. Did my mom know you were coming? She didn't even mention it to me."

"It was a last-minute decision," Rachel said. "I guess Mom didn't get a chance to tell her."

"Well, I hope this means that we'll be seeing more of you from now on."

Rachel nodded. "Almost dying can make you reevaluate your priorities." She looked over at Lindsay, then back at her cousin. "I'd love to stay and visit longer, Brian, but this is my friend's first powwow, and I want to show her around."

"Oh, sure." Brian turned to Lindsay. "I hope you enjoy your first powwow."

"I'm sure I will," Lindsay said. "And it was really nice to meet you, Brian."

As Rachel and Lindsay continued around the circle of vendors, Lindsay noticed that Rachel seemed to know at least half of them. "Why did you stop coming to the reservation when you obviously have so many friends and family here?"

Rachel shrugged. "I didn't do it consciously, really. It just sort of happened. Things happened in my life a few years back that were hard to deal with. I guess I used my work to compensate and refocus. Before I knew it, years had passed, and I was in the hospital wondering why I had let all the people who were close to me slip into the background. That was a real wake-up call. I don't intend to let it happen again."

They continued to walk, and Lindsay was in awe every time they stopped to watch one of the Indian artisans at work. Everywhere she looked, there was incredibly intricate beadwork, leatherwork, and fine silver jewelry. No matter what direction she looked in, there was something made from any number of combinations of leather, feathers, and beads.

"She makes it look so easy," Lindsay said to Rachel as they stopped to watch an older woman who was weaving a basket. She was fascinated as she watched those nimble fingers work their magic.

The woman working on the basket smiled. "It is easy," she said. "Just takes practice."

Rachel nodded. "A lot of practice."

"Do you know how to weave a basket?" Lindsay asked.

"Well, it's been a long time, but I could probably still remember how to make a simple one."

Lindsay grinned. "I'm impressed."

Rachel laughed. "You shouldn't be. Remember, I said probably. It's not a sure thing. Besides, I never did anything like these. Basket weaving was not my thing, but my grandmother insisted I learn."

They started walking again, and Lindsay's nose told her they were approaching the food vendors. Just then Rachel said, "I'm getting hungry. What say we go hunt up my mom's booth, and I'll treat you to that Indian taco I told you about?"

"Sounds great. I'm getting kinda hungry myself." Lindsay spotted the older woman she had seen at the hospital and tapped Rachel on the arm. "Oh, look, there's your mom."

Sanaqua saw them at about the same time, and her face lit up. She rushed over to greet them and embraced Rachel. "I couldn't believe it when Waheya told me you were coming." Then she released her hold on Rachel and turned to Lindsay. "You must be Lindsay. I'm Rachel's aunt Sanaqua. Waheya told me how you saved our Rachel's life. I'm so glad you could come." Before Lindsay could respond, Sanaqua pulled her into a fierce hug. "Bless you, my dear."

Lindsay was sure her surprise showed on her face, and Rachel laughed out loud. "I guess I should have warned you that I have a very demonstrative family."

Sanaqua released her hold on Lindsay and turned back to her niece. "You sure look better than the last time I saw you."

"Well, I should hope so. Last time, I was flat on my back in the hospital."

Sanaqua linked arms with Rachel and Lindsay and walked them toward the booth she and her sister ran. "Waheya tells me that you start back to work on Monday."

Rachel nodded. "I think I've milked all the sympathy I can get out of this leg. Time to get back to work." She rubbed her stomach. "Not to change the subject, but we're hungry. Where's the food?"

This time it was Lindsay's turn to laugh. The Rachel she was seeing today was such a different person than the Rachel she had first met. This one was open and friendly, and she wondered if what Rachel said about reevaluating her priorities had something to do with the change.

Of course, she couldn't really expect a police detective who thought Lindsay was a pedophile to have been open and friendly toward her. She also had to admit that her own attitude had been colored when she had first seen Rachel's tattoo. In fact, it was remarkable that the two of them were friends at all, considering everything that had happened.

"Yeah," Lindsay said, "I can't wait to try my first Native American taco."

Rachel nudged her. "You don't need to be so politically correct."

"Are you sure? I wouldn't want to offend anyone."

"You won't."

"That's right," Sanaqua said." We call ourselves Indians; to hell with political correctness. Now, come on. I wouldn't want to see the two of you waste away right here in front of my eyes. Waheya! Look who I found."

Waheya popped her head around the corner of the canvas and smiled. "It's so nice to see you again." She too welcomed Lindsay with a hug.

"I warned you," Rachel said to Lindsay when Waheya finally let go of her. "Mom, I told Lindsay you'd fix her an Indian taco. She's never eaten fry bread."

"Oh, my. Well, I think it's time we remedied that." Waheya turned back to the booth. "How about a taco and some fried green tomatoes?"

Lindsay stopped short and turned to Rachel. "You eat green tomatoes?"

"Mmm. You're gonna love 'em."

"I'm willing to try them," Lindsay whispered. "But no guarantees."

"Fair enough."

They stopped at the counter in front of the booth, and Lindsay noticed an older woman sitting in the back patting out balls of dough into half-inch patties. Rachel walked behind the counter to the woman and leaned down to kiss her on the cheek, then wrapped her arms around her. "*Gvgeyui, Elisi*," she said.

"*SdvgeyuI*," the old woman replied.

Rachel stood up and motioned for Lindsay to join them. "Elisi, this is my friend Lindsay. I told her you make the best fry bread around."

Lindsay approached respectfully, and the old woman stood up and wiped her flowered hands on her apron. Then once again, Lindsay was pulled in for a hug.

"*Osiyo Quetseli o'gina'li tsilugi. Nihi uwoduhi gigage gitlu,*" Elisi said.

"She said that my friend is welcome," Rachel translated. "She also said that you have beautiful red hair. I must confess that I agree with her."

Lindsay looked at Rachel's grandmother and smiled, then looked back to Rachel. "Could you tell her thank you? And tell her that all of your family has made me feel very welcome."

"You just told her," Rachel said. "She understands English pretty well; she just refuses to speak it." She turned to her grandmother and winked. "It's her way of making sure that her family doesn't forget the language of their people."

Waheya tapped Rachel on the shoulder. "Excuse me, sweetie, but I need you to move so I can get to my tomatoes."

Rachel nodded, bent down, and kissed her grandmother again. "We're going to get out of the way, Elisi. We'll wait out front."

"*Donadagohvi ihedolvi,*" Elisi said and patted Lindsay's arm again. Lindsay looked to Rachel for a translation.

"She said good-bye and she hopes you come back."

"I will. Good-bye." Lindsay smiled at the old woman, then followed her friend out of the booth. She watched Rachel's mother assemble their tacos. "Looks good and smells even better."

"I love this stuff." Rachel eyed the plates heading her way. "But I can't eat like this too often; my cholesterol would soar."

Waheya set two plates of food on the counter. "I hope you enjoy your first taste of Indian cooking, Lindsay." Then she faced

Rachel. "Uncle Bob should be back soon, and I'll have him bring the umbrella over for you."

"Thanks, Mom." Rachel picked up her plate and led the way back to their spot. She dropped onto one of the chairs. "Boy, I was ready to sit down."

"Me too." Lindsay sank into the other seat. She took a bite of her taco and her face lit up. "This is really good." She looked at Rachel's taco and noticed that it had mushrooms. "Yours is different than mine."

"I'm a vegetarian," Rachel said.

"Really? I've never met a vegetarian before."

Rachel stabbed a bite of tomato and grinned. "You probably have and just didn't know it. We're everywhere." She motioned to her plate. "You're welcome to try a bite if you'd like."

"Okay. What the heck. This is a day for trying new things." Lindsay set her plate in her lap and held out her hand.

Rachel handed her plate over and watched as Lindsay took a curious bite of her taco.

"It's good," Lindsay said around a mouthful of food, "but I think I like mine better." She handed the plate back. "Could you pass me a Pepsi?"

Rachel reached into the cooler, grabbed a bottle of water and a can of Pepsi, and handed the Pepsi to Lindsay.

"Thanks." Deciding it was time to try the fried green tomatoes, Lindsay picked one up and took a bite. "Wow, these are great. I never would have thought a green tomato could taste this good."

Rachel's mouth was full, but she nodded her agreement. "I like them raw too," she said when she finally swallowed her bite. "Actually, I like tomatoes any way I can get them."

"Are all your family vegetarians?"

Rachel shook her head. "No, I'm the only one." She took a drink of water, then placed the bottle on the ground beside her chair. "When I was fourteen, one of my grandfather's sows accidentally rolled over onto one of her little ones and broke its hip. He gave her to me to foster and I raised her as a pet. Called her Sally Slop-Bucket. She was smart as a whip and followed me around like a puppy dog when she was finally able to walk. Problem was, when she was grown, her crippled hip wouldn't support her weight properly, and my grandfather butchered her one day while I was at school. I've been a vegetarian ever since."

"That must have been awful."

"Yeah, it was. I don't think my grandfather had any idea just how traumatic it was for me."

A man arrived with a large umbrella and broke the somber mood.

Rachel placed her plate on top of the cooler. "Hey there, Uncle Bob." She stood and grinned at the silver-haired man, ready for an embrace.

"It's about damn well time you came back for a visit," he said and wrapped his arms around her in a bear hug. When he let go, he turned to the cart that held the umbrella. "Where do you want this?"

"Behind the chairs will be great."

He grunted as he hefted the five-gallon tub of cement that was the umbrella's base. "Damn thing weighs a ton." He put the tub down behind the folding chairs and opened up the umbrella. "I swear, it never used to be this heavy. I must be getting old."

"Thanks, Uncle Bob," Rachel said. "You're a lifesaver. I fear my pale little redheaded friend would burn to a crisp without it." She took his arm and led him around to the front of the chairs. "Uncle Bob, this is Lindsay."

"Hello, Lindsay," he said. "It's nice to meet you."

Lindsay smiled. "It's nice to meet you too."

"Well, I've gotta run, ladies. Lots to get done before I have to go change."

"Uncle Bob's the head singer," Rachel said to Lindsay. She pointed to the large drums. "He'll be playing and singing when the dancing starts."

"Are you going to be dancing, Rachel?" Bob asked.

"No, I'm strictly a spectator this time around."

"We've missed you, you know."

"I know."

Bob turned to Lindsay. "You stay under this here umbrella, little lady. Rachel's right about that white skin of yours. Better put on some sunblock too."

Little lady? "Thanks, I put some on a little while ago."

"Well, don't forget to reapply every once in a while," Bob said. "I've seen many a sunburn on people who claimed to be wearing sunblock." He grabbed his cart. "Take care, now. I'll see you later." He tossed a quick wave over his shoulder as he walked away.

Lindsay popped her last bite into her mouth and chewed thoughtfully as she watched Rachel's uncle walk away. All of Rachel's relatives had been warm and friendly, and she decided she could easily like her family very much. "It must be nice to have such a large family." She stuck her plate under her chair until she could find a proper trash receptacle.

"This is just the tip of the iceberg. My dad's side of the family is even larger."

Lindsay sighed. "There's just me and my dad, and I don't have much use for him anymore."

"No siblings?"

"Nope. My mother had five miscarriages before I was born, and the doctor told her she would never carry a baby to full term, but here I am. She called me her little miracle." She looked over at Rachel. "How about you, any brothers or sisters?"

"One of each," Rachel said. "I'm the baby. My sister Nancy is three years older than I am, and Mark is seven years older." She placed her empty plate on top of the cooler, then picked up her water and absentmindedly started peeling the label. "Mark had a hard time moving out here after we lost my dad. He considered this the sticks, and he hated it. He also missed his friends. He convinced Mom to let him go back to New Orleans and stay with our grandparents so he could graduate with his class. He's still there." She smiled. "He's a DJ on one of the local radio stations there."

"What about your sister?"

"She lives in Cherokee and teaches school. She'll be here any time now; she's always late. I never expect to see her before the dancing starts."

"Will she be dancing?"

"Oh, sure. She wouldn't miss it."

Just then, the MC stepped up to the microphone and announced that everyone should stand for the grand entry. There were about eight men around each of the large drums, and when the singing and drumming began, the music reverberated through the crowd. Lindsay stood and watched in awe as the procession started. The flag bearers entered first. Behind them were Indian men dressed in full regalia, and bringing up the rear were the women in all their finery. The sight was breathtaking.

Rachel looked over at her spellbound friend and smiled. "I'm glad you came with me today."

"So am I." Lindsay returned the smile.

Lindsay rang Pat's doorbell and waited impatiently for her to answer. When she didn't, Lindsay knocked on the door, then rang the bell again.

"Hold your horses," Pat called.

As soon as the door was open, Lindsay fairly burst into the room. "I had the most wonderful day yesterday." She grabbed Pat's arm and pulled her toward the couch. "Come sit down and I'll tell you all about it."

"Let me put on a pot of coffee and go pee first," Pat said. "I'm not even awake yet."

Lindsay looked at her watch. "It's past nine. Just be thankful I didn't wake you at seven when I woke up."

Pat rolled her eyes and shuffled to the kitchen. She set up the coffeemaker, then exited for the bathroom. "She better have been damn good in the sack for you to drag me out of bed like this. I was out until the wee hours last night. Be right back."

"She didn't take me to bed last night. She didn't even try to kiss me," Lindsay said as she followed to the bathroom door.

Pat turned around in the bathroom doorway, an incredulous look on her face. "Not even a kiss?" She shook her head. "I don't know, Linds, she seems kind of slow on the uptake to me. You sure she's the one?"

Lindsay flashed a radiant smile. "I'm sure. But I don't want to be too pushy. I don't want to scare her off."

"Hold that thought. We need to talk. Be with you in a minute." Pat rolled her eyes again, then closed the bathroom door.

After her bathroom chores, Pat was definitely awake and ready for Lindsay's story. She walked back to the kitchen, grabbed two mugs, and handed them to Lindsay. "You pour the coffee, and I'll get the milk and sugar."

They both settled down at the kitchen table with appropriately fixed coffees. "Okay, I'm ready." Pat blew a cooling breath across the surface of her coffee. "So tell me, if you didn't even get a kiss, what's all the excitement about?"

"It was just a wonderful day, that's all. Being with her made me happy." Lindsay also blew on her coffee before taking a sip. "She took me to a real Indian powwow, and her mother fed me Indian tacos and green tomatoes."

Pat put her cup down. "Her mother was there?"

"Yep. And her grandmother, sister, cousins, aunts, and uncles."

"No wonder you didn't get a kiss." Pat shook her index finger at Lindsay and laughed.

"Go ahead, make fun; I don't care. I had a wonderful time." Lindsay's face became serious. "You know she's so different now, and it's not just the 'her cop, me stalker' thing either. When she was shot and I was trying to help her, I felt this overwhelming sadness when I touched her. I don't feel that now."

"You think that's because of you?"

"No, not entirely," Lindsay said. "But I think I have something to do with it, and she's grateful. She said to me that getting shot was a blessing in disguise. She told her cousin that it had made her reevaluate what was important in her life." She flicked her hair behind one ear. "Everyone down there was so surprised to see her that I got the feeling that she's been kind of a hermit these past few years, and that's changed." She absently ran her finger around the lip of her cup. "I'm glad things are better for her, but I don't want her to like me just because she's grateful. I want her to like me for me."

"I think she does." Pat reached over and squeezed her hand. "I was there yesterday when she picked you up, remember? She's interested. I'm sure of it."

"How can you be so sure?"

"Didn't you see the way her face lit up when she saw you? Believe me, she's interested."

Lindsay grinned. "I hope you're right."

CHAPTER SEVEN

Rachel sat down at her desk and looked around. It seemed like forever since she'd been there, but it had only been five weeks. So much had changed in her life, but everything at work looked just as she'd left it.

"So, you finally decided to drag your lazy ass back to work, did you?" The tall detective sat on the edge of her desk. "What'd you do, get yourself shot so you could take a vacation?"

Rachel laughed. "Great way to get a nice long vacation, Max. You should try it sometime." She leaned back in her chair. "So, anything new on the case?"

"We put Eddie Dellacroix's DNA through CODIS and connected him to four child rapes."

"And if not for Lindsay, Mandy would have been number five." Rachel shook her head. "I really blew it on this one, Max. If she'd been number five, it would have been my fault."

"We all did, Rachel. Let's just get the bastard off the streets so there won't be a number five." Max got up and strolled across the room to the coffee machine. "Can I get you a cup?" he called to her just as the phone on Rachel's desk rang.

"No thanks," Rachel said and reached for the phone. "Detective Todd." Her whole demeanor changed when she heard Lindsay's voice. "I tried to call you yesterday afternoon, but you weren't home. I would have left a message if you'd had a machine."

"I'm sorry I missed your call," Lindsay said. "I've never needed a machine because no one ever calls me."

"I just wanted to tell you again how much I enjoyed your company on Saturday," Rachel said, and meant it. It was the first time in a long time that she'd felt so relaxed and comfortable with someone.

"I had a great time too. In fact, I had such a great time that I thought I'd invite you over for dinner. I found some vegetarian recipes that I want to try. If you're interested, you can be my guinea pig. Tonight will be lasagna with broccoli and mushrooms."

Rachel laughed. "Where are you finding all these vegetarian recipes?"

"I went to the library and searched the Internet," Lindsay said. "I had no idea there was so much information available at my fingertips."

"You just keep on searching to your heart's delight, and I'll happily volunteer for food-tasting duty."

Lindsay grinned. "Deal."

"I get off work at six; what time do you want me?"

"We'll eat about seven, but you can come over early if you'd like."

"Okay," Rachel said. "I've got a quick stop to make when I get off work, then I'll be over."

Lindsay rearranged the pillows on the couch for the third time, then put them back the way they were before she started fretting over them. *This is silly. Rachel's not coming over to evaluate my decorating skills, she's coming to see me.*

She finished the few dishes she had dirtied to prepare the meal and was drying her hands on a towel when the doorbell rang. Her heart leapt into her throat, and she stood a moment to compose herself. Even though she had spent the entire day on Saturday in the police detective's company, somehow it was different this time. They would be alone. Her palms started to sweat and she wiped them on the towel, then tossed it on the counter. The bell rang again and her frozen feet could finally move. She hurried over and opened the door.

"Hi," Rachel said. She held up a package. "I brought you a present. It's something I thought you could use."

Lindsay took the box and stepped aside so Rachel could come in. "I love surprises," she said, shaking the box. "What is it?"

Rachel shrugged. "Open it and see."

They sat on the couch, and Lindsay ripped the paper off the neatly wrapped package. "Oh!" she said and grinned. "It's an answering machine."

"I wanted to make sure I can leave a message if you're not home."

Lindsay placed the box on the coffee table, her smile growing. "That was really sweet. Thank you. I've never really cared if I missed a call...until now." She looked down at her hands and concentrated on breathing. "I like you a lot. I...I'm attracted to you." She could feel the heat rising in her face and her heart pounding. The silence coming from the other woman was deafening, and she slowly lifted her eyes, afraid of the rejection she might see in Rachel's eyes. Rachel looked uncomfortable, as if she was trying to think of a way to let her down gently. *Damn, why did I have to open my big mouth? She'll probably run screaming into the night.*

"I'm sorry," Lindsay said as she quickly crossed the room. "I didn't mean to make you uncomfortable. If you want to leave, I'll understand." She heard footsteps behind her, then felt a hand on her shoulder.

"I don't want to leave." Rachel gently squeezed Lindsay's shoulder. "Please, come back and sit down. We need to talk."

"There's nothing to talk about," Lindsay said. "It's clear that you don't feel the same way about me. You don't need to try and spare my feelings."

"I'm not trying to spare your feelings, Lindsay, and I am attracted to you. You're the first woman I've wanted to spend time with in a very long time."

Lindsay turned around and saw the pain in Rachel's eyes. "But..."

"But you're moving a little too fast for me, and I'm just not sure I'm ready to jump into a full-blown relationship this quickly." She reached out and cupped Lindsay's cheek in her hand. "I love spending time with you, and I can't deny that I'm very attracted to you. I do care. I don't want to hurt you, but I want you to know where I'm coming from."

"You really are attracted to me?"

Rachel smiled. "Yes, I really am."

"Then I can wait." Excited and pleased, Lindsay managed to remember dinner and headed to the kitchen. "Are you hungry?"

"Starved."

"Come on, then. Dinner's ready."

Lindsay filled the teapot with water and placed it on the stove to heat. It had been almost a week since she had seen Rachel, although she had talked to her several times on the phone. She was making a concerted effort not to say anything that would make Rachel feel rushed. She respected her wish to move slowly and had decided that the next step, if there was a next step, would be Rachel's.

The phone rang and she picked it up, smiling when the caller ID displayed Rachel's number. "Hello."

"Hi there," Rachel said. "Do you bowl?"

Lindsay laughed. "What a way to start a conversation."

"I was in the mood to bowl and thought if you wanted to, we could go bowling."

"I've never bowled before," Lindsay said, "But if you don't mind bowling with a novice, I'd love to go with you."

"Don't worry about that. I haven't been bowling in a very long time, and this limp is going to throw off my approach big-time. It'll be like we're both beginners."

"You're just trying to lull me into a false sense of security before you stomp all over me."

"Would I do that to you?"

"Well," Lindsay said. "I get the feeling that you like to win."

"Oh, I do like to win," Rachel said. "But don't worry. I'll stomp gently. You won't feel a thing."

"In that case, you've got yourself a bowling partner."

"Good," Rachel said. "I'll be over to pick you up in about fifteen minutes."

"Okay, see you then." Lindsay hung up the phone, still grinning. The prospect of spending her Sunday afternoon with

Rachel definitely brightened her mood. The teapot whistled, and she walked to the stove to turn the burner off, then grabbed a teabag. The folded napkin on the counter caught her eye, and she picked it up.

Suddenly, she could see herself back up at the cabin, but this time she was in the grave and Eddie was shoveling dirt on her. She struggled, but her hands and feet were bound with duct tape. She called out to Eddie to stop, but he just laughed and continued to cover her with dirt.

The vision ended, but the fear and panic it engendered did not. Her heart beat frantically as she rushed to her door and turned the dead bolt. Then she checked all the windows, making sure they were locked. Finally satisfied that everything was secure, she collapsed on the couch and buried her face in her hands, letting the tears flow.

She had stopped crying by the time the doorbell rang, but she was far from calm. She walked quietly to the door and peeked through the peephole to make sure it was Rachel. She was terrified that it might be Eddie, even though her logical mind told her that he would not just walk up and ring her bell.

"What's wrong?" Rachel stepped inside quickly and closed the door behind her. Lindsay tried to speak but burst into tears, and Rachel wrapped her arms around her. She held on until Lindsay calmed down enough to talk.

"I'm sorry." Lindsay crossed to the table and pulled a few tissues out of the box. "I didn't mean to break down like that."

"It's okay. Just tell me what happened. You seemed fine when I talked to you a few minutes ago."

Lindsay picked up the napkin off the floor where she had dropped it. "Eddie wrote his number on this napkin for me when I first met him." She placed the napkin on the coffee table, then dropped to the couch. "I picked it up a few minutes ago and saw myself in the grave up at the cabin. I was being buried alive and I tried to get Eddie to stop, but he just laughed." Tears started down her face again, and she wiped them away with a tissue. "I was so scared, but I shouldn't let it get to me like this." She reached over and picked up the napkin again. "I don't know what's different or why I'm getting something now. I've been picking up this damn napkin every day for weeks." She turned to Rachel, who had joined her on the couch. "It's my only link to him and I kept hoping that eventually I'd get something."

Rachel's brow furrowed. "You know I don't know anything about psychic things, and I could be totally wrong here, but perhaps you didn't get anything before because he hasn't been concentrating on a victim. Maybe you're picking up that extra energy he puts out when he's fixating on someone."

"You could be right, I just don't know." Lindsay shrugged. "You know, every time it's ever happened, there were strong emotions involved. And I've never been able to control the visions. Things just come unexpectedly and almost never when I'm trying."

"Maybe you need to stop trying so hard and just relax and let it happen."

"I was relaxed this time. I'd picked it up so often that I wasn't expecting anything." Lindsay took a deep breath and sighed. "I guess he's fixating on me now. He probably blames me for ruining his plans, and he wants me to pay."

Rachel reached over and took her hand. "I'm not about to let that happen." She stood up and pulled Lindsay to her feet. "Go pack a bag. You're coming home with me."

"Coming home with you?"

Rachel nodded. "I don't want you to be alone."

"You don't have to do that. I don't want to be an albatross around your neck."

"You are not an albatross around my neck." Rachel put her hands on Lindsay's cheeks and spoke softly. "I care about you, Lindsay Ryan. I want to keep you safe. Believe me when I tell you that it's not a burden to have you there. Now, this isn't up for further debate. You're coming home with me."

"Thank you," Lindsay said as a shy smile came to her face. "I didn't want to be alone, but I didn't want to push myself on you either."

"I'm glad we've got this settled. Now go get that bag packed."

"Okay, it'll just take me a minute." Lindsay stepped away and noticed something different. "When did you stop using your cane?"

"Today, actually. I knew I couldn't bowl with a cane, so I left it home. I think it's time I tried to get along without it."

The doorbell rang and Lindsay froze.

"You stay back," Rachel said, "I'll go see who it is."

Lindsay nodded and Rachel warily approached the door.

"It's your friend Pat," Rachel said as she opened the door and stepped aside so that Pat could enter.

Pat took one look at Lindsay, then glared at Rachel, her hands balling into fists. "What did you do to her?"

"Pat, please, she didn't do anything to me," Lindsay said. "I had another vision, and this time I was Eddie's victim. It shook me up, that's all."

Pat unclenched her fists and released the breath she was holding. "I'm sorry," she said to Rachel. "I should have known better." She walked over to Lindsay and pulled her into her arms. "It's going to be okay, honey."

A surge of jealousy ran through Rachel at the sight of Lindsay in Pat's arms. "Better go get packed, Lindsay," she said. "We need to get going."

Pat released Lindsay and took a step back. "You're moving out?"

"No, not hardly," Lindsay said. "But I'll be staying with Rachel until we get this Eddie thing over and done with." She turned and hurried to the bedroom. "I'll only be a minute."

Pat watched her disappear into the bedroom, then turned to Rachel. "I don't know if moving Lindsay into your place is such a good idea. She's in love with you, you know."

"I know she cares for me," Rachel said, "and I care for her, but we're not in love. It's too soon for that."

Pat walked over and stood toe to toe with Rachel. "It may not be love to you, but it is to her, and if you hurt her I'll—"

"I have no intention of hurting her. I'm just trying to keep her safe."

"Just doing your cop thing, right?"

"It's more than that," Rachel said, angry that she had to explain her motives to this woman. "I care for her."

"I'm sorry, then." Pat backed away. "I'm just worried about her. I don't want to see her get hurt."

"She's lucky to have a friend like you, Pat."

"Yeah, well, she's special."

Rachel nodded. "Very special."

"Okay, I'm ready." Lindsay carried two large bags into the room and set them down. She looked at Rachel and Pat and cocked her head. "Did I miss something?"

"Not really," Pat said as she turned around and hugged her again. "I'm going to miss you."

"Hey," Rachel said. "It's not like she's going to be in jail. She can have visitors, you know."

"That's right," Lindsay said, "so you'd better come see me."

"Count on it." Pat picked up one of Lindsay's bags.

The three women walked to Rachel's car and deposited the luggage in the trunk.

"I'll call you later," Lindsay said as she slid into the passenger seat. She waved at Pat, then turned to Rachel as they pulled out into traffic. "This should be fun."

Rachel's brow wrinkled. "Hiding out from a deranged man who plans to kill you should be fun?"

"No, silly." Lindsay slapped her arm. "Bowling. Bowling will be fun."

"You still want to go bowling?"

"Of course," Lindsay said. "I'll have one of Asheville's finest with me. I plan to take precautions, but I'm not going to hibernate in a hole like a hermit."

"Okay," Rachel said as they walked into the bowling alley. "I'll go get us a lane. You go over there and rent a pair of shoes."

"Right." Lindsay turned toward the shoe counter.

"What size, ma'am?" the young man behind the counter asked.

"Eight," Lindsay said. She watched him reach down and pull a pair of shoes off the rack. He handed her the shoes, and she sat on a nearby bench and put them on, then handed him the ones she had removed.

He pushed her shoes into the rack and handed her a claim ticket. “That’ll be two dollars, ma’am.”

A tap on her shoulder as she paid him turned her around to find Rachel standing behind her.

“We’re on fifteen,” Rachel said. “It’s this way. Follow me.” They walked to the lane, and Rachel set her bowling bag on the bench. She pointed to the rack along the walkway. “The balls are over there. Check out the ones in the twelve to fourteen pound range and find one that feels good on your hand. I’ll get my shoes on while you find a ball.”

Lindsay checked the numbers on the rack until she found the weight she was looking for. She tried several balls. “I found one,” she said, holding up a green ball. “Now what?”

“Now we throw some practice balls before we start keeping score.” Rachel took her ball out of her bag and placed the bag under the bench with her shoes. “When you pick up your ball, always use both hands.” She looked over at Lindsay, “You’re right-handed?”

Lindsay nodded.

“Then you’ll start with your right foot like I do.” Rachel picked up her ball, walked to about two feet from the end of the approach, and stood facing the pins. She held the ball in front of her chest, with the weight in her left hand, and nodded toward the floor. “See these dots on the floor? Stand with the middle dot between your feet, and when you throw the ball, aim just to the right of the center arrow over there.” She inserted her fingers and thumb into the holes and squared her stance. “Check to make sure no one on either side of you is bowling before you make your approach. You never want to interfere with another bowler.” She glanced from side to side, even though they were alone at their end of the alley.

Lindsay was a study in rapt attention.

“Bend your knees slightly and step off with your right foot and push out with both hands. Lock your elbow and let your arm swing back.” She demonstrated for Lindsay and smoothly released the ball. It rolled down the alley and knocked down all the pins.

She turned back to Lindsay and shook her head. “Wow. That was a fluke. I sure didn’t expect a strike on my first ball. It’s been way too long since I've been bowling." Her astonishment turned into a grin. "Lady Luck must be smiling on me today."

Lindsay grinned back. "You sure made that look easy."

"It is easy. Just remember that you push the ball out with your first step, letting its weight carry it down on the second step. The third step you're swinging back, and the fourth step you swing forward and release. Follow through with your hand and let it point to the first pin. Got that?"

"That's a lot, but I think so." Lindsay picked up her ball and stood where Rachel had indicated. In her head, she kept repeating, *push, drop, swing back, release.* "Here goes nothing." She released the ball and watched it roll about halfway down the alley before it dropped into the right gutter. She looked over at Rachel. "Right, it's easy."

Rachel could barely stifle her amusement.

"This is not my game." Lindsay shook her head.

"It's your first ball, give yourself a break. Now try again, but this time, take a step to the left to compensate."

Lindsay huffed out a breath but picked up her ball again. This time the ball made it all the way down the alley and knocked down six pins. She jumped into the air and clapped her hands. "I did it!"

Rachel smiled. "See, didn't I tell you it was easy?"

"That was really fun," Lindsay said as they walked into Rachel's house. "But I was right; you did stomp all over me."

"Hey, you averaged eighty, and that's not bad at all for your first time out."

"Really?"

Rachel nodded. "Really."

"You still beat me by almost a hundred pins. I thought you said you were going to stomp gently?" Lindsay put her suitcase down and looked around the room. A picture of an adorable toddler caught her eye. "Oh, is that your grandson?"

"Yes, his name is David." Rachel put down the other suitcase, walked over, and picked up the picture, adoration clearly evident in her eyes. She smiled at Lindsay. "I might never have met him if not for you."

"I don't understand."

"It's a long story," Rachel said. "Sit down and make yourself comfortable, and I'll get us something to drink." She put the picture back on the table and headed for the kitchen. "Sorry, I don't have any Pepsi. I've got apple juice, or I could make some tea." She opened the refrigerator and peered inside. "Or beer, I've got beer." She reached in, grabbed a bottle, and held it up.

"Beer sounds good." Lindsay wasn't really sure if she'd like it, but what the heck, it was about time she found out.

Rachel grabbed another bottle and closed the door. "Bottle or glass?"

"Bottle." Lindsay jumped when a fur-covered something leapt onto her shoulder from behind the couch. It sniffed her hair, then bounded down onto the couch beside her. "Who do we have here?"

"That's Miss Kitty." Rachel joined Lindsay on the couch and handed her the beer.

The cat strolled leisurely across the couch and flopped down on Rachel's lap.

"She's lovely," Lindsay said and reached over to pet her. Her eyes tracked back to Rachel's. "You were about to tell me a long story."

Rachel nodded. "As Trish grew into adolescence, she couldn't deal with the embarrassment of having a lesbian for a mother. Kids can be cruel, and I guess they teased her at school." She took a sip of beer, then reached for a coaster and placed the bottle on the table. "She asked me if she could live with her father, and after a long debate, I said yes. I didn't like it, but she was old enough to decide which parent she wanted to live with." She shook her head. "I didn't know she was going to tell all her new friends that his wife was her mother."

Lindsay ventured a sip of her beer and shuddered. Beer was not her drink. "That must have been awful."

"It was. We talked on the phone a lot at first, and I saw her every weekend. Pretty soon she only came home the occasional weekend. It wasn't until she told me she was engaged and I asked to meet him that I found out he thought Betty was her mother. That everyone thought Betty was her mother. She told me she wanted me to come to her wedding, but only if I left Lisa home and didn't tell anyone I was her mother."

"Lisa?"

"Lisa was my partner," Rachel said. "We were together six years when I lost her."

"I'm so sorry." Lindsay felt herself blush. "I didn't mean to bring up painful memories."

"It was a long time ago, but it still hurts. I wasn't sure I would ever be able to forgive Trish, but I have. Things will never be the way they were before all this happened, but we're working on building a relationship again. I love my daughter, and I'm grateful to have her and my grandson back in my life." Rachel picked up her beer and took another long swallow.

"The funny thing about the whole situation is that Trish was such a great kid growing up. We did everything together and I thought our relationship was fine. I told her, when I thought she was old enough to understand, that I was a lesbian. She seemed okay with it until Lisa came to live with us. Lisa and I both really tried to make us a family, but Trish never would accept Lisa. I thought with time she would come around, but she never did."

"You know," Lindsay said, "maybe it wasn't the gay thing as much as having to share you with someone else. She'd had you all to herself until Lisa came. You worked full time, and what little time you had to spend with Trish had to be shared with someone else. Maybe it was jealousy."

"I don't know. Perhaps it was a little bit of both. Whatever the reason, she was lost to me, and if I hadn't been shot, she would never have come and asked if we could start over."

"What an awful thing to have to go through to get your family back."

"It was worth it." Rachel scooted Miss Kitty off her lap, then got up and grabbed Lindsay's suitcase. "Come on, I'll show you where you'll be staying."

Lindsay stood and grabbed the other suitcase, then followed Rachel down the hall.

"You can stay in here. It was Trish's room."

Lindsay walked to the bed and dropped her bag on it. "Thanks. I do feel safer here. I don't think Eddie would ever think I'd be staying with you after all the awful things I told him about you." She looked over and caught a fleeting look in Rachel's eyes. Was it pain? "Of course, that was before I really knew you."

"I know," Rachel said. "It's okay." She turned and started for the door. "You get settled in and I'll see you in the morning. What time do you go to work?"

"I need to be there at eight."

"Okay. I'll call Ben in the morning and let him know what happened. He won't mind my coming in late."

"You don't need to be late," Lindsay said. "You can drop me off at my car as early as you need to."

"No, I'll drive you to work until this is resolved. I don't want you out there alone."

"Now wait just a darn minute." The mood in the room shifted. "I appreciate that you're letting me stay here. I really do. But that doesn't mean that I'm relinquishing control of my life to you." Lindsay put her hands on her hips. "I can drive myself to work."

"Lindsay, be reasonable. It's not safe for you to be alone right now. Let me do this."

Lindsay turned back to the bed and picked up her bag. "This isn't going to work. I think you'd better take me home."

"Okay, you win." Rachel lifted her hands in surrender. "If I take you to get your car in the morning, will you stay?"

"I meant it when I said I wasn't going to hide in a hole, Rachel. If you can accept that, I'd like to stay."

Rachel stuck her hands in her pockets and gazed at the floor. "I can accept it." She turned and left the room, closing the door softly behind her.

Lindsay unlocked the door to Rachel's house and carried her grocery bags inside. She was grateful that the detective had given her a key when they had lunch together earlier. Since Rachel was providing her a place to stay, the least Lindsay could do was feed her.

She set her bags on the kitchen table and stuck a six-pack of Pepsi in the refrigerator. Then she opened cupboards in an attempt to find where to put the rest of her purchases. In no time at all, everything was put away and a vegetarian casserole baked in the oven. To celebrate the completion of her tasks, she pulled a Pepsi from the fridge. At last, there was time to explore her new surroundings. She walked into the living room and examined each of the framed pictures on the sideboard. Most were of Rachel's grandson, David, which evoked a smile.

"Not at all proud of that grandson, are you, Rachel?"

"Did you say something to me?"

Lindsay shrieked and jumped, her heart beating wildly. "God, Rachel, you scared me out of ten years' growth. Don't sneak up on me like that."

Rachel burst out laughing and dropped onto the couch. "You squeaked!"

"I did not."

"Yes, you did, you squeaked." Rachel doubled over in hysterics on the couch, tears running down her cheeks.

Lindsay crossed her arms over her chest and tapped her foot. "Are you done?"

"I'm sorry," Rachel said though gasps of laughter, "but I've never heard anyone make a noise like that before, and it just struck me funny." She sat up, wiped the tears from her eyes, and then noticed Lindsay's stance. "You know, you really are cute when you pout."

"You said that before."

"That's because it's true." The smell of dinner cooking caught Rachel's attention. "What smells so good?" She sniffed the air.

"I've got a creamy vegetable mushroom casserole in the oven."

"Sounds great," Rachel said. "I knew there was a good reason to have you stay here."

"All right then." Lindsay walked over and joined Rachel on the couch. "Tomorrow is your turn to do dinner, and I expect a home-cooked meal. No stopping for fast food on the way home."

Rachel clutched her chest in mock horror. "I'm crushed. I'll have you know I'm an excellent cook."

"If you're such an excellent cook, why didn't you have anything to cook in the house?"

Rachel shrugged her shoulders. "It's no fun to cook for just one person. I used to cook every night when I had a family to cook for."

Lindsay noticed a large photo album on the coffee table and picked it up. "Is it okay if I look at this?"

"Sure, if you want to."

"My turn for payback. Any pictures in here of you as a kid?"

"A few."

Lindsay opened the book and found a picture of a young man and woman. "Is this your mom?"

Rachel scooted closer to view the picture. "Yep, that's her." She pointed to the handsome young black man. "And this is my dad."

"They look like such babies."

"They were," Rachel said. "That was the summer they met. Mom was seventeen and Dad was nineteen."

Lindsay turned the page and found a wedding picture of Rachel's mom and dad. She could recognize a younger version of Rachel's grandmother standing to Waheya's right and assumed the couple standing by her father was her paternal grandparents. The woman was tiny, with hair as red as Lindsay's.

"Those are my dad's parents," Rachel said in answer to Lindsay's unspoken question. "Papa's a doctor, and during World War II, he spent five months in London during the Blitz. Gran came from Scotland to help with the war effort and drove an ambulance. They met on a Thursday and were married the following Sunday. They've been married sixty-four years, and for their sixty-fifth anniversary, Papa's giving her the big wedding he wasn't able to give her then."

The next few pages contained pictures of Rachel and her siblings through the years. There were pictures of large family gatherings at Christmas and Thanksgiving and various birthday parties. Then came pages of Trish—being given her first bath by Rachel, celebrating her first birthday, missing her first teeth. Finally, there were the pictures of Rachel as an adult. Rachel in a softball jersey, Rachel holding up a bowling trophy, Rachel standing by a blonde woman with very short hair. There were several pages of pictures of the blonde woman, and in one, she wore a bathing suit that showed a tattoo on her right breast. It was an ornate heart and in the middle was the script *Rachel*.

"Is this Lisa?"

Rachel nodded. "She died of ovarian cancer."

In the silence of that moment, the timer on the oven buzzed, and Lindsay was glad for the distraction. "I guess it's ready," she said as she got up and walked into the kitchen.

"That was really good." Rachel carried her dishes to the dishwasher.

Lindsay picked up her dishes and took them over as well. "Do you have any plans for tonight?"

Rachel loaded the washer. "Not a thing. What did you have in mind?"

"There's a documentary on warrior women through the ages that I thought you might like. I saw the first part last week and it was really interesting."

"Sounds like a plan."

They settled on the couch and Rachel turned on the TV. The show was almost over when Rachel heard a soft snore and turned her head in the direction of the sound. Lindsay had fallen asleep, and her head was nodding forward.

Rachel briefly considered waking her when Lindsay leaned over and snuggled into her shoulder. Rachel's breath caught as fingers lightly gripped her arm, and she had to accept that it was time to make a choice. End their friendship totally or let things go forward, knowing what was likely to happen. She looked down at the sleeping woman and knew in her heart she didn't want to stop. The feel of Lindsay's body so close against her felt wonderful, and Rachel gazed at her with quiet affection. She closed her eyes and leaned into the warm inviting body, basking in the closeness. *No need to wake her up just yet.*

Lindsay took a deep breath and snuggled closer to something warm and soft. Then it dawned on her that the soft, warm something she was cuddling against was breathing. *Rachel?* She held her breath and slowly opened her eyes, her heart leaping into her throat when she saw Rachel looking back at her. "I'm sorry," she said as she practically fell off the couch in her haste to extricate herself.

"It's okay," Rachel replied. "I didn't mind."

Lindsay's face flushed red. "I didn't realize I was so tired. Guess it's time I hit the hay. Good night."

"Good night. Sweet dreams."

"You too." Lindsay hurriedly walked down the hall to her room. *Damn, I can't believe I did that.*

Rachel watched her go, then glanced at the album on the table. She could almost see Lisa smiling up at her from within those pages. She picked up the book and turned to her favorite picture, kissing her finger and pressing it to Lisa's lips. "I love you, Lisa. You know I do, but I don't want to be lonely anymore. It's time I finally accept that you're gone and move on with my life." She remembered the feel of Lindsay snuggled up against her and smiled. It had felt so good.

"Lindsay's a wonderful woman, Lisa. I know you'd love her. She makes me feel...alive again. It's been so long since I've really felt alive. I died with you, you know. My body kept functioning, but everything else was gone. That's not living. Not really." She closed the book and hugged it close to her chest. "Lindsay makes me feel good. She makes me smile. She stirs things inside me that I thought were gone forever, and she doesn't even have to try. I love that about her."

Lindsay awoke to the smell of coffee brewing. Any other time, it would have been a pleasant way to wake up, but after snuggling into Rachel's breast in her sleep last night, she was afraid to face her this morning. She had been trying so hard not to do anything that would make Rachel regret having invited her to stay, and to wake up like that was a shock. Rachel had made it clear that she wasn't ready for a relationship, and now, after finding out about Lisa, Lindsay understood why. She had seen the longing look in Rachel's eyes when she looked at the dead woman's picture.

She got up and dressed, forgoing her usual morning shower. She needed to talk to someone and decided to drop in on Pat before work.

Upon entering the kitchen, Lindsay found Rachel sitting at the table with her first cup of coffee. "Morning," she said as she walked by Rachel and headed for the door. "I've got to run."

Rachel frowned. "I was hoping we could talk. Don't you have time for a cup of coffee?"

Lindsay shook her head. "Early meeting." She waved her hand and rushed out the door. *She wants to talk? Damn, she's going to ask me to leave. I just know it.*

She chastised herself as she drove, and by the time she reached Pat's, she was in quite a state. She rang the doorbell a couple of times and then started knocking. "Pat!" she called and continued knocking.

When the door finally opened, a very wet Pat stood before her with a towel wrapped around her middle. She pulled her inside and slammed the door. Her eyes were round with fright. "What's wrong?" She pulled the window curtain over far enough to peek out. "Is it Eddie?"

"Uh, no," Lindsay said. "Nothing like that. I just needed to talk."

"God, Lindsay, you scared the shit out of me." Pat looked down at the puddle of water on the floor and groaned. "Go put on the coffee. I'll be back in a minute."

"I'm sorry," Lindsay said. "I just didn't think."

"Mop up this water and all is forgiven."

"Deal." Lindsay set up the coffeepot and had just finished wiping up the puddles when Pat returned.

"Okay, spill," Pat said. "What's going on? Trouble in paradise?"

"I really blew it, Pat." There was a tremble in Lindsay's voice, and Pat melted. She wrapped her arms around Lindsay.

"Come sit down and tell me all about it." Pat ushered her over to the couch and pulled her down beside her. "What did you do?"

"She wanted to talk to me this morning, and I just know she's going to ask me to leave." Lindsay wiped at a tear with the back of her hand.

"I don't understand. Why would she want you to leave?"

"I practically mauled her last night in my sleep."

"You slept with her?"

"No, not like that." Lindsay shook her head. "I was the only one sleeping. We were watching TV, and I fell asleep." She dabbed at her eyes again. "I really don't know what happened, but when I woke up, I was snuggled on her breast with my arm around her middle."

"And?"

"And she's made it clear she's not interested in a relationship. She's in love with someone else."

"Someone else?" Pat looked puzzled. "Must be a very trusting someone to let her move another woman into the house."

"You don't understand," Lindsay said. "She's dead. How can I compete with a dead woman?"

"Okay, you've lost me here. Who's dead?"

"Lisa. Lisa's dead. She was Rachel's partner for six years."

"Hold on now," Pat said. "Just what makes you think she wants you to leave? Wasn't it her idea for you to stay there in the first place?"

"Yes, it was her idea, but that was before last night."

"Huh. I don't see what's so bad about a little snuggling. Jesus, Lindsay, you were asleep. What exactly did she say to make you think it upset her?"

"She said it was okay, that she didn't mind."

Pat rolled her eyes. "If she said she didn't mind, then what's the big deal?"

"You didn't see her looking at those pictures of Lisa. She still loves her."

"Of course she still loves her, sweetie. I'm sure she always will. You don't stop loving someone because they die. That doesn't mean she can never love anyone else." Pat wrapped her arms around Lindsay and pulled her close. "She cares about you. Give her time." She leaned back and looked at Lindsay. "And if she says she didn't mind, believe her. What reason would she have to lie about it?"

"You really think so?"

"I really think so. I've seen the way she looks at you. She cares. Maybe more than she's willing to admit."

Lindsay wrapped her arms around Pat and hugged her tightly. "Thanks, Pat. I always feel better after I talk to you."

"Any time, my friend. Any time."

CHAPTER EIGHT

Rachel stirred the pasta sauce, then put the lid back on the pot and let it simmer. She looked around the kitchen, mentally checking everything off her list to make sure she hadn't forgotten anything. The garlic bread was on the baking sheet, ready to go under the broiler. The salad was waiting in the refrigerator, and the water for the spaghetti was heating on the stove. The broccoli was cleaned and ready to pop into the steamer. Yes, everything was ready. All that remained was for Lindsay to come home. She heard the sound of the key in the lock and turned toward the door.

Lindsay put her purse down on the table by the door. "What smells so good?" She joined Rachel in the kitchen.

"My own special spaghetti sauce," Rachel said. "I hope it meets with your approval. You did say I had to feed you something homemade."

"I'm impressed. You weren't kidding when you said you cook."

"No, I wasn't. And I make a killer spaghetti sauce." Rachel turned back to the stove and gave the sauce another stir.

Lindsay peeked in the pan and grinned. "Looks like you made enough to feed an army."

"Yep. I always make a big batch of sauce. Silly to go to all that trouble for just one meal. I'll freeze the leftovers for later."

The doorbell rang and Rachel's face became somber. She wasn't expecting anyone and briefly wondered if Eddie had figured out that Lindsay was staying with her. *No, that's silly. Eddie wouldn't come up and ring the bell.* She opened the front door and was pleasantly surprised to find Trish and David smiling back at her.

"Happy birthday, Gramma Rachel," David said as he held up a box wrapped in hand-decorated paper.

Rachel scooped him up in her arms and stepped aside so his mother could come in. "Thank you. What a surprise." She looked at Trish. "Why didn't you tell me you were coming over?"

"S'posed to be a surprise," David piped up.

Rachel grinned at him. "Well, it certainly is." She ruffled his hair. "Come on, there's someone in the kitchen that I want you two to meet."

Lindsay had been standing in the kitchen doorway watching Rachel greet her family. "Why didn't you tell me it was your birthday?"

"When you get to be my age you try to forget birthdays." Her eyes sparkled, and she looked down at the child in her arms. "David, this is Gramma's friend Lindsay. Lindsay, this is my daughter, Trish, and my grandson, David."

"It's nice to finally meet you," Lindsay said.

"Same here," Trish replied. "Mom's told me so much about you."

David excitedly tugged on Rachel's sleeve. "Open my present." His grin was huge and full of mischief.

Rachel walked over to one of the kitchen chairs and sat down with David in her lap. She shook the box. "What could it be?" She shook it again. "Hmm, sounds like a car."

David giggled. "A car couldn't fit in there, Gramma."

"It couldn't? Hmm, what could it be?"

"I'll open it for you," David said. He took the box and tore off the paper, then opened it with a flourish.

Rachel looked inside and found a plaster imprint of David's hand. "Oh, what a perfect gift. Much better than a car." She hugged him close. "I know just where I'll put it."

David giggled again. "How old are you, Gramma Rachel?"

"I'm forty-two."

"I'm three." He grinned and held up three fingers.

"Yes, I know. You're getting to be such a big boy." Rachel looked up at Trish. "Can the two of you stay for dinner?"

"No, you weren't expecting us. I don't want to put you out."

David wrapped his arms around Rachel's neck. "I want to stay with my gramma."

"We've got plenty, and I'd like you to stay."

Trish grinned at David. "I guess we're staying."

"They're nice," Lindsay said when Rachel returned from saying good-bye. "I'm glad I finally got to meet them."

"Me too."

Now that they were alone, Lindsay's insecurities returned in a heartbeat, and she decided it was time to make a hasty retreat to her bedroom. "I think I'm going to turn in. Good night." She started down the hall.

"Wait...please."

Lindsay turned and found Rachel standing right behind her. "Yes?"

"I just wanted to give you a proper good night." Rachel captured Lindsay's face in both hands and leaned over to lightly kiss her lips. "I'm glad you're here." She leaned in for one more kiss, then opened Lindsay's door for her. "Good night. Sweet dreams."

As Rachel walked away, Lindsay tried to breathe. *She wants me here.* She reached up and touched her lips. *And she kissed me.* She grinned and hugged herself. *She kissed me!*

Lindsay stepped out of the shower and reached for her towel. Her head was still spinning thinking about what Rachel's kiss the previous night might mean. Everything was different now. All her insecurities had vanished with that sweet encounter in the hall.

She finished toweling off and hung her towel over the shower door to dry. *Damn, I wish I had known about her birthday in time to do something special. It's not too late. I can still do something to make her feel special.* She brushed her teeth while she went over the list of things she wanted to do. *Order a cake, buy forty-two candles, and go shopping for a gift.* So it was a day late.

Better late than never. She had no idea what she wanted to get Rachel, but she had all day to think about it. One thing was for sure. She would need to leave work at least an hour early if she was going to get everything done.

She quickly pulled her clothes on and headed for the kitchen. She grinned when she saw Rachel's face light up when she walked in.

"Morning." Rachel got up and grabbed another cup. "Coffee?"

"Yes, thank you." Lindsay pulled out the chair next to Rachel's and sat down.

Rachel poured the coffee and joined her at the table. "I meant what I said last night. About being glad you're here, I mean. Since I've gotten to know you, I find myself smiling all the time for no reason at all." Rachel cocked her head in thought. "No, that's not true. There is a reason." She lifted her hand and ran her fingers lightly over Lindsay's lips. "It's you."

Lindsay's heart thudded in her breast and in her ears. "I liked it when you kissed me last night," she said. "Do you think we could do that again?"

"I liked it too." Rachel breathed a sigh, and her eyes dropped to Lindsay's mouth. "You have beautiful lips." She leaned over and placed a kiss on them, then her gaze returned to Lindsay's eyes. "Everything about you is beautiful."

"Sweet-talker." Lindsay blushed.

"There's that pretty blush again."

Lindsay's flush deepened and she fanned her face. "I hate when I do this."

"Well, I think it's cute." Rachel carried her empty cup to the sink and rinsed it out. "And that wasn't just sweet talk. I meant every word. You are beautiful." She patted her pocket to make sure she had her keys. "I've got to get going."

Lindsay stood up and intercepted Rachel on her way to the door. She wrapped her arms around her neck. "I can't let you leave without a proper good-bye." She leaned in for a kiss and felt Rachel's arms wrap around her. The kiss was brief, and she took a step back to gaze into Rachel's eyes. "I could get used to this, you know."

Rachel pulled her close again, the hug lingering. "I could too. It feels so good to hold you in my arms, I don't want to let go." Reluctantly, she did let go and stepped away. "But duty calls." She leaned over for one more quick kiss. "See you later," she said, then turned and strode away.

Feeling that her feet barely touched the floor, Lindsay ran to the phone and punched in Pat's number. It was answered on the third ring.

"Hello?"

"She kissed me!"

Pat laughed. "And you doubted me. Didn't I tell you she was interested?"

"Yes, you did," Lindsay said. "And now I need some more advice. Do you know a good bakery? I need to order a cake for tonight."

"Why don't you just bake a cake? You're a wonderful cook."

"Why, thank you, my dear, but I won't have time. I've got to buy a gift, and that's going to take some time. I don't have a clue what I want to get her, but I'm going to take off work a little early to make sure I get everything done. I want to be here waiting when she gets home."

"Is it her birthday?"

"It was yesterday, but I'm going to give her a belated celebration. I'm going to take her out to her favorite restaurant, and have cake and a gift waiting at home. I want to make her feel special."

"Then Ruthie's is the place to go," Pat said. "They make killer cakes."

"The place is called Ruthie's?"

"No, it's called Asheville Bakery, but Ruthie works there. She decorates the cakes. Let me know what you want on it, and I'll give her a call. Just remember, they close at six."

"Oh yeah, I've seen that place," Lindsay said. "I'll be there well before six." She considered a moment. "Just have her put Happy Birthday, Sweet-Talker."

Pat laughed again. "Sweet-talker, huh?"

"Oh, yeah. Very sweet. Thanks, Pat. I owe you big-time."

Eddie stood in the shadows and watched the parking lot across the street. In his hands he held a paper bag and a Slim Jim. That bitch was going to pay for taking his freedom away. It was her fault he was hiding in the shadows and living on the run like this. He glanced around and made sure the street was clear for the moment. The parking lot was quiet, and he quickly walked to Lindsay's car and used the Slim Jim to unlock the door. In a little over an hour, the lot would be full of people leaving work. He climbed into the backseat and crouched down on the floor out of sight.

He pulled a bottle and a rag out of the bag. He wanted everything ready for when the time was right. There couldn't be any slipups, and the sound of the rustling bag might warn her of his presence. He stuffed the bag under the driver's seat and settled in to wait.

Perspiration beaded up on his forehead and upper lip, and he used the rag to wipe it off. *Damn, it's hot.* He knew if she hadn't parked in the shade, he'd never have been able to last an hour hidden in the back of the closed car.

Eddie wiped the sweat out of his eyes and wondered if this was such a good plan. He looked at his watch. It was a little after four. *Damn. It's only been a few minutes and I'm already sweating like a pig. Another hour and she'll smell me when she opens her door.* The sound of footsteps caught his attention and he stiffened.

The footsteps came closer, and he held his breath when he heard the sound of the locks popping open. He sneered. She was an hour early; he'd gotten there barely in time. This made things much easier, though. The plan had been to keep out of sight and wait until she drove to a less public location. Luck was with him, and he wouldn't have to wait. Quietly, he opened the bottle. Holding his breath, he poured a generous amount liquid on the rag.

When Lindsay slid into the driver's seat, he was on her in a heartbeat, holding her with one arm while pressing the rag against her face with the other hand. She struggled for a few moments and then went limp, but he kept the rag in place to make sure she breathed in enough of the fumes to keep her out for a while.

Satisfied that she was not going to come to any time soon, he pulled her into the backseat and covered her with a blanket.

"You're going to be very sorry that you crossed me, bitch. Very sorry."

Rachel frowned when she didn't see Lindsay's car in her driveway. They had an agreement that Lindsay would let her know if she was going anywhere after work. She left her car in the driveway and rushed inside to see if Lindsay had left a note. Finding none, she reached for the phone book and looked up Pat's number.

"Hello?"

"Pat, this is Rachel. Is Lindsay with you?"

"She's not with you?"

"Of course she's not with me. Why would I be calling you if she was with me?"

"Don't panic, Rachel. I talked to her this morning, and she told me she was going out shopping after work."

"She's supposed to let me know if she's going to be late."

"It probably just slipped her mind," Pat said, not wanting to give away the birthday surprise.

"Thanks, Pat. I'll talk to you later." Rachel hung up the phone, walked into the kitchen, and grabbed a cold bottle of water from the fridge. *Damn, I wish you had a cell phone, Lindsay. I hate being out of touch with you when I know Eddie's out there somewhere.* She dropped down onto one of the kitchen chairs and took a sip of her water. Talking to Pat should have reassured her, but Rachel was still uneasy. Something just didn't feel right. She took another sip of water and the phone rang. She glanced at the caller ID and snatched it up.

"Did you hear from her, Pat?"

"No, and now I'm worried. I just got a call from my friend Ruthie. She works at the Asheville Bakery. Lindsay was supposed to pick up a cake before they closed at six. She never showed up."

"I'm going out to look for her," Rachel said. "Take down my cell number and call if you hear from her. I'll call you as soon as I know anything. You have a pen and paper?"

"Yep."

"Okay, it's 555-3232."

"Got it, thanks."

Rachel hung up and rushed to the car. She punched the speed dial to Ben's cell phone as she drove.

"Hello?"

"Ben, this is Rachel. Lindsay's gone missing, and I'm on my way to the cabin."

"If Eddie's got her, I don't want you confronting him alone, Todd. Wait for backup."

"I can't. Just get someone out there as fast as you can." She disconnected the call before he could protest. There was no way she was going to wait when Lindsay's life could be in danger.

"Well, well," Eddie said when Lindsay stirred. "Sleeping Beauty's finally waking up."

Lindsay tried to bring her thoughts into focus. Someone was speaking, but the sound seemed to be coming from a great distance. *Where am I? What happened?* She tried to move and found that her legs would not move and her hands were bound. She was totally disoriented and felt as if she might disgorge the contents of her stomach at any moment.

As consciousness pushed the foggy feeling away from her brain, she finally understood what had happened. She opened her eyes to confirm her suspicions and realized she was lying in a shallow grave, her legs and lower body totally covered in dirt. She spotted Eddie standing above her with a shovel in his hand.

"Why are you doing this?" she asked.

"My, my. I thought you were clever enough to figure it out. It's because of you I'm a wanted man."

"Because of me?" In spite of the situation, Lindsay was incredulous. "They're after you because you prey on innocent little girls. You're sick and you need help."

"I'm not sick, and I don't need help. All those girls loved me. They wanted me. I never did anything but love them."

"You're sick if you call what you did to them love. And what about Mandy, your niece? You were going to kill her. Was that love?"

"I loved Mandy, but she knew who I was. If everything had gone as planned, when the two of you disappeared together, they would have thought you took her. No one would have been looking for me."

"You made mistakes then, and you're making a big one now. This is premeditated murder!"

"You got the premeditation right," Eddie said. "I've been thinking about this a lot. In fact, it's all I've been able to think about for weeks. I've been patient, waiting for you to wake up, and you sure took your sweet time about it. I want you to experience every glorious moment of your demise. I want you to suffer the way you've made me suffer."

He scooped up a shovel full of dirt and tossed it onto her chest. "I liked you, Lindsay. I originally felt bad that you had to die. I'd planned to kill you quickly so you wouldn't have to suffer. But then that cop showed up and you went and sided with her. That's when everything fell apart."

"You'll never get away with it," Lindsay said. "The police are probably already on the way here."

Eddie laughed. "Why would they come here? They'd never expect me to be stupid enough to"—he lifted his fingers into the air to indicate quotation marks—"return to the scene of the crime. That only happens in the movies." He scooped up another shovel full of dirt, but this time tossed it over her face.

Lindsay saw the dirt coming and closed her eyes, bringing her hands up to cover her face as best she could. She wiggled and struggled, but the dirt covering her lower body held her in place. Her thrashing finally caused her stomach to rebel. She lifted her upper body as much as she could and vomited over the dirt that covered her.

"That's disgusting." Eddie quickly tossed dirt over the mess. "I wanted you to be awake for this because I want to see the terror in your eyes when I'm about to toss that last shovel of dirt over your face."

"Don't do this, Eddie. You can still walk away. I won't even tell anyone that I saw you."

"You really expect me to believe that you wouldn't tell anyone?"

"I won't," Lindsay said. "I swear it."

Eddie's maniacal laughter echoed in Lindsay's ears as he tossed another shovel of dirt on her chest.

Rachel's heart pounded furiously as she drove toward the cabin. Lindsay's words about her vision played constantly in her mind. *"I was in the grave up at the cabin and Eddie was burying me alive."* She knew that Lindsay was running out of time. The image of the redhead lying in the grave Rachel had dug weeks before flashed in her mind, and she gasped, her chest aching. "If you hurt her, Eddie, I'll kill you with my bare hands. I swear it." Tears streamed down her face. Just the thought of losing Lindsay filled her with a misery she hadn't felt since Lisa had died. With a shaking hand, she wiped the tears from her face. "Pull yourself together, Todd!" she yelled at herself. "You won't be any good to Lindsay if you fall apart."

The drive seemed to take forever, but finally, she pulled up in front of the cabin and saw Lindsay's car. She leapt from her car, service revolver in hand, and started running. Adrenaline gave her feet wings as she raced for the grave site. Her worst fears were realized as she rounded the corner of the cabin and saw Eddie tossing dirt onto the grave.

"Police! Put down the shovel and drop to the ground, hands behind your back!"

Eddie turned and advanced on her with the shovel. "You're too late. She's dead. And you're gonna die too." He hadn't taken more than a couple of steps when something slammed into his body. Then he was on the ground clutching at the hole in his chest and writhing in pain. "It hurts."

"Ask me if I care." Rachel rushed past him and saw that the grave was completely filled with dirt. Frantically, she started digging with her hands, afraid she would hurt Lindsay if she used the shovel. *Unelanuhi, let me be in time. I'll never ask for anything again, I swear it.*

She heard the sound of running feet and glanced up to see Ben and four other police officers running toward her. "Hurry! We have to get her out. She's suffocating!"

All the officers dropped to their knees around the grave and pawed the loose dirt. Rachel dug until she felt something she recognized as flesh. Quickly, she cleared the dirt away to find that it was Lindsay's hands. They were taped together at the wrists, and it was clear Lindsay had been using them to keep the dirt away from her face. Rachel lifted the hands away and placed her fingers in front of Lindsay's nose.

Nothing.

"She's not breathing!" Rachel worked her hands under Lindsay's arms and pulled. Most of the loose dirt fell away, and she slid out easily.

"I...told...you, you were...too...late," Eddie gasped.

Rachel ignored him and started rescue breathing, desperately hoping that the cupped hands over Lindsay's face had trapped enough air to allow her to breathe for a while after she had been entombed. It couldn't have been long, but perhaps it was long enough.

Rachel's tears were flowing freely now as she breathed into Lindsay's mouth. They dripped onto Lindsay's face and made muddy streaks down her dirt-encrusted cheeks. "Please breathe," Rachel begged. She continued until, miraculously, Lindsay did start breathing on her own.

"*Wado, Unelanuhi, Wado.*" Rachel pulled Lindsay up, cradling her against her body. When Lindsay flailed her arms in panic, Rachel pulled her in closer, rocking gently. "It's okay, I've got you." She pressed her face against Lindsay's cheek and hummed softly. The gentle rocking and soft melody seemed to calm Lindsay and she stopped struggling.

Lindsay's eyes fluttered open, and she gazed at the woman who held her so tightly. "I knew you'd come," she whispered as she wrapped her arms around Rachel. "But your timing sucks."

Rachel was physically and mentally exhausted when she unlocked her front door, and she could only imagine how much worse Lindsay must feel. "I still think you should have let me take you to get checked out."

"I don't need to be checked out. I'm fine."

Lindsay's tone was sharp, and Rachel held up her hands in surrender. "I'm sorry. It's just that I'm worried about you.

"I'm sorry too. I didn't mean to snap at you."

"I know."

They stood a moment in awkward silence. "I think I need a drink," Rachel said. "How about you?"

"Maybe later. I just want to get in the shower and clean up."

"I know what you mean." Rachel looked at her dirt-covered hands and arms. "I'm filthy too." She watched Lindsay disappear down the hall, then walked into the kitchen and turned on the water, soaping and rinsing herself twice before she dried off and grabbed a beer. The adrenaline that had kept her going earlier had finally deserted her, and she collapsed on the couch. Her body felt weak and shaky, but her mind was racing. Sleep would not come easy that night. She took another swallow of beer and ran her fingers through her hair. "That was too damn close."

Suddenly, Rachel remembered her promise to call Pat and forced herself to get up and find her phone. She punched in the number and this time the phone was answered in one ring.

"It's about time," Pat said. "Did you find her?"

Rachel dropped back down onto the couch and put her feet up on the table. "I found her."

"What happened?"

"Eddie grabbed her when she got off work and buried her in a shallow grave up at the cabin." Rachel's voice cracked, and she felt the same raw emotions she had felt earlier welling up inside. She ran her fingers through her hair again and took a deep breath, working to control her shaky voice.

"Buried her? Oh my God! Is she okay?"

"Physically, I think she's fine. We got there in just the nick of time," Rachel said. She started peeling the label off her beer bottle. "I'm worried, though. We haven't talked about what happened at all, and if I bring it up, she changes the subject."

"Maybe she just needs time."

Rachel shrugged. "Maybe." She looked up as Lindsay walked into the room dressed in her bathrobe.

"Damn, that's better," Lindsay said. "I feel human again."

"Well, I don't." Rachel handed the phone to Lindsay. "You and Pat can talk while I get cleaned up." She tilted her bottle up and drained it dry, then set it on the table.

"Hey, Pat," Lindsay said as she walked to the kitchen and helped herself to a beer. She didn't like beer, but she needed something to settle her nerves and hoped it would do the trick.

"Hey, yourself."

"Hold on a second, Pat." Lindsay set the phone down and opened her beer, then sat down at the table. "I'm back," she said, "needed both hands to open a bottle."

"Rachel tells me that you had a run-in with Eddie. What happened?"

"He was waiting in my car when I left work, but Rachel took care of him. He won't be bothering anyone again."

"Rachel's worried about you, you know."

"She doesn't need to worry, and neither do you. I'm fine." Lindsay brought the bottle to her lips and took a large swallow, wincing as the beer made its way down her throat. *God, that's awful.* She forced herself to take several more swallows before setting the bottle back down on the table. *The more I drink, the worse it tastes.*

"When are you coming home?" Pat asked.

"I'm not sure, probably after work tomorrow. I'm too tired tonight."

"Good. I'll be glad to have you close again. I like having you as a neighbor. And, Lindsay, if you need to talk about what happened, I'll be there."

"Why is it that everyone wants to talk about Eddie? That's over. I need to move on."

"If by everyone, you mean Rachel and me, it's because we care about you."

"And I'll say it again, I'm fine." She picked up her beer and drained the bottle. "Listen, Pat, I'm dead tired. I think I'm going to turn in. I'll see you tomorrow."

"Okay, see you tomorrow."

Why can't they just let it alone? The last thing Lindsay wanted to think about was the horror of being buried alive. *Can't they understand that? I want to forget, and they keep bringing it up.* She hoped that telling them she was fine would put an end to the subject, once and for all. She sighed and put her head in her hands, leaning forward on her elbows. She had to find something to deaden the pain, but what? Beer wasn't working. Perhaps if she could drink enough, it might, but she didn't think she could get past the taste to drink enough to do the trick.

Then she remembered she had seen a bottle of some kind of liquor stuck in the back of the pantry and decided to give it a try. *Anything has to be better than beer.* She got up and moved things around so she could get to it. She pulled it out and found it to be bourbon. The bottle was very dusty, and it was obvious that it hadn't been touched in a very long time.

Lindsay opened the cupboard and pulled out a glass. She wasn't sure how much bourbon it would take, so she filled the glass about half full and took a swallow. She choked as the strong liquor burned its way to her stomach, then wiped her mouth and shuddered. That wasn't going to work either. She walked to the refrigerator and pulled out a can of Pepsi. She added enough cola to fill her glass the rest of the way. This time when she took a swallow, it was tolerable. Not particularly good, but she could drink it.

Lindsay returned to her seat and forced herself to finish the drink. Her mind became hazy as the booze took effect. *Good. A little more, and it will all be gone. At least for a while.* She picked up the bottle of bourbon and started to pour another drink when the queasiness in her stomach hit. She hadn't eaten anything but a pastry that morning, and her body was urgently telling her that she had exceeded its limits. "Oh no," she whispered, feeling her stomach roil.

She rushed to the bathroom and leaned her forehead against the closed door. "Rachel!" she called. "I need to get in."

"The door's not locked," Rachel called back. "Come on in."

Lindsay made it to the toilet, but not in time to lift the seat before her stomach rebelled.

Rachel pulled back the shower curtain to find Lindsay on her knees with her head hanging over the toilet. "Are you okay?" She grabbed her towel and quickly wrapped it around herself. Then she grabbed another towel, wet it, and handed it to Lindsay when she stopped vomiting.

"Thanks," Lindsay said as she wiped her face with the damp towel. Her head pounded, and she closed her eyes and sat down flat on the floor, leaning back against the side of the tub. "I thought I'd have a drink to settle my nerves, but I forgot I haven't eaten since this morning, and I guess my stomach wasn't happy with that plan." She ran her fingers through her hair. "God, I feel like shit." She opened her eyes and took in the mess she had made and reached over with the towel to wipe it up.

Rachel took the towel from her. "Go rinse your mouth out, hon. I'll clean this up." She reached down with her other hand to help Lindsay up.

Lindsay felt too bad to protest and simply nodded, allowing Rachel to pull her to her feet. "Thanks," she said again, then went to the sink and rinsed her mouth several times with mouthwash before going to her room and collapsing on the bed. A few minutes later, Rachel came in and sat on her bed, still wrapped in a towel.

"I'm sorry I made such a mess for you to clean up."

"That's okay." Rachel brushed the damp hair off Lindsay's forehead. "Are you okay?"

"Yeah," Lindsay said. "My stomach's feeling a bit better now. I think I'll live."

"You try to get some rest and I'll see you in the morning." Rachel leaned down and brushed her lips softly over Lindsay's. "Sweet dreams." She got up and turned off Lindsay's light on the way out.

Lindsay sat up in bed, her body drenched in sweat. She had wakened to the nightmare of her body weighed down with dirt, gasping for breath. She looked at the door, knowing that Rachel was only a few steps away. Then she glanced at the clock and sighed. *Rachel will kill me if I wake her up at three in the morning.*

Afraid to face the possibility of another nightmare, she got up, tiptoed into the living room, and dropped down on the couch. She picked up the remote and turned on the TV, turning the volume down so as not to disturb Rachel. "Poop," she said as she flipped through the channels, finding nothing that captured her interest. She turned off the television and tossed the remote on the table. This was going to be a long night.

Rachel yawned as she walked into the kitchen and set up the coffeepot. She silently cursed herself for not remembering to do it the night before. She liked to have hot coffee waiting when she got up. God, she was tired. She heard footsteps and turned to see Lindsay walk into the kitchen. From the dark circles under her eyes, she hadn't gotten much sleep either.

"Morning," Rachel said. "Coffee's almost ready."

"Great. I could sure use a cup about now." Lindsay sat down and crossed her arms, placing them on the table, and leaning heavily against them. "I guess this means I can move back home now."

"Yeah, I guess it does." The coffee finished dripping. Rachel poured two cups and joined Lindsay at the table. She supposed it was inevitable that once the danger was over, Lindsay would want to go back home, but Rachel had really enjoyed her brief stay and was not eager to see it end. It was very early in their relationship, and she knew that under other, more normal, circumstances, she would never have even considered moving someone into her home until she felt secure. Perhaps this was for the best. Although she had tried, she still hadn't completely accepted the possibility of anyone other than Lisa truly owning her heart. "When will you be leaving?"

Lindsay kept her expression neutral. "I'll take my stuff with me this morning when I go to work." Lindsay was silent for a moment. "Oh, I guess I need to pick up my car. Would you mind taking me to work, then driving me out to the cabin this evening?"

"Sure," Rachel said. "Why don't you just take it easy today, and I'll drive you to get the car this evening when you've rested up a bit. You can miss a day's work, can't you?"

"No. I think I want to go to work. I need to keep busy." Lindsay took a sip of her coffee, then set the mug down on the table and stood to leave. "I'll hurry so you won't be too late."

"You don't need to rush. Sit down and finish your coffee. Ben'll understand if I'm a little late."

"You sure? I wouldn't want you getting in trouble because of me."

"I wouldn't have said it if I wasn't sure. Now sit down and drink your coffee."

Rachel started up the walk to Lindsay's apartment, carrying a bouquet of mixed flowers. It had been a week since Lindsay had moved back into her apartment, and she kept insisting that she was doing fine. But every time Rachel visited, she saw the telltale dark shadows under Lindsay's eyes and could tell that she wasn't sleeping well.

She rang the doorbell and stood to wait. When the door opened, she thrust the flowers forward. "I saw these on the way over, and they were so pretty I had to get them for you."

"Thank you." Lindsay grinned and took the flowers. She brought them up to her face and inhaled their fragrance. "They're beautiful."

Rachel leaned over for a quick hug and kiss. "Almost as beautiful as you." They walked into the apartment together, and Lindsay took the flowers into the kitchen to find a vase. Rachel followed and wrapped her arms around Lindsay from behind, then leaned her chin on Lindsay's shoulder and watched her arrange the flowers in the vase. "You feel good in my arms. You know that?"

Flowers set to her satisfaction, Lindsay put the vase down on the kitchen counter and turned around, wrapping her arms around Rachel's neck. "If it feels half as good as this does, then yes." She leaned in for a kiss.

Rachel tightened her hold and deepened the kiss. When they came up for air, she said, "I'm going to New Orleans for my grandparents' anniversary. It's next weekend. I was supposed to fly out on Thursday with the rest of the family, but I think—I think I'd like to drive, if you'll come with me." She smiled. "I want you to meet my brother and my grandparents."

Lindsay returned the smile. "I'd like that. But are you sure your grandparents won't mind an outsider horning in on such a special occasion?"

"I'm sure." Rachel took Lindsay's hand, led her into the living room, and pulled her down to sit beside her on the couch. "I'm so glad you're coming with me. I think we need to get away from everything that's happened. We've never been able to be together without something hanging over our heads."

"I know," Lindsay said. "It's not been the easiest way to start a relationship. I'm looking forward to the trip. I really like your family. I've always envied anyone with a big family. There was just me and my mom and dad."

Rachel shook her head. "I can't imagine what that would be like. There were just three of us kids, but I have nieces, nephews, aunts, uncles, and cousins coming out my ears."

Lindsay leaned over to examine Rachel's ear. "Awfully crowded in there."

"You are such a smart-aleck."

"How long will it take us to get there?"

"If we drive straight through, it's about eleven or twelve hours of driving. I've done it in ten, but that's a killer."

"When are we leaving? I'll have to arrange it with work."

"I'll drop Miss Kitty off at the vet's and pick you up around eight tomorrow morning. We can stop and get something to eat, then head out."

Shock was evident on Lindsay's face. "Tomorrow morning? I thought you said it was only a one-day drive."

"It is, but I thought we could take a few days. You know, take it easy, stop when we feel like it, and get there when we get there. We're not on a timetable. As long as I'm there by Thursday when the family arrives, it's cool. I want to be there when my grandparents meet David. I can't wait to show him off."

Lindsay wrapped her arms around Rachel. "I can't think of anything I need more right now than a few days away from here with you." She started to lean over for another kiss when the doorbell rang. With a sigh, she halted a breath from waiting lips. "Hold that thought. Someone has poor timing." She opened it to Pat, grabbed her hand, and pulled her into the apartment.

"Guess what?" Excitement showed clearly on Lindsay's face. "Rachel and I are taking a road trip. Just the two of us." She looked over at Rachel and grinned.

"That's great. Where are you going?"

"New Orleans, but we plan to stop along the way."

"How long will you be gone?"

"I don't know." Lindsay looked at Rachel with the question. "We hadn't got that far in our plans yet."

"I've scheduled two weeks off," Rachel said. "So as far as I'm concerned, we don't need to be back until weekend after next.

But if you want to come home next weekend, that's okay too. I'm easy."

"Easy, huh?" Pat wiggled her eyebrows.

"Watch it," Lindsay said. "She's taken."

Pat laughed. "My, my, aren't we the possessive one."

Rachel crossed the room purposefully and wrapped her arms around Lindsay. "Yes, we are," she said, leaning over for a quick kiss. She leaned back but kept her arms around Lindsay. "Have you thought about how long you want to be gone?"

"I want the whole two weeks, but I need to go call Michael and see if he'll let me off that long." She wiggled out of Rachel's arms, picked up the phone, then went in search of her purse for her boss's after-hours emergency phone number. "Be right back." She disappeared into the bedroom, clutching the phone.

"I sure hope her boss will let her have the time off," Pat said. "She really does need to get away. She told me she hasn't been sleeping well, and I know she's not letting on how much the kidnapping scared her."

Rachel nodded. "I know. I talked to her boss and explained everything to him before I asked her to go with me. He's going to give her all the time she needs. I didn't tell her I talked to him, because I don't want her to think I'm butting in, but he needed to know what's going on."

The bedroom door burst open and Lindsay rushed out. "It's all set," she said to Rachel. "I'm all yours for the next two weeks."

CHAPTER NINE

Rachel smiled when she felt a hand settle on her thigh. She covered the hand and squeezed. "I'm glad you wanted to make this trip with me. I think we both needed it."

Lindsay nodded. "I've never been on a real vacation."

"Never?"

"Nope. My dad never kept a steady job, and if we did manage to save a little of the money my mom earned, he'd lose it in another one of his get-rich-quick schemes." She sighed. "My mom worked so hard and he just blew it."

"Why did she stay with him?"

"I really don't know. I mean, I know she loved him, but I never would have stayed with him if I'd been her. In my opinion, he wasn't worthy to shine her shoes, but she stuck by him through thick and thin. Then when she needed him most, he left. I'll never forgive him for that." She looked over at Rachel with a wistful expression. "I wish you could have known her."

"Me too," Rachel said. "She sounds like someone I would respect. And if she was half as sweet as her daughter, I know I would have liked her a lot."

Rachel's stomach growled loudly, and Lindsay laughed. "I think that stomach of yours is trying to tell us something."

"Mmm, think you're right. I'm starving. Let's keep an eye out for a place to eat."

"What's that?" Lindsay pointed as they crested the top of a small rise, opening a wide vista. "Oh, oh, it's a carnival!" She immediately picked out a Ferris wheel and grabbed Rachel's arm, her face lighting up like a child's on Christmas morning. "I want to go."

"Do you want to eat first?"

"We can eat there. Part of the carnival experience is to fill up on yummy junk food." Rachel didn't respond. "Or we can eat first if you want. That's okay with me."

Rachel turned to her with an indulgent smile. "If you want carnival junk food, we'll get carnival junk food. I'm sure I can find something to eat. Who knows, they may even have veggie dogs."

It was two o'clock by the time they parked and arrived at the food vending area. Rachel was pleased to find that one vendor did have a veggie version of their hot dogs.

"Oh, look," Rachel said. "They have those giant pretzels. I want one of those too."

With food in hand, they searched around for an empty table. Finding none, Rachel headed for a table for four with two empty seats and an older couple occupying the other two. "Do you mind if we join you?"

"Not at all," the man said. "I'm John, and this is my wife, Edna."

"Thank you." Rachel returned the introductions. "This is Lindsay, and I'm Rachel."

"Yes, thank you." Lindsay put her food on the table and sat down. "I thought we were going to have to eat standing up."

"Well, I'm glad you could join us," Edna said. "Have you been having fun today?"

"We just got here," Rachel said. "We're on our way to New Orleans for my grandparents' wedding anniversary and just happened upon the carnival. It sounded like fun, so here we are. We're on a spur-of-the-moment vacation and don't have anything planned."

"You know, it's too bad your trip didn't take you through here next week." John stroked his chin. "We have a little place out on the lake that we rent out to vacationers. It's booked for most of the summer, but we had a cancellation."

"We'll take it," Rachel and Lindsay said in unison, then looked at each other and laughed.

"Actually, we'll be driving back this way next Monday," Rachel said.

"Well, good. Then it's settled." Edna turned to John. "Give them one of your cards, honey."

John reached in his pocket, pulled out a business card, and handed it to Rachel. "You just give us a call when you get in on Monday, and we'll give you directions to our house so you can pick up the key."

"Thanks." Rachel took the card and stuck it in her pocket.

"I was just admiring your hair," Edna said to Lindsay. "I always wanted to be a redhead, but it just doesn't look good on me. You have to have the right coloring or it looks brassy."

"You're probably right." Rachel grinned at Lindsay. "I don't think I'd look good with it either. But on you, it's perfect."

Lindsay flushed. "And here I always wished I could get rid of it."

"You women," John said, shaking his head. "Never happy with the way you look. I've been telling Edna for fifty-seven years how beautiful she is, but she never believes me."

"I've got eyes, old man. I know what I look like."

"So do I, old woman. Truth be told, I know what I like, and you're it. So just shut up and take an honest compliment when it's given."

Edna patted his hand and kissed him on the cheek. With a smile, she confided to Rachel and Lindsay, "Blind as a bat, he is, that's why I keep him around." She looked back to John. "You ready to go, Mr. Magoo? I'm plumb wore out."

John nodded and stood to help her up. "It was nice meeting you, ladies."

"It was nice meeting you too," Lindsay said.

"Yes, it was," Rachel added. "Thanks for letting us join you."

"It was our pleasure, my dear." Edna stood and gingerly moved to her walker. "Bye now."

Lindsay watched them leave, then turned to Rachel. "They were just too cute." She rested her chin on her hands. "Can you imagine being with someone for fifty-seven years?"

"With the right person, yes, I can."

"Was Lisa the right person?"

"Yes, she was, but sometimes things don't work out even if it is the right person. Some things are just beyond our control." Rachel smiled wistfully. "I'm glad we had the time we did. I wouldn't give up the good years to avoid the pain at the end."

"Does it bother you to talk about her?"

"No, not anymore." Rachel looked down at the tattoo on the back of her hand, her finger lightly tracing over it. "I knew by our fourth date that I wanted to make a life with her. I told her I wanted us to live together, but she had been badly hurt in her last relationship and was afraid to risk loving again." Rachel held up her hand. "She drew this and said that all she could promise was that we would be together until the ink faded. I went out the next day and had it tattooed on. I wanted to make damn sure the ink wouldn't fade."

"What was she like?"

"She was a real outdoorswoman. Life was an adventure. She loved camping and rock climbing. She loved working with her hands, and we were building a log cabin on some property we owned. Doing everything ourselves. That was her pet project." Rachel looked down at her hands. "We never finished it. I haven't been back there since she died."

"I'm sorry," Lindsay said. "I shouldn't have brought her up."

Rachel reached over and covered Lindsay's hand. "It's okay. It doesn't hurt to think of her anymore. They're good memories, and I wanted to share them with you." The corner of her mouth lifted in a half-smile. "I think you would have liked her, and I'm sure she would have liked you." She squeezed Lindsay's hand. "I mean, what's not to like."

When they were finished eating, Rachel leaned back in her chair and patted her stomach. "That hit the spot. Now I'm ready to play. What do you want to do first?"

"I don't know." Lindsay gathered up her trash and headed to the nearest receptacle. "How about we just wander around and see what strikes our fancy."

"Sounds good to me." Rachel slam-dunked her trash and followed Lindsay toward the midway. Movement off to her left caught her eye—a person careening toward the ground suspended by a single cord. A giant crane supported a platform and the other end of the cord. The person sprung up toward the platform like a loosed slingshot, then he was falling again. "Bungee jumping!" She grabbed Lindsay's arm and pointed. "They have bungee jumping." She pulled Lindsay in that direction. "I've always wanted to try that. Let's do it."

"Are you crazy?" Lindsay planted her feet and pulled her to a stop.

"Perhaps," Rachel turned back and shrugged, "but I still want to do it."

Lindsay looked up at the crane and shook her head. "Fine. You're on your own, pal. You're not getting me up there."

"Okay, you can stay safely on the ground, but I'm jumping." Rachel turned around and started toward the crane again, with Lindsay following reluctantly behind. When they joined the line of daredevils awaiting their turn to jump, a woman handed them each a clipboard.

"This is a dangerous sport," she said. "We can't guarantee that you won't get hammered by the cord or strain a muscle or two. Most people come out unscathed, but you just never know. Read this over. It outlines the risks involved. If you still want to jump, then sign the release at the bottom that you are jumping at your own risk. The cost is thirty dollars per jump."

Lindsay handed the clipboard back and shook her head. "Not me. I'm just here for moral support."

Rachel read the document through and signed her name, then handed the clipboard back. She reached into her pocket, pulled out her money, and counted out the correct amount.

The woman took the cash and pointed to a scale. "Step on the scale, please." Rachel did as she was told, and the woman wrote her weight on her right hand.

Rachel grinned at Lindsay. "I can't believe I'm really doing this."

"Neither can I. And I still think you're crazy."

Rachel stood on the high platform, looking down at the tiny people on the ground below. Her heart beat double time and sweat beaded on her upper lip. Adrenaline pumped through her body and she tingled all over. *I can't do it*, she thought as a man bound her ankles.

"I'll count you up to five," the man said. "On five, jump away from the platform, arms away from your body."

Rachel looked down and blind panic filled her body. Her mouth was dry, making it hard to swallow. *Can I do this?*

"One..."

I can't do it.

"Two..."

Rachel closed her eyes so she couldn't see the ground below. Her body was trembling, and she thought her knees would give out on her. There was a ringing in her ears and she barely heard as the man continued to count.

"Four..."

I really can't do this.

"Five."

Rachel dived off the edge and spread her arms, thrilling at the feel of wind rushing past her. Then the ground was approaching fast. Too fast, and she was sure she would not stop before she hit it. The cord began to slow her descent and then flung her back up toward the platform, and she was falling again.

Below, Lindsay watched as Rachel plummeted toward earth. She couldn't believe that anyone would possibly think that was fun. After bouncing up and down a few times, Rachel finally just hung there upside down, swinging gently. Then a rope ladder was lowered, and Rachel grabbed on to it, allowing several strong men to pull her back to the top of the crane.

Lindsay shook her head again. "She's certifiable." She stood stock-still and waited until Rachel was on the ground again and walking toward her, a silly grin plastered on her face.

"That was great," Rachel said when she reached her. "I was scared shitless, but it was great."

The carnival had been fun, but Rachel was glad when they got to the motel. She limped noticeably and wished that she had brought her cane with her.

"Are you sure you're okay? I do notice the limp, you know."

"I'm fine. All I need is to get off my feet for a while. Tomorrow I'll be good as new. You stay here and I'll go get us a room."

Lindsay nodded and smiled. *One room. She's getting us one room.* She waited until she saw Rachel emerge from the office, then she got out of the car, pulled their bags out, and set them on the ground. The ice chest followed, and she opened it up and dumped out the water. "What are we going to do with this lunch meat? There's no more ice."

"Toss it. I don't even know why you brought it, we've been eating out."

"There were only a couple of slices left, and I figured they would spoil before I got back home."

"We're over here." Rachel grabbed the handle to the wheeled ice chest and one of the bags and headed down the walkway. Lindsay picked up her bag and followed along. Rachel stopped in front of the first door and unlocked it, flipping on the lights as she stepped inside.

She glanced around the room. "Not too bad. Oh look, we have a refrigerator." It was one of those tiny, under-the-counter models, but it was fine for their needs. She stowed their drinks and Lindsay's lunch meat. "Good thing we don't have much stuff." Chore done, she grabbed her suitcase and placed it on one of the beds. "I'll take this one. That okay with you?"

Lindsay nodded.

"Right." Rachel pulled out a T-shirt and a pair of boxer shorts from her bag, then headed for the bathroom.

Silently, Lindsay sighed as Rachel disappeared behind the closed door. She had hoped that they would share a bed. She rummaged through her bag, pulled out her nightclothes, and waited her turn for the bathroom. It had been a wonderful day, and she wasn't going to let a little thing like sleeping alone ruin it.

When they had both finished their bathroom routines, Lindsay crawled into bed and pulled up the covers. Rachel walked to her and smiled. "Sweet dreams," she murmured, then leaned over and kissed her. "Good night."

Lindsay had her eyes squeezed shut, her hands covering her nose and mouth. The weight of the dirt pressed down on her chest, making it hard to breathe what little air she had trapped with her hands.

Her lungs were screaming for oxygen and there was none to be had. Rachel!

Rachel awoke to the sound of first whimpering, then panicked shouts as Lindsay called her name. She jumped out of bed and leaned over Lindsay. "Wake up, honey, it's just a dream."

Lindsay's eyes flew open and her hands came up to cover her face. "No!" she screamed.

"It's okay, Lindsay." Rachel grabbed her shoulders and pulled her close. "It's me, Rachel. I won't let anything hurt you."

"Rachel?" Lindsay wrapped her arms around Rachel and started to sob. "I was so scared. I thought it was happening again."

Rachel pulled away from her and took her tear-stained face in her hands. "He can't hurt you again. I promise. I won't let anyone hurt you again." She pulled Lindsay back into her arms and held her until the sobbing stopped. "Are you okay?"

Lindsay nodded, but she got out of bed, went to the bathroom, and closed the door.

Lindsay looked distraught when she came out of the bathroom moments later. "Are you sure you're okay?" Rachel asked.

"Honest, I'm fine. It was nothing."

"You know," Rachel came forward and put her hands on Lindsay's shoulders, "you piss me off when you say things like that. It *was* something. A very big something. And there's nothing wrong with being upset over what happened." She pulled Lindsay close and hugged her tightly. "It's killing you to hold all the pain inside, Lindsay. Tonight you let a little out, and that's a good thing. Please don't go back to holding it in. I'm here, and I'll share it with you if you'll let me."

Lindsay buried her face in Rachel's neck and started to cry again. "I didn't want you to think I'm a wimp," she sobbed. "You're so strong. I want to be like that."

"You're wrong. I'd lose it too if I'd been through what you have." Rachel pulled away so she could look in Lindsay's eyes. "And you're not a wimp." She wiped the tears away with her thumbs, then gave her a quick kiss. "Okay?"

"Okay." Lindsay turned and went back to her bed. "Could you sleep with me? I don't want to be alone right now."

Rachel smiled. "Sure." She waited for Lindsay to climb into bed and then slid in beside her.

"Thanks," Lindsay said.

"Does this happen often?"

Lindsay nodded. "I'm afraid to go to sleep at night, but I feel safer knowing that I can just reach out and touch you."

"C'mere." Rachel opened her arms in invitation.

Lindsay turned over and snuggled into Rachel's shoulder. "This is nice."

"Yes, it is."

When Lindsay wrapped her arm around Rachel's middle and her bent leg settled across Rachel's thighs, Rachel stifled a groan as her body responded to the beautiful body wrapped around her. She ached for more, thought she was ready for more, yet there was still that small part of her that kept reminding that these feelings for Lindsay were wrong. That she was being unfaithful to Lisa. Her rational mind told her that Lisa was gone and she would want her to move on, to be happy. She wanted to be able to totally surrender herself to Lindsay, but now was not the time, and she wondered if there would ever be a right time.

Rachel woke early to find herself spooned around Lindsay. She lay still for a moment, just listening to her breathe. It almost felt too good to move, but there were things to do. She slipped out of bed carefully, so as not to wake her slumbering friend. If she hurried, she could go out and get some more drinks and a bag of ice before Lindsay woke up. That would get them on their way sooner. She quickly made her bathroom stop and pulled on her clothes. The sound of barking made her frown, and she slipped out the door and went in search of the dog. If it kept up the racket, the noise would wake Lindsay before she returned.

Around the corner of the building, she found a scruffy-looking brown dog in a small cage. "No," she said sharply, hoping that the dog had been trained to obey the command. It just barked louder. She shook her head. "Damn yappy little dog." Why anyone would want one of those annoying little pests was beyond her. *I hope Lindsay's a sound sleeper*, she thought as she headed for the car.

Lindsay awoke to the sound of barking. She sat up and looked around the empty room. "Rachel?" She got up and found a note from the detective telling her she would be right back. In the bathroom, the sound of barking seemed to be much closer. She opened the window, peeked out, and spied a little dog locked in a cage. She was about to close the window when she saw a man come into view and kick the cage violently, sliding it about two feet across the ground.

"Shut the fuck up! Aunt Maud may have coddled you, you little shit, but she's dead and soon you will be too. When Jessie gets here to relieve me, I'm taking you to get the big sleep shot." He kicked the cage again and the little dog cowered. "That's right. Keep that yap of yours shut." With that, he turned and stomped back into the motel office, slamming the door behind him.

Lindsay dressed quickly and walked outside and around the corner of the building. The little dog was still shaking and cowering when she got to the cage. "It's okay," she said softly, as she squatted down in front of the cage. "I won't hurt you." She put her hand against the cage and let the dog sniff it. Covertly, first making sure no one was watching, she opened the cage and pulled the dog out. "He's not going to kill you."

Once she and the dog were in her room, Lindsay sat it down on the bed. "Are you hungry?"

The little dog just cocked its head and looked at her warily.

"Of course you are. Let me see what I've got that you might like to eat." She noticed a tag that was barely visible in the thick hair around the dog's neck. "Maybe this will tell me something." She lifted the tag and read the name. "So, your name's Gypsy, huh?"

Lindsay crossed the room and bent over to look inside the refrigerator. There was only one slice of turkey lunch meat, but considering the size of the dog, that would probably tide it over for a while. She pulled off a bit of the meat and held it out. "Here you go, Gypsy."

The dog snatched it out of her hand and swallowed it down before Lindsay even had a chance to blink. Then it sat down on its haunches and lifted its front paws in the air, begging for more.

"Smart little whip, aren't you? How long's it been since you had a good meal?" Lindsay pulled off another chunk and handed it to the dog. Gypsy finished the lunchmeat, and Lindsay went to the sink and filled up a glass with water. "I know this isn't a proper dish, but it's all I've got." She held the glass down below the edge of the bed so Gypsy could reach the water. When the dog had drunk its fill, Lindsay put the glass on the table and sat on the bed.

The dog didn't hesitate to crawl onto her lap and seemed to sigh as it laid its head against Lindsay's belly. Brown eyes looked up at her adoringly. Then the little dog snuggled into her lap and closed her eyes. Lindsay ran her hand over the dirty, matted fur and shook her head. "What am I going to do with you?"

Gypsy lifted her head at the sound of her voice. The dog licked Lindsay's hand, then settled back down and closed its eyes again.

A sound at the door brought the little dog to her feet. To her dismay, she watched the woman who had yelled at her earlier come into the room. She barked heartily, determined to scare this rude woman away from her new friend.

"Shh, no barking, Gypsy," Lindsay said. "We don't want the big sleep man to hear you."

The little dog stopped barking, but she kept a watchful eye on Rachel. She wanted to please her new lady, but this intruder had yelled at her earlier. She was not to be trusted.

"What's that dog doing in here?" Rachel stopped in her tracks. "And who's this big sleep man?"

"I stole her."

"You what?"

"The guy in the motel office was gong to put her to sleep. I had to do it. I couldn't let him kill her, could I?"

Rachel walked to the table, put her bag down, and put her hands on her hips. "Couldn't you just have asked him if you could have her?"

Lindsay shook her head. "You didn't see him kick the cage, Rachel. He hates her. I was afraid if I asked and he said no, I'd lose my chance to get her away from him."

"If he wants to get rid of her, why would he say no?"

"Because he's just plain mean and he wants her dead."

"Well, what are we going to do with her?"

"I don't know, but I'm not leaving her here."

"Okay," Rachel said. "I'm reluctant, but we'll take her with us. Maybe one of the family in New Orleans will take her off our hands." That settled, Rachel turned to the cooler and dumped ice into it, then settled the drinks into the ice. "I'll get us checked out and then bring the car over here. I don't want anyone to see you smuggling that dog out of here." She rolled her eyes. "I can't believe I'm actually helping you steal someone's dog."

"Maybe Trish will let David have her." Rachel was fairly sure that neither she nor Lindsay was keeping the dog.

She and Lindsay walked toward the pet groomer. Lindsay had insisted they stop and get Gypsy bathed.

"I don't think Gypsy is the kind of dog you give to a small child," Lindsay said. "David might hurt her."

"He wouldn't hurt her."

"I didn't mean he'd hurt her on purpose. It's just that Gypsy's so little, he could hurt her without even realizing it."

Rachel shrugged. "I guess." She opened the door to the Pampered Pooch Parlor and held it open for Lindsay.

Lindsay paused before going through the door. "You really don't like dogs much, do you?"

"I like dogs okay, just not the little yappy ones. They're so annoying. Besides, she doesn't like me either."

"Give her a chance, will ya?" Lindsay walked by Rachel and into the shop. "Because I think I'm keeping her." She smiled at the woman behind the counter. "Is Gypsy ready yet?"

Rachel inwardly cringed at the thought of having the annoying little dog along for the whole trip. She had hoped they could palm her off on someone in New Orleans.

"That she is," the woman said. "I had to clip her pretty short. Those burrs were really matted into her fur."

"That's okay," Lindsay said. "As long as they're gone and she's clean, that's all I care about."

When the woman handed the little dog to Lindsay, Gypsy almost wiggled out of her arms, she was so excited to see her. It took a moment for her to calm down and let Lindsay get a good look at her. She was shaved almost all the way down to her skin, so it was easy to see how tiny she really was.

Lindsay looked over at Rachel. "I didn't realize how much of her was hair. There's nothing left." She looked back at the groomer. "How much do you think she weighs?"

"Probably about seven or eight pounds," the woman answered.

"Good grief. My cat weighs more than that." Rachel rolled her eyes.

Lindsay smiled at the dog. "I bet you feel better now, huh, Gypsy girl?" She leaned down and sniffed her. "And you smell better too."

The dog seemed to understand that Lindsay was praising her, and her tongue snaked out to lick Lindsay's face.

Lindsay reached into her purse and pulled out her money. "Thanks," she said. "She looks great."

"Bring her back any time," the groomer replied. "It's a pleasure to work on such a well-mannered dog."

"You're such a good girl, you deserve a treat. Wait till you see what we got for you." Lindsay carried the dog out to the car and set her on the seat while she rummaged through the bags of dog supplies they had purchased while Gypsy was being groomed. She grabbed a package of jerky treats and opened it. The smell of the treats wafted out of the package, and Gypsy sat up and did her cute puppy trick. Lindsay handed her one of the treats, and she dropped down to the seat, held it between her front paws, and began to chew on it.

Rachel watched the dog chew on the jerky, and her own stomach growled. "I'm starved." *Hmm, now we are three.* They would not be able to go into a restaurant with that dog along, and they couldn't leave her in the car. It was going to have to be a stay-in-the-room night. "What say we find a place to stay for the night that has cable TV? We can order in a pizza and find a movie to watch."

"Works for me." Lindsay picked up Gypsy from the seat, climbed into the car, and placed the dog on her lap.

Rachel pulled out of the parking lot and started up the highway. "Watch for a place that advertises TV in the rooms."

Lindsay saluted. "Aye, aye, Cap'n."

"This is good," Lindsay said around a mouthful of pizza. She felt a tapping on her thigh and looked down to find Gypsy nudging her leg. As soon as the dog knew she had Lindsay's attention, she dropped down on her butt and lifted her front paws in the air again. "You already had your dinner, silly." Just as she looked away and took another bite of pizza, the tapping came on her leg again. The minute she looked at Gypsy, down she went on her butt again, front paws up in the air. Lindsay was delighted and laughed. "Okay," she said. "I can't say no when you ask like that. It's too cute." She pulled off a small piece and gave it to the dog.

"You shouldn't feed her that, you know," Rachel said, then took a bit of her own pizza.

"I don't see what it hurts to give her a little pizza."

"People food's not good for her. I read somewhere that onions are very bad for dogs." Rachel held up her slice of pizza that was covered in onions and mushrooms.

"I suppose you're right." Lindsay looked down at Gypsy, who was already sitting up for another bite. "No more," she said, and the dog cocked her head. "No," Lindsay repeated, and Gypsy flopped down on the floor and sighed. "Now she thinks I'm mean."

"Give her one of her dog treats," Rachel said. "That's what we bought them for, isn't it?"

Lindsay put down her slice and grabbed the bag of Pup-Peroni. "Here you go, sweetie." She held a treat out to Gypsy.

Rachel picked up the TV remote and began flipping through the guide menu. "Anything look good to you?" She paused at a title. "Oh, darn. *Steel Magnolias* is just ending. I would've liked to see that one again."

"Is it good?"

Rachel nodded. "I loved it. It's a real tearjerker, though."

"We'll have to rent the DVD one of these days and watch it," Lindsay said.

Rachel nodded and took another bite, then continued scrolling through the guide. "This looks interesting." She read aloud the synopsis for *Bend It Like Beckham.* She glanced at Lindsay. "Starts in half an hour. What do you think?"

"Sounds like a plan."

Rachel brought up the channel and muted the TV. "All set," she said, then picked up her pizza and took another bite. "We can get ready for bed when we finish eating and then watch it in bed."

Lindsay put down her pizza and leaned on the table, watching Rachel eat. "You know," she said. "I never would have pegged you as a tearjerker kind of gal."

"Really?" Rachel lifted an eyebrow, "And just what kind of gal would you have pegged me as?"

"Action, adventure."

"I like those too. But I love a good movie that touches me," Rachel tapped her chest, "in here."

Lindsay grinned. "Me too."

They finished their meal and got ready for bed just in time for the movie to start. "Perfect timing," Rachel said as she climbed into bed. Lindsay picked Gypsy up and climbed in beside her. "Does she have to sleep with us?"

"Sorry, Gypsy," Lindsay said. "But Miss Meany-Pants over there doesn't want you on the bed." She leaned over and placed the dog on the floor, then settled back to watch the movie.

Rachel rolled over in her sleep and wrapped her arm around the warm body next to her. "Hmm," she hummed happily, nuzzling into the curly red hair. "Yeow! What the...?" She sat up and pulled her fingers to her chest.

"Huh? What?" Lindsay mumbled, as she lifted her head and looked over her shoulder at her bed partner.

"That dog doesn't like me," Rachel grumbled, holding her injured digits up for Lindsay to see. "She bit me."

"I'm sorry." Lindsay turned on the light, then rolled over onto her back and pulled the hand in question over to examine it. "You big baby, the skin's not even broken."

"Well, it still hurt."

Lindsay shook her finger at the dog curled up against her. "Bad girl."

"That's all you're going to do?" Rachel frowned at the dog. "And what's she doing up on the bed? I thought we left her on the floor last night."

Lindsay put the dog off the bed. "Better?" She smiled at Rachel.

"Much," Rachel said. "So, what would you like to do today?" She glanced at the dog. "We're going to be limited now that we've got a dog with us."

"I know," Lindsay said, "but I couldn't just leave her there to die, could I?"

Rachel shook her head, aware of the brown eyes glaring at her from across the room. "Of course you couldn't. I wasn't saying you shouldn't have saved her." She looked at her hand. "But I think that tiny terror of yours is plotting to get me."

"I don't know why she did that. Give her time and she'll be eating out of your hand."

"I have a feeling she'd rather eat my hand than eat out of it," Rachel said. "Come on, it's almost eight. You take a shower first and I'll start the coffee."

"Okay, I'll be quick."

"Good, we're wasting daylight. What say we get on the road and see what looks interesting?"

Lindsay nodded and started for the bathroom, the little dog falling in step beside her. "Good morning, Gypsy. How's my sweetie today?"

"That's right, keep the mutt occupied while I make my escape." Rachel climbed off the bed and headed for the coffeemaker. She glanced down at her shirt, which lay on the floor. *I know I put that on the chair when I took it off last night.* She reached to pick it up and paused. "Uh, Lindsay?"

"Yeah?"

"Your precious pet left a present on my shirt." She carefully picked it up so the small pile would not fall on the floor. "I told you she hates me."

Lindsay looked down at the little dog wagging her tail innocently at her. "Gypsy, did you do that?"

"No, I got up in the middle of the night and did it," Rachel groused. "Of course she did it. And she had to put in some effort to get my shirt off the chair to use as her toilet."

"At least she didn't use the rug."

Rachel rolled her eyes.

"I didn't mean that it was good she pooped on your shirt," Lindsay said. "I just meant that if she stains up the rug, they might make us pay to clean the carpet."

"Yeah, well, tonight we lock her in the bathroom. That way we don't have to worry about her messing up the carpet."

"I'm sure she won't do it again," Lindsay said. "I'll make sure to take her out for a nice long walk before we go to bed."

"Just the same, I think she should stay in the bathroom. I don't want to take any chances with someone else's carpet. When you get her home, it's your carpet you have to worry about. That's different."

Suddenly, Lindsay got a stricken look on her face. "What if they won't let me keep her there? I didn't have a dog when I moved in, so I didn't think to check on the pet policy."

"So what's the big deal? It's not like you've had her for years. I'm sure we can find someone to take her if they won't let you keep her."

Lindsay picked Gypsy up and hugged her close. "I don't want to find her another home. She loves me, and I want to keep her."

"Okay, okay. Let's not worry before we have to. I'm sure it'll work out." Rachel hadn't realized until then just how attached Lindsay had grown to the little brown dog.

CHAPTER TEN

Rachel pulled into her grandparents' driveway and parked the car. "This is it. Papa and Gran have lived in this house for thirty-nine years."

They got out of the car and Lindsay let her eyes wander over the yard. The home itself was beautiful, but the yard was breathtaking. To the left of her were lilacs in glorious bloom. There was a planter on either side of the front door filled with flowers of every imaginable hue. Off to the right was a small rose garden, and the walkway to the house was completely arched with a trellis covered in flowering vines.

"Oh, Rachel," she said. "It's beautiful." She touched one of the hanging clusters. "What is this?"

"It's wisteria. Gran planted those the year they moved in."

"I don't think I've ever seen a more colorful yard. It's breathtaking."

Rachel grinned. "Be sure to tell Gran. This yard is her pride and joy."

The front door opened and a woman appeared in the doorway. "Is that you, Peanut?" The older woman squinted her eyes, trying to focus on them.

"You lose your glasses again, Aunt Nelda?" Rachel asked.

Nelda grinned when she heard Rachel's voice. "Get up here and let me get a good look at you, darlin'. It's been way too long since you paid us a visit."

"How've you been, Aunt Nelda?" Rachel walked through the yard and up the steps to the door.

"Fair to middlin'," Nelda said. She pulled Rachel into her arms. "Besides, it wouldn't do no good to complain, now, would it?"

"No," Rachel agreed. "I guess it wouldn't. When did you and Uncle Albert get here?"

"Yesterday morning."

Lindsay stayed where she was; she didn't want to intrude on the reunion. Aunt Nelda was a round black woman who looked to be in her sixties, with salt-and-pepper hair that was cropped close to her head. Burgundy lipstick complemented skin that was several shades darker than Rachel's, and large hoop earrings dangled from her ears. Lindsay watched them chat for a moment, wondering if she should go up and join them or wait to be invited.

"Lindsay," Rachel called to her. "Come up here; there's someone I want you to meet."

Lindsay clipped the new leash on Gypsy and joined them on the porch.

"Lindsay, this is my Aunt Nelda."

"It's very nice to meet you," Lindsay said, holding out her hand. "I hope I'm not intruding."

"Nonsense." Nelda took Lindsay's hand and squeezed it. "Any friend of our Peanut is always welcome." She turned and beckoned them into the house.

Lindsay looked at Rachel. "Shouldn't we get our bags first?"

Nelda shook her head. "Y'all come on in and sit a spell first. Them bags can wait. You must be tired after that long trip. Bring that little chit of a dog with you. It's okay. Just make yourself at home, and I'll bring you something cold to drink."

Lindsay picked up Gypsy and followed them into the house. Two children eager to see the dog in her arms immediately greeted her.

"Hanna, Joseph," Nelda said. "Where are your manners?" The children stopped and looked at Nelda.

"We just wanted to see the dog," Joseph said.

"We greet people first," Nelda said, "so say hello to your aunt Rachel and her friend, Lindsay."

Rachel shook her head. "This can't be Hanna and Joseph," she said. "The last time I saw them they were babies."

"We're six." Hanna lifted her hands to display the appropriate number of fingers. Joseph stood beside her and nodded.

Rachel squatted down and pulled the twins in for a hug, then looked up at Lindsay and smiled. "These are my brother's grandchildren."

"And this is Gypsy," Lindsay said with a smile, pointing at the dog.

"Can we play with her?" Joseph asked.

"Please," Hanna said.

"I don't know," Lindsay said. "I'm not sure how she is around children. I wouldn't want her to bite you."

Hanna stuck out her hand for the little dog to sniff. A soft tongue snaked out and licked the small fingers. "See, she likes me."

Rachel shook her head. "Oh, great. She likes everyone but me. I must be special."

"You are special," Lindsay said. "Give her time and she'll see that." She turned back to the children. "Okay, we'll give it a try, but only in the yard. You can't take her off anywhere."

"We won't," the children said in unison.

Lindsay placed Gypsy on the floor and handed the lead to Hanna. "Hold tight to the leash. I don't want her running off. And no running and pulling her around. Remember, your legs are much longer than hers are."

They watched the twins march happily away with the dog and then followed Nelda into the kitchen.

"Where is everyone?" Rachel asked.

"Lawanda took Mom to do some last-minute shopping, and Dad dragged Albert to the golf course. We didn't expect anyone to get here until later tonight."

"Lawanda is my brother's daughter," Rachel explained to Lindsay. She turned back to Nelda and beamed. "I wanted to make sure I got here before Trish arrived. I just had to be here to introduce David to the family."

Nelda reached over and patted Rachel's cheek. "Oh, Peanut, you don't know how glad we all were that things worked out between you and Trish. Now, you two sit down and let me get you something to drink, then we can do some catching up."

Rachel pulled out a chair and sat down, but Lindsay looked back at the door, worry showing plainly on her face. "I hope Gypsy doesn't get scared and try to run away from them."

"I'm sure she'll be fine."

"Just the same, I think I'll go check while you and your aunt catch up."

Rachel shrugged. "Okay, I'll be out in a bit to help bring in the bags."

Lindsay sat on the front porch and watched Hanna and Joseph play with Gypsy. Joseph had found a small ball that he was tossing for her. The sixteen-foot retractable leash allowed the little dog to dash after the ball, but to the children's frustration, she would bring it to Lindsay every time she retrieved it. "You're supposed to take it back to Joseph," Lindsay said as she accepted the ball from the dog and tossed it to the little boy.

"We have a swing," Hanna said to Lindsay. "Ya wanna see?"

"Sure."

Hanna reached up for her hand, and Lindsay noticed the contrast between the small brown hand and her own pale skin. They started off around the side of the house, Joseph and Gypsy following along behind. The backyard was large, and a massive tree with a tire swing stood off to one side.

"Papa made this swing for us," Joseph said. "Isn't it cool?"

Lindsay nodded. "Very cool."

"You can swing on it if you like."

"Maybe later. I think I better go get our bags out of the car and take them in the house. You take good care of Gypsy for me, and I'll be back in a little while." Lindsay turned to walk back around to the front of the house, and the little dog trotted along at her side until she reached the end of her leash. Lindsay kept walking and when she came around to the front of the house, she could see that Rachel was already heading to the car. She started to call out to her when a car pulled into the driveway next door, and the driver waived at Rachel. The detective turned and waved back, then headed to meet the woman in the car.

When the woman emerged, Lindsay could see that she was stunning in a red and white silk suit. Her cocoa skin was smooth and blemish free, and Lindsay was sure she could be a supermodel if she wanted. Rachel pulled her into her arms and Lindsay felt her gut clench. Everything about the woman was perfect, and Lindsay couldn't help the insecurity that spread through her when she saw how loving and comfortable she and Rachel seemed together. Then they turned toward the house next door, and the woman laced her arm through Rachel's as they walked inside.

Lindsay felt hot all over, and her stomach was tied in knots. *She went inside with her!* She leaned against the side of the house and tried to calm herself down. *You're being silly. Rachel's probably known her most of her life. They're old friends, nothing more.* But her gut still clenched. How could she compete with someone like that? The woman was drop-dead gorgeous. If only they hadn't seemed so close. If only they hadn't walked off together, arm in arm.

Lindsay's mind was still reeling with the possibility of Rachel rekindling some kind of old romance when they emerged from the house, the woman having changed into shorts and a tank top. They walked to Rachel's car and Rachel opened the trunk, then went around and opened the back door and pulled out the cooler. From that angle, she noticed Lindsay and waved at her.

"Great, you're here." Rachel grinned and beckoned. "Come on over, there's someone I want you to meet."

Lindsay took a deep breath and pushed off from the wall she had been supporting. When she joined them at the car, she forced a smile.

"Lynn, this is Lindsay," Rachel said.

Lynn extended her hand in greeting, and Lindsay could see that her hands were perfect too. Long tapered fingers with perfectly manicured nails. "It's nice to meet you," she said as she gripped Lynn's hand.

"Nana!" Hanna and Joseph came running around the side of the house.

Nana? She's their nana? Lindsay watched Lynn squat down to greet the children.

"What have we got here?" Lynn indicated the little dog following along behind them.

"This is Lindsay's dog," Hanna answered. "Her name's Gypsy."

"What kind of dog is it?" Lynn asked.

"We really don't know," Rachel answered. "We ripped her off from some guy at a motel we stayed at."

Lynn stood up. "Ripped off?" Her eyes tracked from Lindsay to Rachel. "You took someone's dog?"

"He was going to have her put down for no good reason," Lindsay said. "I couldn't let him do that."

Lynn just laughed. "I can't believe Ms. Law-and-Order participated in ripping something off, no matter what the reason."

"You going to prosecute me, Ms. A-D-A?"

"ADA?" Lindsay's anxiety rose.

Lynn reached into her pocket and pulled out a business card holder, handing one of her cards to Lindsay. The card read Lynndell Todd, Assistant District Attorney.

"She and my brother met when they were both students at Tulane Law School."

"I thought your brother was a DJ?"

"He is," Rachel said. "He hated being a lawyer. Come on, let's get this stuff inside."

Lynn nodded and picked up the cooler while Lindsay and Rachel grabbed the bags from the trunk. Lindsay breathed a sigh of relief to realize that if Lynn was the children's nana, then she must be Rachel's sister-in-law. Suddenly everything was all right again. She shook her head and smiled as she followed them into the house.

Lindsay quietly watched Rachel interact with her family. Everyone was kind to her, but still she felt like an outsider.

"You okay?" Rachel asked as she dropped down beside her on the couch.

"Sure," she answered. "Why do you ask?"

"I don't know. You seem so quiet. It's not like you."

"I just don't want to intrude. I know you haven't seen your family in a long time. I'm happy just to sit back and watch."

"You're not intruding." Rachel reached over and squeezed Lindsay's hand. "I love having you here with me. It was my idea for you to come. Remember?"

Lindsay grinned and nodded. "I remember."

"Good."

The front door flew open, signaling another bustle of activity, and a young black woman walked in, her arms loaded down with shopping bags. Behind her, an elderly woman appeared, and Rachel's eyes lit up.

"Gran!" Rachel was on her feet in an instant, striding across the room to greet her. "I'm sorry it's been so long since I visited." She pulled her grandmother in for a hug. "I've missed you all so much." She released her and took the bags from Lawanda, set them on the table by the door, then wrapped her arms around her. "Hey there, sweetie. I almost didn't even recognize Hanna and Joseph, they've grown so much." She escorted the women over to where Lindsay was sitting on the couch. "Gran, Lawanda, this is my friend, Lindsay."

Lindsay stood up and extended her hand. "It's very nice to meet you, Mrs. Todd, Lawanda." She looked at Rachel's grandmother. "I've been admiring your house, especially your beautiful yard. It's breathtaking."

"Thank you, my dear." She patted Lindsay's hand and smiled. "I do love to putter around in my garden. It's a passion of mine. It's a bit harder to get up and down out there these days, but I don't let that stop me. And please, call me Gran, everyone does, or Jeannie if you prefer, but not Mrs. Todd. Formalities just don't sit well with me."

It was clear that Jeannie Todd had once been a flaming redhead. Her eyebrows were still red but her hair was snow white, with a few strands of red still sprinkled through the back. Lindsay was totally charmed by her lilting Scottish brogue, somewhat softened with time but still there. Somehow, it didn't feel right to call her Jeannie, so Lindsay settled for Gran.

"I have a bit of a passion myself for gardening," Lindsay said, "but I live in an apartment and don't get much chance to try my hand at it anymore." She extended her hand to Lawanda. "I met your children earlier. You should be proud of them, they're so well behaved."

Lawanda beamed with maternal pride. "Thank you. They can be a handful at times." She looked around for the twins, but they were nowhere in sight. "Where are the little buggers?"

"They're out in the back playing with my dog," Lindsay replied.

Lawanda laughed. "We may not see them for hours."

The sound of the garage door opening caught Rachel's ear and she stood up. "Papa and Uncle Albert are home," she said, striding across the kitchen to the door that led into the garage. She opened the door, and her grandfather saw her as he got out of the car.

"Peanut!" He opened his arms wide. Rachel fairly flew across the garage and into his welcoming arms.

Lindsay watched the joyous reunion between Rachel and her grandfather. He was taller than he looked in his pictures, and he had a little more gray, but to Lindsay's mind, he looked far younger than she knew he was. She addressed Nelda. "I've been wondering, why does everyone call Rachel Peanut?"

"Oh, my. That name goes way back to when she was just a bit of a thing," Nelda said, "maybe two or three years old. My Albert was courting me in those days. I never could understand why an educated city man like him was interested in a country gal like me. Anyway, the whole family came down our way to visit the county fair and Albert insisted they stop by to meet me. He asked me to go with them, but I had to finish planting the peanuts before I could go.

"Everyone pitched in, and Rachel was following along behind her daddy, picking up the peanuts he dropped and eating them." She shook her head and smiled. "We been callin' her Peanut ever since."

Rachel paced back and forth in front of the house. "They should be here by now." She glanced at her watch, suspicious that the timepiece was faulty.

"It hasn't been that long since Waheya called," Lindsay said. "They'll be here soon."

"I know." Rachel sighed. "I'm being silly; it's just I've waited so long to be able to introduce David to Gran and Papa. For a long time, I thought it would never happen."

A sound drew her attention, and a large SUV pulled up. Rachel's face lit up when she saw Nancy and her husband, Sam, in the front seats. She wasted no time opening the side sliding door. She reached out to give her mother a hand while she stepped down.

"Gramma Rachel," David called out when he saw her. "I got to go up in the sky!"

"You did?" Rachel lifted him up.

The little boy nodded excitedly and pointed up in the air. "Higher than the clouds."

"Oh, my goodness," Rachel said in mock surprise. "Did you have to flap your arms really hard to get up there?"

David laughed and shook his head. "You're silly, Gramma. We went in a plane, and I could look out the window and see the clouds, and they looked like snow, but Mama said you can't walk on them because you would fall right down to the ground, so we stayed in the plane."

Trish climbed out of the SUV, followed by Nancy's son, Todd, and his wife, Julie. Julie was about six months pregnant, but she was already huge. Rachel moved David to her hip and gave each one of them a one-armed hug, then turned to Lindsay to make the introductions. When she came to Julie, she patted her niece's stomach and said, "And in here we have Justin and Robert."

"More twins?" Lindsay was astonished. "You sure have a lot of twins in this family."

"What's twins?" David asked.

"That's when two babies are born at the same time," Rachel answered. "Usually mommies only have one baby in their tummies at a time, but sometimes there are more. If there are two, we call them twins. Your cousin Julie has two babies in her tummy."

David looked at Julie's stomach. He shook his head. "Two babies couldn't fit in there."

"They curl up in a little ball so they can fit," Trish said.

David still looked skeptical, but he took his mother's word for it.

As the entourage started for the house, the front door opened, and Jeannie and Marcus stepped out on the porch.

"David," Rachel said, "These are your great-great-grandparents. This is Gran, and this is Papa."

Marcus reached out and took the boy into his arms, and Jeannie beckoned Trish to join them. She put one arm around Trish and one around Marcus and pulled them all into a group hug, with David in the middle.

Rachel watched the scene and grinned. She had never thought she would see all of them together, and her eyes stung with happy tears.

"You're squishing me!" David called out, and everyone burst out laughing. When the group separated, Rachel could see that Trish was in tears too.

"What's everyone doing standing around out there?" Nelda held the door open. "Come on in."

As everyone walked inside, David studied his great-great-grandfather. He reached out and traced one of the lines in his face. "You're kind of old."

"David!" Trish squeaked, embarrassment flushing her cheeks.

Marcus patted her hand. "It's okay, sweetie. David's right, I am old. And I've earned every gray hair on this old head."

Hanna and Joseph arrived with Gypsy, and David wiggled to get down. He obviously couldn't wait to get his hands on the little dog. Marcus put him down, and he rushed for Gypsy. But before he reached her, she had tucked her tail and run for the safety of her new mom.

Trish caught his hand and pulled him back. "We never run up to a strange dog," she said. "We wait to be introduced. If you scare her, she might bite you." She walked David slowly over to where Gypsy hid behind Lindsay's legs. "Now hold out your hand and let her smell you."

David obediently held out his hand. "Why does she want to smell me?"

"That's how dogs get to know each other."

David looked up, puzzled. "But I'm not a dog." Gypsy inched over to his outstretched hand and carefully sniffed, then licked it. David giggled. "See, Mama, she likes me." He patted her head, and the little dog's tail wagged.

Rachel squatted down and smiled. "David, these are your cousins." She pointed to the boy who was still holding onto Gypsy's leash. "This is Joseph."

Before she could get to Hanna, Joseph grinned and pointed to his sister. "This is my sister, Hanna. We're twins."

"I know what a twin is," David said.

"You wanna come play with us?" Hanna asked.

David nodded and marched off with his new cousins as if he had known them forever.

Lindsay sat on one of the twin beds in the room she and Rachel were to share while they were in New Orleans. Rachel's family was nice, but it was a bit overwhelming being introduced into such a large family all at once. It had been such a long time since Rachel had visited with them, and Lindsay felt that she should just fade into the background and let her be with her family. But now that she was up in the room by herself, she felt lonely. Perhaps she should go down, get Gypsy, and take her for a walk through the neighborhood. Anything was better than sitting up there alone. Being alone was different at home. She had things to do, but this visiting family thing had her in uncharted water.

A knock came at the door and Lindsay called, "Come in."

The door opened and Waheya stepped inside. "I thought I might find you here." She sat on the bed next to Lindsay. "Is everything okay with you and Rachel?"

"Everything's fine. Um, did Rachel say something?"

Waheya patted Lindsay's hand. "No, my dear, nothing like that. You've been so quiet, and then you just disappeared. I was worried something might be wrong."

Lindsay sighed. "I don't think anything's wrong, but with Rachel it's hard to tell. As far as friends go, we're fine. If you mean romantically, I'm just not sure. One day she gives me the impression that she wants to take our relationship further, and the next day she backs off. I get so many mixed signals from her that I'm not sure about anything anymore."

"Do you love her?"

Lindsay nodded. "I didn't set out to love her. In fact, when we first met, I didn't like her at all. I'm not sure when I fell in love, I only know I have. I knew she didn't want it at the time, but I couldn't help myself." She averted her eyes. "I still can't."

"That daughter of mine can be slow at times," Waheya said, "but I know that she cares deeply for you. I haven't seen her this relaxed and happy in years. I like the effect you've had on her. Don't give up on her, Lindsay. Let her know how you feel."

"I'm afraid I'll scare her off if I push. The last time I did that she told me to back off."

"I've seen the way she looks at you. I don't think she'd tell you to back off now."

The door opened and Rachel walked in. "There you are," she said to Lindsay. "I've been looking all over for you. Mark's here and I want you to meet him."

"Think about it," Waheya said softly as Lindsay stood to follow Rachel.

Lindsay looked back at her and smiled. "I will," she said, and then she was gone.

When they got downstairs, there were twice as many people as when Lindsay had left. "Don't tell me these are all your family," she said.

Rachel glanced around the room and nodded. "Most of them, yes. I told you I had a big family." Grinning, she grabbed Lindsay's hand and pulled her across the room toward a man standing with his arm around Lynn. "Mark, this is my friend, Lindsay."

A smile lit up Mark's face.

Lindsay smiled back, but inside she was hurt that Rachel always introduced her as her friend. She knew Rachel was not in the closet with her family, so the term "friend" simply proved to her that she and Rachel were not in the same place when it came to categorizing their relationship. She wanted more than friendship. Much more.

"It's nice to finally meet you," she said.

"It's nice to meet you too." He nodded at Lynn. "We were just talking about starting up a couple of tables of pitch. You up for a game?"

"Pitch? I've never head of it."

"Well," Mark said, "If you're going to spend much time around this family, you have to learn. It's the card game we always play when we get together."

"Oh, a card game," Lindsay said. "I don't know how to play. I haven't played many card games."

"It's easy," Rachel said. "I'll teach you. There are way too many people here, so we have to play rise and fly. We can sit out and watch for a while till you think you're ready to jump in and play."

"Which are we playing first?" Lindsay was befuddled. "Pitch, or rise and fly? And what is rise and fly?"

Rachel laughed. "We're playing pitch. Rise and fly means that the losers rise and fly, and the winners stay to play the next set of partners. We only have two tables going, and there are four people per table. So, at the end of each game, two new people sit to play the winners, and the losers wait for their turn to come again."

"I'm crushed," Lynn said to Rachel. "My partner has deserted me." She turned to Lindsay. "I'll have you know that when Rachel and I team up, we almost never have to rise and fly. We hold the table."

"Maybe I should sit out and just watch," Lindsay said. "Whoever is stuck with me is sure to lose."

"Don't be silly," Waheya said as she walked up behind them. "Of course you'll play. You can be my partner." She chuckled. "That way, they won't have to draw straws to see who gets stuck with me this time." She put her arms around Mark and hugged him. "Hello, sweetie."

Mark kissed her forehead and squeezed back, then looked at Lindsay and laughed. "I love her, but she's wild when it comes to bidding."

"You can't win if you don't bid." Waheya turned to Lindsay. "We may lose, but we'll have fun doing it."

Lindsay grinned. "You've got yourself a partner."

Lindsay stood and raised her glass when Rachel gave a toast to her grandparents. The wedding celebrating their sixty-fifth anniversary had been lovely, and she had enjoyed the last two days with Rachel's family. They hadn't seemed quite as intimidating once she got to know them. They were a warm and welcoming bunch, but she was anxious for the family part of the trip to be over so she could be alone with Rachel again.

She had taken Waheya's advice to heart, given her relationship with Rachel a lot of thought, and realized Waheya was right. Lindsay needed to let Rachel know how she felt about her. But there, surrounded by the Todd family, was not the place or time to try to take her relationship with Rachel to the next level, especially when Rachel still seemed hesitant to do so. In fact, Rachel seemed quite content the way things were.

Everyone sat back down, and Rachel flashed Lindsay a breathtaking smile. Lindsay couldn't remember ever seeing Rachel so happy. Her heart skipped a beat just looking at her.

Suddenly, the panicked voice of a teenaged girl interrupted the celebration. "Mrs. Davies!"

Sheila Davies stood up, panic clearly in her eyes. Everyone turned to see what was going on. The girl was Dawn Reilly, and she was supposed to be two doors down taking care of Sheila's eighteen-month-old daughter.

"Where's Jenny?" Sheila whispered.

Dawn burst into tears. "I don't know," she managed through her sobs. "She was there one minute, and then she was gone. I found the back door open and figured she went out. I went around the neighborhood and couldn't find her."

"Did you check everywhere in the house?"

Dawn nodded. "She's not there. She's vanished."

Rachel pushed her way through the concerned crowd gathered around the teen. "How long has she been gone?"

"She doesn't know," Lindsay said, and everyone turned to her, all speaking at once.

"How do you—"

"What—"

"You weren't even—"

"—could possibly—"

"—at the table—"

"She was..." Lindsay hesitated, trying to decide how much to tell. Dawn and her boyfriend had been having sex, but that was more information than a room full of people needed to know. "She was entertaining her boyfriend," Lindsay finally said.

"That's a lie," Dawn yelped.

"How could you know that?" Sheila asked Lindsay. "You've been here with us."

"You can trust what Lindsay says," Waheya said. "She has the gift of sight."

Sheila looked puzzled. "The gift of sight? What does that mean?"

"That's my mom's way of saying that she's psychic," Rachel said. "She can see things we can't see. I've seen her do it."

Sheila turned and glared at Dawn. "You left my baby alone while you entertained your boyfriend in my home?"

Dawn buried her face in her hands and sobbed. "I'm so sorry."

"I'll deal with you later." Sheila turned pleading eyes to Lindsay. "Do you know where my Jenny is?"

"Sorry, no." Lindsay shook her head. "I can't see her."

"Then we're wasting time," Sheila said. "We've got to start looking for her."

Waheya interrupted the moving crowd. "Give Lindsay a chance first. She's our best chance for finding your baby quickly."

"I don't know if I'll get anything. But I'll certainly try." Lindsay turned to Sheila. "I need something of hers."

"Come on," Sheila said, and led the way to her house. She went up to Jenny's room, brought back a stuffed flop-eared bunny, and handed it to Lindsay. "It's my baby's favorite."

Lindsay took the toy and sat down with it on the couch. She was clutching the rabbit so tightly that her hands were trembling. *I have to be able to do this. Another little child is at risk.*

Waheya sat down next to her and spoke quietly. "Don't try so hard, Lindsay, just relax and let it come." She hummed softly.

Waheya's gentle voice had a calming effect on Lindsay. Taking a deep breath, she tried to relax her tense body. She held the bunny to her chest and stroked the soft fur, taking more deep, calming breaths. *I can feel it! But I don't see anything. Where is the child?* She saw nothing but darkness. About ready to give up, she saw an image in the darkness. It was Jenny. She was asleep on what appeared to be carpet. Was she in a carpeted box? The cover seemed to be no more than an inch above the sleeping child.

"I see her," Lindsay said, but she kept her eyes closed and continued to stroke the bunny.

Sheila burst into tears. "Is she okay?"

"She's sleeping. She's in a box, I think." Lindsay paused. "Do you have a box with pink carpet on the bottom?"

"A box with carpet?" Sheila couldn't believe the question. "I have mauve carpet in my bedroom, but no box."

Lindsay continued to stroke the toy. Something else came into focus. She strained to make out what it was. It looked like a curtain. *A curtain? In a box?* Then it came to her. "Do you have a dust ruffle on your bed?"

"Why, yes."

Lindsay opened her eyes and looked calmly at Sheila. "I think she's asleep under your bed."

Sheila gave a strangled cry and bolted up the stairs to her bedroom with Lindsay right behind her. She dropped to her knees and peeked under the bed, and there she found Jenny, sleeping peacefully. She gently pulled the toddler out and clutched her tightly to her chest, kissing the small head as tears streamed down her face. When she heard the sounds of footsteps coming down the hall, she saw that everyone had followed her up, but her brimming eyes only sought Lindsay. "Thank you."

Lindsay felt incredible. Maybe this vision thing wasn't the curse she'd believed it to be for so long. Perhaps it really was a gift. *I don't feel helpless anymore.* Whatever it was, she was glad that she'd been able to help. Plus, she had confirmed Waheya and Rachel's faith in her. She looked over at Rachel and found that she was grinning at her, and it warmed her heart. God, she wanted that woman to love her. *Maybe if I relax and let it unfold, like my vision.* She knew she couldn't make it happen, but somehow, she just knew in her heart, it would happen.

CHAPTER ELEVEN

Rachel packed the last of their things in the car and walked back into the house to start her good-byes. Lindsay was in the backyard collecting Gypsy from Hanna, Joseph, and David. When Trish wrapped her arms around her, Rachel kissed the top of her head. It had been good to spend several days with Trish and David, and it had given her a chance to really get to know her grandson better.

"Uncle Al is getting his tail whipped in there," Mark said as he walked in from the kitchen.

"You'd think he'd know by now that he can't beat Papa when it comes to cribbage," Lynn said.

Mark laughed. "One of these days he'll do it and we'll never hear the end of it."

"Uncle Albert gloat?" Rachel joined in the laughter.

"Don't you wait so long between visits," Jeannie admonished as Rachel walked into the living room. "I'm not getting any younger, you know."

"I promise." Rachel squatted down in front of her grandmother's chair, then leaned over for a hug and a kiss. "I love you, Gran."

"I love you too."

"You gettin' ready to head out, Peanut?" Nelda entered from the kitchen, where she had been watching the mismatch with Papa and Albert.

"Yep," Rachel said. "Soon as I collect Lindsay and the dog." She stood up and walked over and gave Nelda a hug, then started for the kitchen. Lindsay showed up at the back door about that time with Gypsy in tow. "You ready?" Rachel asked, and received a nod in reply.

Albert and Marcus stood, and Marcus wrapped his arms around Rachel, squeezing her in a big bear hug.

"I love you, Papa." When Marcus released his grip, Rachel turned to Albert. "Love you too, Uncle Albert."

Nelda appeared again, carrying a brown paper bag. She handed it to Rachel. "Thought you could use some snacks for the road."

Rachel nodded. "We sure could." She opened the bag, peeked inside, and found two sandwiches and two pieces of her aunt Nelda's famous peanut-butter fudge. "Mmm, thank you." She kissed Nelda on the cheek.

Lynn and Mark followed them out to the car, and there were more hugs all around.

"You take care of my little sister," Mark whispered to Lindsay in a quick good-bye embrace.

Lindsay wasn't sure what he meant by that, but she nodded. "I will."

Once on the road, Lindsay peeked into the bag that Rachel had placed between them. "Yum." She pulled out a large piece of Nelda's fudge. "Your aunt makes about the best fudge I've ever eaten." She broke off a piece and fed it to Rachel, then took a bite herself. "I really like your family."

Rachel smiled. "They liked you too. Thanks for coming with me. Next time we come, I want to show you the sights. New Orleans is an interesting and entertaining city." She glanced down at her watch. "I told Edna that we'd be there by seven, but if this traffic doesn't lighten up, we're going to be late."

The traffic did ease up, and they made good time, pulling up in front of John and Edna's house at just after seven. Rachel had developed a pounding headache during the trip and Lindsay had driven the last hour.

"We need to stop by a drug store before we head to the cabin," she said. "This headache is a killer."

Lindsay sighed. She hated to see Rachel in pain, and she hated that her plans for a romantic evening had gone up in smoke. At the door, they knocked and were greeted by a smiling John.

"Hi, there. You folks hungry? We've got plenty of food we can warm up."

"That's very kind of you to offer," Lindsay answered for them. "I'm afraid Rachel's not feeling well. We need to pick up the key and then find a drugstore so she can get some pain medication."

"Come on in and I'll get it."

They followed John into the house and waited while he went to get the key. Edna padded in from the kitchen with her walker and smiled when she saw them. "I didn't even hear you come in. You kids hungry?"

"I just asked 'em that," John said as he returned. "Rachel's feelin' poorly and they need to get some pills in her."

"Oh, I'm sorry to hear that. What's wrong?"

"Killer headache," Lindsay answered for Rachel again.

"John," Edna said. "Go fetch them pills the doctor gave me when I got out of the hospital. They're on the bottom shelf in the medicine cabinet. I think the date's still good." She looked at Rachel. "I had this hip replaced and they gave me a bottle of pills, but I didn't finish 'em. That was around Thanksgiving, so they should still be good."

John returned with a pill bottle. "This it?" He held it up.

"Did you get it off the bottom shelf?"

"Yes."

"Then that's it."

John handed the bottle to Rachel.

"Don't just stand there, you old poop. Get her some water so she can take one."

John looked at Lindsay and smiled. "That old woman's lucky she's got me to fetch and carry for her."

"Good thing, too," Edna said. "It's kind of hard to fetch and carry when you're walking around with one of these things." She indicated her walker. "But the old coot loves me." She smiled in his direction. "I'm a lucky woman for sure."

"That you are," Lindsay answered. She wondered what it would be like to live with someone for that many years and still be in love.

John returned with the water and handed it to Rachel.

"Thanks." Rachel took the medication. "I think you better drive," she said to Lindsay. "Vicodin knocks me on my butt."

John handed Lindsay the key and directions to the cabin, and they were on their way. It only took about twenty minutes to get there, but the medication was already kicking in. Lindsay handed Rachel the key. "You go in and lie down. I'll bring in the bags."

"I can help."

"I don't need any help. Now get in there and lie down. That's an order."

"Yes, ma'am."

By the time Lindsay walked the dog and carried in their things, Rachel was out cold on the couch. She smiled at the sleeping woman, then grabbed one of the blankets off the bed in the bedroom and brought it in to cover her. "Sleep well," she said as she leaned down and lightly kissed her lips.

Lindsay opened the back door and stepped out onto the large porch that faced the lake and found a rested and refreshed Rachel sitting at a small table with her morning coffee. It was a beautiful morning and Lindsay sighed as she took in the view. "Good morning. It's so peaceful here I could stay forever." She set her coffee down on the table and took the seat next to Rachel.

Gypsy trotted over, carrying the small ball that Hanna had given her. She dropped it at Lindsay's feet and sat up on her hind legs, begging her to toss it.

"Okay," Lindsay said, and picked up the ball. She tossed it and Gypsy dashed off across the grass to chase it down. The ball kept going until it was in the lake.

The little dog didn't let that deter her and jumped in after it. When she tried to climb back onto shore, however, the wet ground kept falling away.

Seeing Gypsy in distress, Lindsay jumped up and ran to retrieve her from the water. But when her feet hit the slick mud at the edge, she slipped down the incline and ended up in the lake with Gypsy. She disappeared under the water and emerged sputtering and spitting.

Rachel's coffee spewed from her mouth, and she doubled over laughing. Lindsay glared at her, but she couldn't stop. "I'm sorry," Rachel said, "but if you could have seen yourself, you'd be laughing too."

Gypsy paddled over to Lindsay, grateful to be rescued. The water wasn't very deep that close to shore, and Lindsay was sitting on the bottom with water lapping at her chin. She shook her head, sending drops of water in all directions, then grabbed the dog and stood, her wet nightshirt clinging to her body.

She saw Rachel's expression change instantly, so she looked down and saw that the thin cotton shirt had become almost transparent, leaving nothing to the imagination. She made her way slowly up the slight grade and placed Gypsy on the ground, aware that Rachel hadn't blinked. She smiled and started for the deck, determined to find out if the look in Rachel's eye was what she thought it was.

Shielding her eyes from the sun, Rachel squinted at her. "It's not nice to tease," she warned playfully.

"No?" Lindsay feigned innocence. "Why not?"

"Play with fire and you might get burned."

"I can't get burned unless there's a flame," Lindsay said as she walked toward Rachel. She placed her hands on her hips and raised one eyebrow. "So tell me, Rachel, is there a fire burning? Do you feel heat?"

Rachel's eyes shifted from Lindsay's face to her breasts, then back to her face again. Desire burned in her hungry eyes as she answered, "An inferno," amazed at how shaky her voice sounded.

Lindsay leaned over, resting her hands on the armrests of the chair. "When you look at me like that, you make me feel sexy."

"You are sexy."

Lindsay straightened up and held out her hand.

Without a word, Rachel reached up and took it, allowing herself to be pulled to her feet, then led to the cabin. In the bedroom, Lindsay shut the door on a puzzled Gypsy. Then Rachel watched as Lindsay peeled the wet nightshirt off and tossed it over a chair, revealing wet skin that glistened in the morning light, nipples firm and erect.

"You're so beautiful, you take my breath away." Rachel could feel the fine hairs on her arms stand up, and a slight tremor shook her body. She thought her heart would pound its way out of her chest as she strode purposefully across the room and pulled Lindsay into her arms. Her blood sizzling, she captured waiting lips, and her passion exploded when Lindsay moaned into her mouth and thrust her hips against Rachel's. She dropped her lips to Lindsay's throat, biting lightly against her skin, leaving small marks in her wake.

Lindsay groaned but pushed Rachel away while reaching for her shirt. "I want you out of these clothes." She unzipped Rachel's shorts and slipped them, along with her underwear, off the detective's slender hips. "I need to feel your skin against me."

Rachel stepped out of the shorts and pulled her shirt over her head. While her arms were still up in the air, Lindsay slipped her hands under the sports bra Rachel wore and pulled it off as well. "I want you so much." She turned and led Rachel to the bed. "So much."

Rachel's eyes closed instantly, her back arching, when she felt soft lips close around her nipple. Her fingers twined in the red hair, holding Lindsay's lips right where they were. It had been so long. "Yes..." she whispered, her legs parting as a searching hand slipped into her wet curls.

With a sigh, Lindsay lifted her head from Rachel's breast, gazed into eyes full of passion, and lost herself in the love she saw there. She slid down Rachel's body, kissing and nipping the smooth flesh of her belly. Each whimper from Rachel sent a shiver through her, and she nuzzled into dark, curly hair, breathing in a scent so intoxicating that it made her head spin. Tentative fingers stroked swollen lips and were rewarded when Rachel's hips thrust up to meet them. She was overwhelmed by her all-consuming desire for the woman beneath her. She hungered for the taste of her and nudged Rachel's legs further apart so she could slip between them.

Rachel went completely rigid at the feel of Lindsay's tongue against her flesh. She felt her breath rip through her lungs in short, aching gasps and tried to slow the powerful orgasm she felt building far too quickly. She wanted this ecstasy to last longer, but there was no stopping it. The force of it took her completely by surprise as her resolve shattered into a million shards of light.

Eyes still closed, Rachel smiled, pulled Lindsay up, and clutched her tightly, burying her nose in the soft strands of red hair. "God, what you do to me," she murmured, kissing Lindsay's neck.

Lindsay grinned, her fingers still combing gently through Rachel's wet curls. "I should have tried to seduce you sooner."

"I'm not sure it would have worked sooner," Rachel said. "I wasn't ready."

"But you are now?" Lindsay's fingers stilled. "I don't think I could bear it if this is just a fling."

Rachel rolled them over and looked deeply into Lindsay's eyes as she ran her fingers gently along her jaw. "I don't do flings. This is the real thing for me." Her fingers continued to move, tracing over trembling lips. "I never thought I could feel this way again, but I do." She leaned down and gave her a kiss, then pulled back slightly. "I love you, Lindsay."

Lindsay grinned and wrapped her arms around Rachel's neck, pulling her down for another kiss. "You don't know how I've longed to hear you say those words."

Rachel wiggled around so her cheek was resting on the warm softness of Lindsay's belly. "I like this," she sighed happily. She felt Lindsay's hand stroking her hair. "You make a nice pillow."

Lindsay's fingers continued to comb through Rachel's hair. "I don't think I've ever been this happy."

Rachel moved back up and turned on her side, propping her head up with one arm. She didn't say a word as she gazed at Lindsay.

"What?"

"I just like to look at you. You're so beautiful." Rachel leaned over and kissed Lindsay, then tucked a few unruly curls behind her ear. "We could conserve water and shower together," she offered hopefully, earning a smile from Lindsay.

"You're incorrigible, you know that? We spent practically all of yesterday in bed, with only a couple of breaks to feed the dog, and at this rate we won't get out of the cabin again today."

"And that would be bad?" Rachel winked at her. "You, me, another day of staying in bed making love. Sounds like a splendid idea to me."

"Nothing wrong with your libido," Lindsay said playfully.

"Must have something to do with the company I've been keeping lately."

Lindsay turned over on her side too. "Ya think so?"

"Oh yeah." Rachel wrapped her free arm around Lindsay and pulled her tight against her. She nipped at her neck and then nuzzled into her hair. "I can't seem to get enough of you."

A knock sounded on the outside door, which set Gypsy to barking, and Rachel turned over to see the travel clock on the table by the bed. It read eleven thirty a.m., and she was surprised at how late it was. The knocking sounded again, and she called out, "Be right there," above the barking. "You don't suppose Edna and John have decided to come over and pay us a visit, do you?"

Lindsay got up and grabbed her shorts, stepping into them and reaching for her shirt. "I don't know who else it could be. We don't know anyone around here."

Rachel followed suit and dressed quickly. "We really shouldn't be greeting guests like this, you know."

Hesitating at the door, Lindsay looked at her with a puzzled expression on her face.

Rachel shrugged. "Take a whiff, darlin', we smell like an orgy."

"Omigod. We do!" Lindsay burst out laughing. "Nothing like wafting what we've been doing for the last twenty-four hours under their noses. What can we do?"

Rachel grabbed her travel bag, scrounged around inside, and pulled out a bottle of cologne. She gave herself a few good squirts, then handed it to Lindsay. "Put it on heavy and I think it'll do the trick."

"Oh, honey." Lindsay took a step back and fanned the air. "Now you really smell like a brothel. Sex and cheap perfume."

Rachel put her hands on her hips. "How would you know what a brothel smells like?" Then she put the bottle up to her nose and sniffed. "Does it really smell cheap?"

Lindsay started laughing again and nodded. She grabbed her robe and slipped it on over her clothes. "You stay here. I'll tell them we're not dressed yet."

Lindsay picked up the barking Gypsy near the front door and opened it a crack to peek out. She was surprised to find two men she had never seen before. They were rather nice looking, but she wondered what they were doing at her door. "Yes?"

The shorter man smiled. "Hi, I'm Luke. John and Edna's grandson," he added, turning to his friend, "and this here's my friend, Ryan. My grandmother told us you girls rented the cabin this week. She thought you might like to have some fun while you're here. Tonight is line dancing at Charlie's Tavern if y'all would like to go with us?" He looked at her expectantly. "Two single ladies like yourselves shouldn't be sittin' out here all alone. We'd like to show you a good time."

Lindsay didn't know what to say. Edna and John were such a sweet old couple. They'd been so nice to rent them the cabin on short notice, and she didn't want to hurt their feelings. Still, she wanted to spend her time there with Rachel. "That was sweet of them to think of us," she said, "but I'm afraid I'm going to have to decline. Rachel and I are not single ladies."

"Oh, I see. Just vacationing without your husbands. I'm sorry for the misunderstanding, ma'am. We meant no disrespect. We'll just be on our way, then."

Lindsay returned to the bedroom with Gypsy right on her heels. "It wasn't John and Edna. It was their grandson, Luke, and he had a friend with him. They invited us to go dancing. I think Edna's trying to play matchmaker."

Rachel frowned. "Great, just what we need." She put her hands on her hips. "Please tell me you sent them packing."

"Yep. Though they misunderstood my saying that we're not single ladies. They thought we left our husbands home."

"Just as well." Rachel's stomach growled. "Hey, I'm starving. I haven't had anything to eat since yesterday morning." She wiggled her eyebrows. "No food, anyway."

"Be good." Lindsay smacked her arm.

"I am good." Rachel tackled Lindsay, and they fell onto the bed. Her fingers dug into Lindsay's ribs, tickling mercilessly, while Gypsy barked and jumped at the edge of the bed.

Lindsay shrieked and wiggled. "Stop!" she called through her giggles. "Stop!"

"Not until you say I'm good."

"You're good, you're good!" Tears were streaming down Lindsay's face from all the laughing.

Rachel used her thumbs to brush them away, then leaned down for a quick kiss. "Protect me from that vicious dog of yours, darlin', and I'll go fix us something to eat."

Lindsay shrieked when she saw a spider scurrying across the hardwood bedroom floor. She grabbed the first thing at hand—the bottle of perfume that Rachel had given her earlier. Afraid to take her eyes off the spider, she accidentally squirted herself in the mouth in her haste to spray it.

She sputtered at the awful taste and turned the bottle around so that the nozzle was facing the proper direction. She was just about to spray again when Rachel rushed in to see what the screaming was about.

Lindsay pushed the perfume nozzle down, and a fine mist squirted out toward a spider, who put on a burst of speed when it felt the moisture.

Rachel squatted down and placed her hand on the floor, allowing the fleeing spider to climb up on it. Then she quickly covered it with her other hand. "Open the door for me," she said as she started for the front door.

Lindsay shuddered when she saw Rachel pick up the spider. "Are you going to kill it?"

"No, I'm going to put it outside."

Lindsay rushed ahead and opened the door, glad to have the eight-legged intruder out of the cabin.

Rachel let the spider crawl off her hand and onto a shrub, then turned back to find Lindsay standing in the doorway, the perfume bottle still in her hand. "What were you going to do, drown it with my perfume?" She took the bottle out of Lindsay's hand.

"It was all I could find."

Rachel wrapped her arms around Lindsay. "Darlin', it was just a harmless little old house spider. Nothing to be afraid of."

Lindsay shuddered again. "I know it's irrational, but I have a horror of spiders. They scare me senseless, and I don't want them anywhere near me."

"Just call me and I'll take care of them for you." Rachel leaned over and kissed Lindsay, then wrinkled her nose. "What's that on your lips? It tastes terrible." She wiped her mouth on her arm. "Ugh."

"It's your perfume." Lindsay grinned. "When I tried to spray the spider the first time, the nozzle was facing the wrong way."

Rachel laughed and took her hand. "Let's go rinse it off." She led her to a small wooden dock about fifty feet away, then released her hand and started to strip off her clothes.

"You're not going in naked, are you?"

"Why not, there's no one around." Rachel stepped out of her pants and tossed them on top of the rest of her clothes. "Haven't you ever gone skinny-dipping?"

Lindsay shook her head. "What if someone comes?"

"I'll tell them to go away." Rachel dove off the dock and swam toward a swimming platform floating about thirty yards from shore. When she reached the platform, she pulled herself up and stretched out on the smooth surface. "Come on," she called to Lindsay, who was still standing on the dock. "Live dangerously."

"What the hell," Lindsay said and stripped.

When Lindsay jumped in the water, Gypsy started to bark and run back and forth on the bank. After her brief venture into the lake, she was afraid of the water and wanted her lady to come back out where it was safe.

Rachel sat up and watched Lindsay paddle toward her. She extended her hand when she reached the platform and helped her climb out of the water. "Much better," she said as she kissed Lindsay without tasting perfume on her lips.

Lindsay stretched out on her stomach and Rachel lay on her side with her head propped up with her hand. She ran her other hand down Lindsay's back and let it rest on her luminous white behind. She looked at her brown hand resting atop the pale flesh and marveled at the contrast in color. Lindsay was fair, even with a bit of a tan, but her backside was amazingly white. It was clear that it had never been exposed to the sun. "We'd better not stay out here too long, darlin', or this pretty little ass of yours will turn as red as your hair."

Lindsay rolled onto her back and pulled Rachel over on top of her. "There, I'm covered. Now I won't get burned."

Rachel leaned down and kissed her. "You sure?"

"Well, not by the sun anyway. The fire you ignite when you kiss me like that is quite a different matter."

Rachel loaded the last bag in the car and sighed. She wished they could have had more time alone out there. She watched Lindsay lock the cabin door and pick up Gypsy. "You sure we've got everything?" she asked as Lindsay opened the passenger door and climbed in.

Lindsay nodded. "I did a final check before I locked up." She buckled her seat belt and settled Gypsy on her lap.

They pulled out on the road and drove a few minutes in companionable silence. Lindsay was happy and it showed. She looked over at Rachel.

Rachel could feel Lindsay watching her. "What?"

"You're beautiful."

"No, I'm not." Rachel flushed. "My nose is too big."

"Your nose isn't too big. It's perfect."

Rachel smiled. "I'm glad you think so, but it is too big." Uncomfortable with the close scrutiny, she changed the subject. "How would you like to come here next summer?"

"I'd love to." Lindsay grinned. "We could make it an annual event. But no skinny-dipping next year."

"I thought you enjoyed our skinny-dipping."

"I did, but next year, there'll be a cabin across the lake. We won't be alone out there."

"Did you have a vision?"

Lindsay laughed. "No, silly. When Luke and his friend were leaving I heard his friend tell him that his parents are breaking ground on a cabin out here next month. Nothing psychic about it."

"Have you always known you were psychic?"

"I've always known that I was different than other people. It wasn't until I was older that I had a name for it. The first time I had a vision that anyone was aware of was when I was about three or four." Lindsay took a swallow of her Pepsi, leaning her head back against the headrest. "I don't remember it, but apparently it caused people to think I had the power to put curses on them."

Rachel's brow lifted. "Curses?"

Lindsay nodded. "My father was between jobs again, and we'd fallen behind in the rent. The landlord had come over several times to try to collect and had decided to toss us out. I guess I told him the last time he came over that he couldn't go home because his house was on fire. The next day his house burned down."

"He thought you put a curse on his house?"

"Mmm, well, his wife did. He accused my dad of setting the fire until the arson investigators proved it was faulty wiring. But his wife believed I cursed their house because they were evicting us from ours. A house for a house, so to speak. I don't really remember any of it. But it did give me a reputation that followed me around. I was a little kid and people were actually afraid of me."

Rachel took Lindsay's hand and squeezed it. "That must have been hard."

"It was. My mom told me not to let anyone know that I could see things; that it would be our secret. It was too late for that, though. People already knew. But I tried. I tried so hard not to see things, to push them away."

"Perhaps that's why you're only now learning to use your gift."

"I don't know. Maybe."

Pat was picking up her mail when she saw Rachel's car drive up. She grinned and waved, detouring toward the car to help carry Lindsay's things inside. She waited as Lindsay climbed out of the car and placed a small dog on the ground. Then she embraced her. "How was the trip?" The little dog yipped at her, and she jumped back. "What's that?" She pointed at Gypsy.

Lindsay rolled her eyes. "It's a dog, silly." She reached down and scooped Gypsy up into her arms.

"I can see that, but where did it come from?"

"We stole it," Rachel said as she joined them on the sidewalk.

Lindsay turned and swatted at Rachel's arm. "Would you please stop telling people we stole her."

Rachel dodged out of the way and laughed. "Well, we did."

"I prefer to say we rescued her. It sounds better."

Rachel opened the trunk and pulled out bags. "Semantics." She mouthed to Pat, "We stole her."

Pat picked up one of the bags and headed for Lindsay's apartment. "Okay, Bonnie and Clyde, I want the whole story."

"It's simple really." Lindsay grabbed Gypsy's treats and her overnight bag. "Her owner died and the guy who had her was an ass. He was going to have her put down. Can you believe it? We had to take her."

Lindsay caught up with Pat, who was waiting at her door. "I mean, look at her face." Gypsy seemed to know she was talking about her and licked Lindsay's face. "No licking," Lindsay said and put Gypsy down so she could rummage in her purse for her keys. "How could anyone look at that sweet little face and not fall in love with her?"

Pat looked down at the little dog. "Well—"

"Not you too?" Lindsay unlocked the door and stepped aside so Pat and Rachel could enter.

"I didn't mean I'd put her down," Pat said. "I'm just not a dog person."

Lindsay emptied her hands and started opening windows. The apartment was hot and stuffy after being closed up for two weeks.

Rachel put down the bag she was carrying and started for the kitchen. "You have anything cold in your fridge?"

"I've got Pepsi or water. Take your pick and grab me a Pepsi." Lindsay looked at Pat. "How about you?"

Pat shook her head. "I'm good."

Lindsay picked up one of her bags and started for the bedroom.

For a scant moment, Pat and Rachel were alone. "Are there still nightmares?"

"No," Rachel whispered. "Believe it or not, the rescue of that damn little dog gave her back some feeling of control."

"Good." Pat went into the bedroom and grabbed Lindsay's arm, turning her around. "So?" She looked at Lindsay expectantly. "Was the trip what you hoped for? I'm dying to know."

Lindsay's face lit up. "It was wonderful. She loves me, Pat."

"I told you that before you left."

"I know, but I had to be sure."

"And now you are? No doubts?"

Lindsay shook her head. "No doubts."

Pat pulled her in for a hug. "I'm so happy for you, sweetie." Rachel appeared in the doorway with their drinks, and Pat stepped quickly away. "I was just telling her how happy I am for her...for both of you."

Rachel grinned. "Thanks, and don't worry, I'm not the jealous type." She glanced at her watch. "I've got to go spring Miss Kitty and see if she's still speaking to me." She leaned over and kissed Lindsay. "I'll see you a little later, darlin'." They kissed again.

Lindsay grinned, and Gypsy barked. "I like it when you call me darlin'."

Rachel leaned closer. "Do you?"

"Mmm."

"Good, because you're going to be hearing it for a long, long time. Tell the mutt to get used to it."

About the Author

Verda Foster has worked in and around the art and crafts industry for twenty years, and is often found judging at one of the many ceramic and craft shows held throughout Southern California .

She has been teaching the art of painting statuary for thirteen or fourteen years, and enjoys seeing a student's eyes light up when they see a piece of white-ware come to life in their hands.

She wrote her first story in 1999 and was hooked. Her first book, The Chosen, was published in September of 2000 and will be re-released by Cavalier Press in 2004.

She has collaborated with BL Miller on several stories, and loves working with this wonderful writer. Their first published novel, Graceful Waters, can be purchased from StarCrossed Productions, and their next offering, Crystal's Heart, will be published by Cavalier Press in 2004, and can be purchased from StarCrossed Productions.

New Releases From Intaglio Publications

Gloria's Inn
by Robin Alexander
ISBN 1-933133-01-4

Hayden Tate suddenly found herself in a world unlike any other, when she inherited half of an inn nestled away on Cat Island in the Bahamas. Expecting something like the resorts found in Nassau, Hayden was shocked and a little disappointed to find herself on a beautiful tropical island undiscovered by tourism. Hayden reluctantly begins to adapt to a simpler way of life found on the island, and her conversion is often comical.

Not only did Hayden's aunt leave her an inn, but the company of her former business partner as well. Strange as she is beautiful, Adrienne turns Hayden's world upside down in many ways. Hayden quickly learns that being with Adrienne will always be an adventure.

The tranquility of the island is shattered with the disappearance of a mysterious guest. Hayden and Adrienne soon find themselves at the center of a murder investigation, fearing for their own safety and the lives of their guests. Eager to rid themselves and the island of a ruthless killer, Adrienne and Hayden decide to conduct their own investigation. The eclectic mixture of guests and staff make their efforts both interesting and humorous.

***Infinite Pleasures:* An Anthology of Lesbian Erotica**
Stacia Seaman (Editor), Nann Dunne (Editor)
ISBN 1-933113-00-6

Hot, edgy, beyond-the-envelope erotica from over thirty of the best lesbian authors writing today. This no-holds barred, tell it like you wish it could be collection is guaranteed to rocket your senses into overload and ratchet your body up to high-burn. This is NOT a book to be read in one sitting—savor, simmer, and let yourself be seduced by these Infinite Pleasures from Ali Vali, C Paradee, Cate Swannell, CN Winters, DS Bauden, Gabrielle Goldsby, Georgia Beers, JP Mercer, Jean Stewart, Jennifer Fulton, Jessica Casavant, K Darblyne, K Stoley, Karin Kallmaker, Katlyn, Kelly Zarembski, KG MacGregor, Leslea Newman, Lois Cloarec Hart, Lynn Ames, NM Hill, Nann Dunne, Radclyffe, S. Anne Gardner, Sarah Bradbury, Stacia Seaman, SX Meagher, Therese Szymanski, Trish Kocialski, Trish Shields, Vada Foster, and Verda Foster.

The Cost Of Commitment
by Lynn Ames
ISBN 1-933133-02-2

"ABSORBING"

Lynn Ame's first novel, The Price of Fame, has been called "absorbing and filled with romance" (Lori. L. Lake, Midwest Book Review). Now Ames is back with the second installment in the lives of Katherine Kyle and Jamison Parker.

SPINE-TINGLING SUSPENSE

Kate and Jay want nothing more than to focus on their love. But as Kate settles in to a new profession, she and Jay become caught up in the middle of a deadly scheme—pawns in a larger game in which the stakes are nothing less than control of the country.

OUTSTANDING ACTION

In her new novel of corruption, greed, romance, and danger, Lynn Ames takes us on an unforgettable journey of harrowing conspiracy—and establishes herself as a mistress of suspense.

THE COST OF COMMITMENT

It could be everything...